THE WARS

TIMOTHY FINDLEY

LAUREL

A LAUREL/SEYMOUR LAWRENCE EDITION

A LAUREL BOOK

Published by
Dell Publishing Co., Inc.
1 Dag Hammarskjold Plaza
New York, New York 10017

Originally published in Canada by Clarke, Irwin & Company Limited, Toronto/Vancouver.

ISBN: 0-440-39239-X

Reprinted by arrangement with
Delacorte Press/Seymour Lawrence

Printed in the United States of America
First Laurel printing—March 1983

For: My Father and Mother
and
P. M. Findley
and
in memory of
T. I. F.

"Never that which is shall die"
Euripides

ACKNOWLEDGEMENTS:

Novels rarely contain acknowledgements, but this one could not have been written without the encouragement, consideration and help of the following: Graham Brogan, Nancy Colbert, Stanley Colbert, Nora Joyce, Alma Lee, Buffalo Brad Nicholson, Beverley Roberts and William Whitehead. I must also thank Alan Walker for his expertise in the matter of fire arms, Ellen Powers for typing the manuscript and Juliet Mannock for reading it with an eye to English and historical detail. Lastly, I want to thank M. for the midnight 'phone calls and the letters from which the photographs fell.

T. F.

PART ONE

In such dangerous things as war the errors which proceed from a spirit of benevolence are the worst.

von Clausewitz

Prologue

She was standing in the middle of the railroad tracks. Her head was bowed and her right front hoof was raised as if she rested. Her reins hung down to the ground and her saddle had slipped to one side. Behind her, a warehouse filled with medical supplies had just caught fire. Lying beside her there was a dog with its head between its paws and its ears erect and listening.

Twenty feet away, Robert sat on his haunches watching them. His pistol hung down from his fingers between his knees. He still wore his uniform with its torn lapels and burned sleeves. In the firelight, his eyes were very bright. His lips were slightly parted. He could not breathe through his nose. It was broken. His face and the backs of his hands were streaked with clay and sweat. His hair hung down across his forehead. He was absolutely still. He had wandered now for over a week.

Behind him, the railroad track stretched back towards the town. In front of him, it reached out through the fire towards the open countryside and the road to Magdalene Wood. On one of the sidings was a train. Its engineer and crew had either abandoned it, or else they had been killed. It could not be told. Robert appeared to be the sole survivor.

He stood up. The engine hissed and rumbled. The train was about a dozen cars—no more. They appeared to be cattle cars. Robert walked to the horse.

He had feared she might be lame, but as soon as he approached she put her hoof back down on the cinders and raised her head. Robert petted her, slipping his arm around her neck and drawing the reins back over her ears. She greeted him with a snuffling noise and looked around to watch him as he adjusted her saddle and tightened her cinch. The dog, in the meantime, had got to his feet and was wagging his tail. It was as if both dog and horse had been waiting for Robert to come for them.

The horse was a fine black mare, standing about sixteen hands. She had been well cared for up till now and someone had obviously ridden her every day. She was in superb condition. The dog apparently was used to her company and she to his. They moved in tandem. The dog was also black. One of his ears fell forward in an odd way, giving the appearance of a jaunty cap. Robert did not know what sort of dog he was, but he was about the size of a Labrador retriever. Before mounting, Robert reached down and rubbed his hand across the dog's back. Then he said: "let's go" and swung up into the saddle.

They rode down the track towards the road to Magdalene Wood passing, as they went, the engine on the siding. When they got to the first of the cars—the horse stopped. She threw her head up and whinnied. Other horses answered from inside the car. "All right," Robert said. "Then we shall all go together."

Half an hour later, the twelve cars stood quite empty and Robert was riding along the tracks behind a hundred and thirty horses with the dog trotting beside him.

They were on the road to Magdalene Wood by 1:00 a.m. This was when the moon rose—red.

1: All of this happened a long time ago. But not so long ago that everyone who played a part in it is dead. Some can still be met in dark old rooms with nurses in attendance. They look at you and rearrange their thoughts. They say: "I don't remember." The occupants of memory have to be protected from strangers. Ask what happened, they say: "I don't know." Mention Robert Ross—they look away. "He's dead," they tell you. This is not news. "Tell me about the horses," you ask. Sometimes, they weep at this. Other times they say: "that bastard!" Then the nurses nod at you, much as to say—you see? It's best to go away and find your information somewhere else. In the end, the only facts you have are public. Out of these you make what you can, knowing that one thing leads to another. Sometime, someone will forget himself and say too much or else the corner of a picture will reveal the whole. What you have to accept at the outset is this: many men have died like Robert Ross, obscured by violence. Lawrence was hurled against a wall—Scott entombed in ice and wind—Mallory blasted on the face of Everest. Lost. We're told Euripides was killed by dogs—and this is all we know. The flesh was torn and scattered—eaten. Ross was consumed by fire. These are like statements: *"pay attention!"* People can only be found in what they do.

2: You begin at the archives with photographs. Robert and Rowena—rabbits and wheelchairs—children, dogs and horses. Barbara d'Orsey—the *S.S. Massanabie*—Magdalene Wood. Boxes and boxes of snapshots and portraits; maps and letters; cablegrams and clippings from the papers. All you have to do is sign them out and carry them across the room. Spread over table tops, a whole age lies in fragments underneath the lamps. *The war to end all wars.* All you can hear is the wristwatch on your arm. Outside, it snows. The dark comes early. The archivist is gazing from her desk. She coughs. The boxes smell of yellow dust. You hold your breath. As the past moves under your fingertips, part of it crumbles. Other parts, you know you'll never find. This is what you have.

3: 1915.

The year itself looks sepia and soiled—muddied like its pictures. In the snapshots everyone at first seems timid—lost—irresolute. Boys and men stand squinting at the camera. Women turn away suspicious. They still maintain a public reticence.

Part of what you see you recognize. Here for the first time, the old Edwardian elegance falters. Style is neither this nor that—unless you could say it was "apologetic." The men wear caps and shapeless overcoats to work, jamming their hands deep into pockets. Imitation uniforms spring up everywhere: girls wear "middy's"—boys are dressed in sailor suits. Women wear a sort of great coat and flat brimmed hats with rosette badges. Ladies no longer wear their furs; they drape them from their arms with all the foxtail trophies hanging down like scalps. No one smiles. Life is dangerous. Summer induces the parasol—winter the galosh. Some of the photographs are blurred. Even though the figures freeze—the dark machines that fill the roads move on.

Here is the Boys' Brigade with band. Backyard minstrels, got up in cork, bang their tambourines and strut across a lawn on Admiral Road. Every parlour has its piano: here are soldiers, arm in arm and singing: "*Keep Your Head Down, Fritzie Boy*!" Tea-Dance partners do the Castlewalk to orchestras of brass cornets and silver saxophones. Violins have been retired.

This is the age of motorized portation. Over one thousand makes of motorcar can be had. Backyard blacksmiths build them to custom. ASK THE MAN WHO OWNS ONE! Here are families, sitting overdressed in Packards—posed aloof in the backs of Chevrolets and Russell Knights. Everyone, it seems, is journeying around the block. Children vie to blow the horns.

Then something happens. April. Ypres. Six thousand dead and wounded. The war that was meant to end by Christmas might not end till summer. Maybe even fall. This is where the pictures alter—fill up with soldiers—horses—wagons. Everyone is waving either at the soldiers or the cameras. More and more people want to be remembered. Hundreds—thousands crowd into frame.

Here come the troops down Yonge Street! Women abandon all their former reticence and rush out into the roadway, throwing flowers and waving flags. Here come the 48th Highlanders!! Kilts and drums and leopard skins. Boys race after them on bikes. Little girls, whose mouths hang open, hardly dare to follow. Older men remove their hats. There is Sir Hughes standing on the dais, taking the farewell salute. "GOD SAVE THE KING!!!" (a banner). Everywhere you look, trains are pulling out of stations, ships are sailing out of ports.

Music drowns the long hurrah. Everyone is focused, now, shading their eyes against the sun. Everyone is watching with an outstretched arm—silenced at the edge of wharves and time.

Robert Ross comes riding straight toward the camera. His hat has fallen off. His hands are knotted to the reins. They bleed. The horse is black and wet and falling. Robert's lips are parted. He leans along the horse's neck. His eyes are blank. There is mud on his cheeks and forehead and his uniform is burning—long, bright tails of flames are streaming out behind him. He leaps through memory without a sound. The archivist sighs. Her eyes are lowered above some book. There is a strand of hair in her mouth. She brushes it aside and turns the page. You lay the fiery image back in your mind and let it rest. You know it will obtrude again and again until you find its meaning—here.

A Band is assembled on the Band Shell—red coats and white gloves. They serenade the crowd with "Soldiers of the Queen." You turn them over—wondering if they'll spill—and you read on the back in the faintest ink in a feminine hand: "*Robert.*" But where? You look again and all you see is the crowd. And the Band is still playing—quite undisturbed—and far from spilled. Then you see him: Robert Ross. Standing on the sidelines with pocketed hands—feet apart and narrowed eyes. His hair falls sideways across his forehead. He wears a checkered cap and dark blue suit. He watches with a dubious expression; half admiring—half reluctant to admire. He's old enough to go to war. He hasn't gone. He doubts the validity in all this martialling of men but the doubt is inarticulate. It stammers in his brain. He puts his hand out sideways: turns. He reaches for the wicker back of a wheelchair. "Come on, Rowena. There's still the rest of the park to sit in."

* * *

Thomas Ross and Family stand beside a new Ford Truck. The new Ford Truck is parked before the gates of RAYMOND ROSS INDUSTRIES, where farm machinery is made. This picture will appear in the Toronto *Mail and Empire* with a banner headline, stating that the truck is being turned over to RAYMOND ROSS Field Surgery Hospital behind the lines in France. Large red crosses adorn its sides. The "family" consists of Mister and Mrs Ross and three of their children: Robert, Peggy and Stuart. Rowena, the eldest, is not shown. She is never in photographs that are apt to be seen by the public. In fact, she is not much admitted into the pressence of a camera. Robert has her picture on his bureau.

Rowena is seated in her scalloped wicker chair with the high, double wheels. She wears a white dress. Her hair is curly and short. Her shoulders are perpetually hunched. Her head is large and adult but her body is that of a ten-year-old child. She is twenty-five years old. She is what is called *hydrocephalic*—which in plain language means she was born with water on the brain. Her expression is lovely and pensive. She wears a wide and colourful sash. In her lap she holds a large white rabbit. Robert told her once, she was the first human being he remembered seeing. He was lying in his crib and, waking from a nap through half-closed eyes, he saw his sister gliding in her chair across the room and coming to rest beside him. She stared at him for a long, long time and he stared back. When she smiled, he thought she was his mother. Later, when he came to realize she couldn't walk and never left the chair, he became her guardian. It was for her he learned to run.

Mother and Miss Davenport, wearing their canteen aprons, stand on the platform at Sunnyside Station handing out chocolate bars to the soldiers who are leaning out of trains. They do this every Thursday afternoon. Robert wishes his mother wouldn't do such things because he's shy and thinks she appears too much in public. But Mrs Ross is adamant. Such things have to be done . . . someone has to do them. The leaders of society are dutybound—and what would people say . . . ? Etc. Etc. All the while, Miss Davenport is nodding and smiling: agreeing with every word. But not one word of it is true. Mrs Ross performs her duties Thursday afternoons because of dreams.

Here is *Meg—a Patriotic Pony*, draped in bunting, standing in a garden. Her ears lie flat. She is either angry or frightened. Meg is very old. Just at the edge of the picture. Stuart can be seen squinting at the sun. He wears an Indian headdress and he holds a baseball bat.

This is *Peggy Ross with Clinton Brown from Harvard*!!! Nothing in Clinton Brown from Harvard's appearance warrants three exclamation points. He was only one of Peggy's many beaux. Robert is in this picture too, seated on the steps of the South Drive house along with a girl called Heather Lawson. Robert was supposed to be "interested" in Heather Lawson but the fact was it was she who was interested in him. Not that Robert didn't like her—only that he wasn't interested. "Interested" led to marriage and this is what Heather Lawson wanted. So did her parents. Robert was a fine catch for any girl. He was a scholar and an athlete. Besides—he had money.

One summer the Rosses crossed to England on the *S.S. Minnetonka* in order to spend a holiday with the RAYMOND/ROSS British representative, whose name was

Mister Hawkins. All through the month of June they languished on the beaches of the Isle of Wight. In late July they came home on the *Minnetonka's* sister-ship the *S.S. Minnewanka.* From the decks of this ship, early one mornning, one of the Rosses (it was not clear which)—took a photograph of the ocean. Whoever it was, later drew an arrow—pointing to a small white dot on the far horizon. The small white dot can barely be seen. Nothing else is visible but sea and sky. Just above the arrow, written in bold black ink is the question: "WHAT IS THIS?" All too clearly, the small white dot is an iceberg. Why whoever took the picture failed to verify this fact remains a mystery. The thing is dated August 4th but no year is given.

Shuffle these cards and lay them out: this is the hand that Robert Ross was born with. Mister and Mrs Ross—Peggy and Stuart—rabbits and Rowena. Also a dog named Bimbo and a clipping from the paper, reading: "LONGBOAT WINS THE MARATHON!" Meg and Miss Davenport—Heather Lawson and the iceberg. And Clinton Brown from Harvard, who died a hero's death at the battle for Belleau Wood in June of 1918—worthy of an exclamation point at last.

This is perhaps a good place to introduce Miss Turner, whose importance lies at the end of this story but whose insights throw some light on its beginnings.

Marian Turner was a nurse in the Great World War and she remembers Robert vividly. It was she who received him and cared for him after he'd been arrested and brought into the hospital at *Bois de Madeleine.* She has given (on tape) the only first-hand account of him we have aside from that of Lady Juliet d'Orsey. Here is part of what Miss Turner has to say. She is over eighty now, but still robust and she speaks with a good deal of energy, sprinkling her conversation with laughter and offerings of sherry in a wide, green apartment overlooking a park.

Transcript: Marian Turner—1:

"You will understand, from what took place, why I cannot tell you what he looked like. I suppose such things are of interest. Well—of course they are! (LAUGHTER) Everyone wants to know what people look like. Somehow it seems to say so much about a person's possibilities. Do you know what I mean? What I can say is that Lady Barbara d'Orsey was in love with him—and that all her other men were smashing! So I dare say Ross was, too. Anyway, because of what happened I can't remark about the face—but my impression was of someone extremely well made who cared about his body. At least that's my memory of it—the way it was. You get them all mixed up, after so long a time; and every boy they brought to us seemed such a handsome lad. You never hear that any more: *he was a handsome lad*! But we were always saying so in all the letters we wrote to their families. I guess you saw them all as beautiful because you couldn't bear to see them broken. The human body—well—it's like the mind I guess; terribly impressive till you put it in jeopardy. Then it becomes such a delicate thing—like glass. Robert Ross? Well—it was just so tragic. When you think that nowdays so many people—young people especially—might've known what he was all about. But then . . . (PAUSE) My opinion was—he was a hero. Not your everyday Sergeant York or Billy Bishop, mind you! (LAUGHTER) But a hero nonetheless. You see, he did the thing that no one else would even dare to think of doing. And that to me's as good a definition of a 'hero' as you'll get. Even when the thing that's done is something of which you disapprove. He was *un homme unique*—and that's much more of a compliment in French than it is in English. Oh, he was . . . (PAUSE) . . . Fire, you know—there's nothing worse than fire. Even after all I've seen. And the story of the horses is something I'd rather never have known had happened. Oh, I quite understand why you feel it must be told—but . . . (MISS TURNER TURNED TO LOOK OUT THE WINDOW AT THIS POINT. THERE IS QUITE A LONG PAUSE ON THE TAPE) . . . Well. It was the war that was crazy, I guess. Not Robert Ross or what he did. You'll say that's trite, of course. But is it? Looking back, I hardly believe what happened. That the people in that park are there because we all went mad. Yes. He was unique. But you have to be careful, searching his story out. I've been through it all, you know—(LAUGHTER)—the whole of this extraordinary century—and it's not the extraordinary people who've prevailed upon its madness. Quite the opposite. Oh—far from it! It's the *ordinary* men and women who've made us what we are. Monstrous, complacent and mad. Remember that. Even if I do sound a moralizing fool, I'll risk it. After all—I'm pretty old. (LAUGHTER) I could be gone tomorrow! There may not be anybody else who'll say this to you. Everyone's so sophisticated these days they can't stand the hot lights. Eh? Well—I saw both wars. And I'm here to tell you the passions involved were as ordinary as me and my sister Bessie fighting over who's going to cook the dinner. And who won't! (LAUGHTER) Those people in the park—you—me—every one—the greatest mistake we made was to imagine something magical separated us from Ludendorff and Kitchener and Foch.

Our leaders, you see. Well—Churchill and Hitler, for that matter! (LAUGHTER) Why, such men are just the butcher and the grocer—selling us meat and potatoes across the country. That's what binds us together. They appeal to our basest instincts. The lowest common denominator. And then we turn around and call them *extraordinary*! (HERE SHE TAPPED THE TABLE, RATTLING THE SHERRY GLASSES) See what I mean? You have to be awfully careful how you define the extraordinary. Especially nowadays. Robert Ross was no Hitler. That was his problem."

4: Easter was early in 1915. Good Friday fell on April 2nd. It snowed. Robert got off a train that morning in Kingston, Ontario. He carried a brand new suitcase and wore his checkered cap. His raincoat—also new—was of a style that soon would be known as the "Trench Coat." Its buttons were made of criss-crossed strips of leather and its salient feature was that it was short: short enough for you to wade in water up to your knees.

Robert stood alone to one side, watching the engine from under the eaves of the station. He was watching the stoker feed the flames with rattling shovelfuls of coal. He watched with his hands in his pockets—shoulders hunched and his toes pressed hard against his suitcase. At school he'd been taught that hunching the shoulders was an ungallant posture; still he maintained it while the engine bellowed and hissed. Great clouds of steam billowed out around its wheels. The "*fire horse*": that's what the Indians called it. Robert looked to one side from under the peak of his cap, hoping that no one had seen him flinch from the steam or stepping back from the fire. He was wishing they would leave. His shoulders hurt. His arm was sore. There were bruises on his back. He ached. He wanted all the others who had got off the train to depart the station before him. There must have been three dozen —forty or fifty men—all coming down from Toronto together—joining others from as far away as Winnipeg and Saskatoon. Most of them had swaggered up and down the cars like braggarts—smoking cigarettes and drinking out of silver flasks. Robert avoided them all through the journey—wanting to protect the last of his privacy. Now they were drifting away in groups of three and four—joshing and pushing one another—calling out names and throwing snowballs—singing songs.

Robert looked the other way down the platform where he saw three women. Two of them were young and smiling. The other was older and wore a nurse's uniform and cape. The younger ones were dressed in neat blue coats and one of them was watching him. Robert turned away, annoyed and confused. He was shy of girls, just now—disturbing them and wondering why they had to look at you and make you think you wanted them. Only a few weeks ago he had discovered he was not in love with Heather Lawson. Heather had behaved so inexplicably. What did women mean to do with men? At a party—in his own house—she'd told him that someone else was in love with her. Robert was not disturbed by this at all. What had someone else's being in love with her to do with him? But Heather Lawson wanted him to be disturbed. "All right," Robert said, "who is it? Maybe then I'll be disturbed." (He'd smiled.) "It's Tom Bryant," Heather said, "and I think you ought to fight him." Robert didn't understand. *Bryant?* Who was he? Did Heather Lawson love him? "No," she had said, "of course not."

"Then why should I fight him?" Robert had asked. "Because he *loves* me," she said. She spoke as if Robert were stupid. It all made perfect sense to Heather, but Robert thought it was idiotic and said so. Heather wailed out loud at that. Wailed and railed and paled. And fainted. In short—she made "a scene" of the sort then popular in the books of Booth Tarkington. All the guests at Robert's party left. There were even social complications for his parents in the aftermath and Heather said she never, never, never wanted Robert in her sight again. All because he wouldn't fight a man she didn't love and whom he'd never seen.

The matron snapped her fingers and the final cab was hailed. After their luggage had been lashed to the roof, the two young women made for the open door. One, not looking back, got in beside the matron but the other—just for an instant—turned and looked in Robert's direction. He was handsome—no question—even though his ears stuck out a bit too far and his jaw was unfashionably wide in an age of pointed features. Something in the way he stood alone appealed to her. But the matron's hand reached out and the girl was snapped inside like a folded doll and the cab was driven away. Looking back—her expression said "goodbye" and she was gone.

Twenty minutes later, Robert still stood there with his suitcase—immobile. He stood so resolutely still the Station Master came and asked him if he'd missed the train. Robert said no—that he was fine and if there was another cab, he'd hire it. But the Station Master said there were no more cabs. Just the standard quota and these days that was never enough, what with everyone coming and going all hours of every day and any day. The week had no more meaning. Even holy days of abstinence and sober significance like Sundays and Easter, the trains came and went and the people got on and off laughing just as if the world wasn't going to end.

"I suppose you've come down here like all them others to join with the Field Artillery, hunh?" he asked.

"Yes," said Robert.

"Well—I wish you luck, young man. The way they pile 'em in and outa here, it seems to me they're lookin' for a long, long wars."

"Yes, I guess they are," said Robert.

The Station Master went about his business, slowly making his retreat into the warmth of the Telegraph Office and Robert could see him talking to the Key Operator—chucking his thumb in Robert's direction—probably saying: "there's a queer young lad out there who doesn't seem to want to leave. . . ."

Robert picked up his suitcase and turned away towards the Station Yard. His shoulders ached. The bruises bore the brunt of the shift in weight every time he moved his arms. The yard was wide and wet. An old white dog was walking across the cinders toward the gate. Robert had stood so long, the snow had turned to rain. Off in the town, the Easter Passing Bells began to toll and Robert looked at his Oxford boots and gauged the width and depth of the nearest puddle brimming off the edge of the platform. Staring down expressionless, he watched as his reflection was beaten into submission by the rain. He turned his collar up and pulled the peak of his cap right down to the bridge of his nose. He closed his eyes and took a deep breath. The melting snow began to turn to mist and the mist was filled with rabbits and Rowena and his father and his mother and the whole of his past life

—birth and death and childhood. He could breathe them in and breathe them out.

Right to the very last second—hearing an approaching train that might have taken him home—he did not know in which direction he would go: down into the puddle and up to the town or back along the platform. The dog beyond the gate, bedraggled and lost, sat down to watch him. Maybe some decision of its own depended on which way Robert went. Then Robert closed his eyes and made his choice. He stepped down into the puddle and stood there.

How could he move?

Rowena had been buried the day before.

5: She fell. It was Sunday.

Stuart was meant to be watching her and so it was Stuart's fault but no—it wasn't Stuart's fault. It was Robert's fault. Robert was her guardian and he was locked in his bedroom. Making love to his pillows.

Jesus.

She fell.

It was Sunday.

Robert wasn't there.

6: She died on the Monday, never regaining consciousness. Mrs Ross wore a large, black hat. Robert wore an armband. People who only knew them from a distance saw them walking down the street and thought they must have lost someone they loved in the war.

Mister and Mrs Ross fell silent. They loved their children—all of them. Still, they were prepared for this. Children like Rowena weren't expected to live. The miracle was that she had lived so long as she had. Hydrocephalics had a life expectancy of ten to fifteen years at most. Rowena had been given ten years of grace.

Why had she fallen?

I don't know, said Stuart.

Why weren't you watching her?

I was playing with Meggy. (Teasing her—making her ears lie flat by whirling the baseball bat above her head.)

Didn't Rowena call you for help?

Nope.

Et cetera.

Nothing would be had from this line of questioning. Nothing would be had from any line of questioning. The thing was—she was dead.

It had happened in the stable, where she'd gone with Stuart to play with her rabbits and feed them. Stuart had dutifully pushed her through the snow and slush and past the neat manure pile and in through the double doors onto the brand new concrete floor that had been poured two weeks before so the Reo Run-about could share the stables with Meg and the rabbits. The rabbits were ranged in hutches down one side—the hutches built especially so Rowena could reach them from her chair. There were ten of them. Robert made them, late in the summer holidays three years before. In those days, the floor was just hard packed earth and everything smelled of hay and oats and pony manure. Rowena would sit with the doors wide open and take the rabbits one by one in her arms and hold them on her lap. Robert did his exercises, standing in the yard where she could see him. Indian clubs—a chinning bar and shadow boxing. Really, he was a long distance runner—but he did these other things to keep in shape. His hero was the great Tom Longboat—winner of the marathon. After the exercises, he and Rowena would take the rabbits out on the lawn and let them eat the grass.

Why had she fallen?

I don't know, said Stuart.

Weren't you watching her?

I was playing with Meggy.

Everyone's back was turned.

"Robert?"

"Yes, Rowena?"

"Will you stay with me forever?"

"Yes, Rowena."

"Can the rabbits stay forever, too?"

"Yes, Rowena."

This was forever. Now the rabbits had to be killed.

7: "Why do the rabbits have to be killed?"

"Because they were hers."

"But that can't possibly make any sense."

"Nonetheless, they must be killed."

"I'll look after them."

"Don't be ridiculous, Robert. Gracious! You're a grown up man."

"Can't we give them away?"

"Who to? Ten rabbits? Surely you can't be serious."

"What about Stuart? Why can't he look after them?"

"Knowing Stuart, I can't imagine why you ask that question."

"I'll take care of them. PLEASE!!!"

"Robert—control yourself."

Silence.

"Who's going to kill them, then?"

"You are."

Robert did not reply. He left his mother sitting in the wide bay windows where the ferns gave off the smell of summer. After he'd gone, she looked around the room and sighed. It seemed such a long, long way from where she sat to the other end . . . of everything.

8: Mrs Ross retired to her bedroom.

Mister Ross went up and knocked at the door.

No, she said.

9: The rest all happened on the one day. The Thursday.

Rowena was buried in the morning. Under the trees in frozen earth they had to split with axes. All the time the minister eulogized and all the time they prayed, it snowed. The coffin was white when they threw down the flowers. Robert looked over at his mother's face. Her mouth was set. She stood apart—refusing to be touched or supported. Miss Davenport was the only one who wept. Her hat was on crooked. Mister Ross kept his eyes closed the whole service.

Peggy's current beau was in uniform. He stood at attention. Robert envied him because he could go away when this was over and surround himself with space. (It was then, perhaps, the first inkling came that it was time for Robert to join the army. But he didn't think it consciously.) All he knew was that his hands felt empty. In his mind, they kept reaching out for the back of Rowena's chair. When they got back home, he moved it up to his room and sat there in it with his knees drawn up till the guests had left the parlour and the clock struck two.

Downstairs, his family sat at the dining room table waiting for him to appear. The subject of the rabbits floated to the top of the conversation. Robert could hear it vaguely through the floor. His mother was adamant. The rabbits had to die—and Robert had to do it. Mister Ross was inclined to be more lenient. Surely the rabbits could be killed somewhere else, he said. Maybe the butcher would want them. No, Robert's mother said. *It must be here and he must do it.*

"Why?"

"BECAUSE HE LOVED HER."

A chair fell over.

Footsteps.

Now his mother would be drinking in her bedroom. But no one would mention it.

A man called Teddy Budge was telephoned (unbeknownst to Robert—who was still in his overcoat seated in Rowena's chair.) This was at three o'clock or thereabouts. Teddy Budge was a large and mindless man who worked at the factory. There was nothing unkind or cruel in his nature—that was not the point. It was just that he would do what he was told. He was also very strong and could shift a rock as large as his arms could embrace, which Robert had seen him do in a contest once on Queen Victoria's birthday. Mister Ross placed the phone call—and even sent the Reo

Runabout down to the factory (driven by Peggy's beau) to bring Teddy Budge to the South Drive house.

Robert heard the car depart—and a good while later return. It sat in the driveway, idling, while Mister Ross went out and stood on the running board talking to Teddy Budge, who sat up high in the seat in his workman's clothes as if he was the King. Then he got down and made for the stables. Robert saw all this from his window.

It took him thirty seconds to emerge from his pain and to realize why Teddy Budge was there. He leapt up out of the chair and ran downstairs unthinking. Only knowing.

Stuart raced after.

Peggy said: "why is everybody running?"

Mister Ross was coming into the house and Robert pushed him aside, almost knocking him down going through the back door.

Robert's feet began to slip and to slide in the slush and the mud of the yard. He fell against the side of the car and part of his sight took in the soldier standing there, lighting a cigarette—and Robert yelled at him something like: "you bastard! Bastard! What are soldiers for?"—while the other part of his sight could see the open stable doors and the wide, Neanderthal back of Teddy Budge.

Robert regained his feet and lunged, butting his head like a battering ram between the giant's shoulder blades. Teddy only knew that he was being attacked. He couldn't see who by and he couldn't imagine why. His reaction was immediate and sensible, under the circumstances. He reached up over his head and grasped the only thing that came to hand. One of Robert's Indian clubs. With this he struck out blindly at the figure in the overcoat, whose face he could not see.

Well. The soldier and the father and the brother pulled the rock embracer away and prevented human murder. They carried Robert into the house—(more or less carried him: his feet were dragged along the ground) and at the door the father turned back and gave the man in the stable the signal to proceed with the business for which he had been summoned.

All these actors were obeying some kind of fate we call "revenge." Because a girl had died—and her rabbits had survived her.

10: That night Robert was lying in the bathtub, soothing his aches and bruises with water that was almost scalding hot. He'd rubbed wherever he could reach on his back with eucalyptus oil. His mother knocked at the door and before he could say: "who's there?" she had entered and closed the door behind her.

The room was full of steam. Mrs Ross was wearing a pale opal dress and long black mourning beads. On one side, her hair had loosened and it hung down in loops across her cheek. The other side was perfectly coiffed and pinned. She was smoking a cigarette and carrying an empty glass. For a moment she stood there, holding her hands in tight against her body as if for some reason Robert might take these possessions away from her. The glass and the cigarette were perhaps some sort of tangible evidence she was alive. Robert watched her with his arms hanging over the sides of the tub and the only sound was the dripping of the taps and the plash of a washcloth sliding into the water like something from the sea—afraid.

Mrs Ross—closing the toilet seat—sat down. She used the sink as an ashtray, carefully rolling the ashes off along its edge and watching them fall down the porcelain slopes like mountain climbers tumbling to their death. She shivered.

Robert looked away. His thoughts—that had seemed so consecutive and wise a moment before—began to stutter and shuffle to a halt. He sat there blank.

Mrs Ross said: "did he hurt you very badly?"

Robert said "no."

"There's such a large blue mark just above your shoulder blades," she said with a smile. "You look as if you'd gone to sea and had yourself tattooed."

"Yes. I could see it in the mirror."

"Do you want me to . . . help in any way?"

"No." Beat. "Thank you."

Mrs Ross tumbled another climber down the slope. "Once," she said, "when you were just a child . . ."

Robert closed his eyes. He hated the way she used his childhood—everyone's childhood as a weapon.

"You fell down. Skating."

"I fell down a lot."

"Yes. But this time you were skating. You bruised so easily. Your elbows and your knees swelled up—worse than Uncle Harry with the gout!" She laughed. "And your arms and thighs and your shins were simply *black* with bruises. Black and blue and yellow. Just like a savage painted for the wars. How alarmed we always were—every time you fell. . . ."

"Yes."

Suddenly Mrs Ross threw her head back and laughed. Robert looked at her to see what might be wrong. She laughed and laughed and laughed until the tears rolled down her cheeks and the cigarette fell from her fingers and she had to bend to pick it up. But the laughter was not hysterical, as Robert had feared. He waited for it to stop—and, finally, she explained.

"If only you'd seen yourself. Wearing those crazy

skates!" she said. "You were such a *serious* child. Everything was done with such great *concentration.*" Laughter. "Thump! Thump! Thump! You were coming up the walk. I don't know where you'd been—but you were walking on your ankles. Absolutely right down flat on your ankles wearing those crazy skates! And you had this great big stick in your hand. You were wearing a sweater—god knows whose it was!—but it was twice your size and the sleeves hung down like the arms of an ape and the waist came down to your knees! You were five years old and your hat had fallen off. Your hair was standing straight on end."

She set the empty glass on the floor and re-assembled herself—using toilet paper to wipe her eyes. After this she sighed and crossed her legs—looking as if she always came and sat in the bathroom with her son while he bathed. "You must've come a long, long way," she said. "That day. Your expression was so intent. And the ankles of your skates were almost worn right through. Do you remember that? I can even hear the sound of the blades as you scraped them over the bricks. Like someone sharpening knives." She blinked. "Still you persevered—and later you were captain of the Team."

Robert moved his legs around and the water lapped at the edges of the tub. His mother watched him—all the laughter fading from her eyes. If Robert had turned to look, the expression on her face might have frightened him. Yet people tend to look most often like themselves when no one else is watching. Her lips, at the corners, drew back involuntarily. Her mouth was dry. Her eyelids drooped. She watched her son with Delphic concentration while the smoke from her cigarette looped up and curled across her face. "Funny," she said; "how most people fall down and nothing happens. Some people bruise like apples. But most people—nothing."

"Yes."

While others die.

After a long, long silence Mrs Ross dropped the cigarette and used her toe to squash it out—grinding and twisting it into the tiles until it was just a mess of juice and paper, torn beyond recognition. For a moment she looked at what she'd done and then, without looking up, she spoke in a voice as passionless as sleep: "you think Rowena belonged to you. Well I'm here to tell you, Robert, no one belongs to anyone. We're all cut off at birth with a knife and left at the mercy of strangers. You hear that? *Strangers.* I know what you want to do. I know you're going to go away and be a soldier. Well—you can go to hell. I'm not responsible. I'm just another stranger. Birth I can give you—but life I cannot. I can't keep anyone alive. Not any more."

Robert sat frozen.

Mrs Ross stared at her empty glass. How long had it been empty? Hours? Minutes? Years? She stood up. She sat down. Nothing more was said. Each one faded from the other through the steam. This was the last time they breathed in one another's presence. In the morning he was gone before she woke.

11: So Robert Ross was admitted to the army, 2nd of April, 1915. Almost at once he was dispatched to join the 30th Battery, C.F.A. in training at Lethbridge, Alberta. He was studious and careful: exact. He watched the men around him from a distance. Some of them were friends from school. To these he was polite but he found excuses to keep them at bay. He wanted no attachments yet. What he wanted was a model. Someone who could teach him, by example, how to kill. Robert had never aimed a gun at anything. It was a foreign state of mind. So what he wanted was someone else who had acquired that state of mind: who killed as an exercise of the will.

The days were made of maps and horses: of stable drill and artillery range. They drilled from dawn to suppertime—wagons and limbers—rigs and harnesses—mountings and emplacements—dress parades and lines of fire. It was much like school: roll call and messhall. Even the pranks were the same—applepie beds and water bombs. Anyone who'd been to boarding school was well conditioned to rank. Someone shouted at you and you jumped. The difference was that, as you rose towards your commission, you were given a good deal more opportunity to shout back. Robert had been a cadet at St. Andrew's but he'd never enjoyed being an officer there. It offended him to raise his voice. Telling other people what to do made him laugh. Just as being told what to do made him angry. Consequently, on parade he was prone to a lot of blushing. For awhile he was known as "Red." This was the source, perhaps, of Robert's popularity. In spite of his aloofness—no one could dislike a man who blushed.

Evenings, Robert would sit on the stoop at the rear of the barracks' kitchen, wearing an old torn pair of flannels and a white shirt with a frayed collar and he would stare at the prairie, deciding which direction to run in. He knew if he stood on the roof he could turn 360 degrees sighting nothing but a distant barn or a dark green bluff of trees. These might be his destination on some of the runs—but he most often made for the horizon.

He would put on his shoes with the rubber soles—

(he never wore socks to run in)—tie his cardigan around his waist and start out walking. He didn't like to run inside the compound. It seemed undignified—perhaps it was too much like being told to run around the quad at school. But walking was an impediment. By the time he reached the gates he was already loping and beyond the gates the lope became the long, instinctive stride that was his natural gait. He kept his eyes cast down. He never watched the sky. He lost all sense of time. There was nothing to be won but distance.

12: One night, Robert ran with a coyote. At first he thought it was a dog until he realized no dog he'd ever seen had legs that long. It was running ahead of him when Robert first saw it—really little more than trotting. Its tail was down and its ears were laid back, which meant it had a destination. Robert had never seen an animal so thin. He wondered why it wasn't hunting and he thought perhaps there must be a place it went to hunt—some valley or slough that Robert hadn't yet discovered where there might be squirrels and rabbits. Robert decided to follow. He would not pick up his pace unless the distance between them was threatened. He recognized the coyote had no inkling of his presence simply because it made no attempt to alter its gait. They ran this way for almost half-an-hour.

Every once in a while the coyote would throw in an extra step—dancing to one side either around some hole in the ground or a stone. The holes in the ground didn't seem to interest it. Perhaps it knew they were dead. Maybe it knew every hole in the prairie and which ones had already offered up their suppers and breakfasts of gophers and sand owls. This was Robert's first thought—but then ahead of them he saw two gophers sitting upright—rising and falling—whistling to one another. The coyote must've seen them, too, but it didn't vary its pace at all—it didn't even come down off its toes. And when it came to the place where the gophers had been sitting, neither did it pause to scuffle the burrows or even to sniff at them. It just went right on trotting—forward towards its goal.

Soon after they'd passed the gopher holes the coyote broke from the trot to a canter. Robert adjusted his stride accordingly and, at first, he found there was little difficulty keeping pace. The previous pace had been so leisurely and steady that neither his lungs nor his legs were tired.

Since the race had begun to quicken, Robert imagined the coyote's destination must be within striking distance and he began to scan the prairie for a likely landmark. There was nothing—not even a mound of stones.

Then suddenly—the coyote disappeared. Vanished. Robert—at the most—had blinked and the beast was gone. He slowed his pace, thinking perhaps the animal would reappear; that maybe there was sweat in his eyes—or a den so perfectly camouflaged that in seconds he would trip at its door. But there was nothing.

Robert ran faster.

His cardigan began to slip down over his thighs. He pulled it off and knotted the arms around his neck. In front of him, as if the world were tipping in his face, he saw the blue-green leaves of trees. The branches seemingly rose straight out of the ground. Robert had come to a valley—as sudden as a pit.

He stopped at the edge, looking down. The valley

was neither wide nor long and was no more than forty or fifty feet deep at its centre. The sides dropped away in sharply incised runnels that indicated the ice age had played some part in forming it. The trees were gathered like whispering conspirators around the edges of a bright sheet of water. The coyote drank at the brink.

This was June and almost the summer solstice. The sun was still two hours from setting, though it was now about seven o'clock. The heat had deserted the day and the water sent a cool shock up the walls of the valley, striking at Robert as if a wind had risen. He put on his cardigan and hunkered down to watch the coyote drinking. It was below him, now—about sixty feet away with its back to him. This was why they'd come the distance. A rendezvous with water. Robert thought when the coyote had finished he would go down himself and maybe even swim. He hadn't been swimming in such a long time he couldn't remember when or where it had been, though it must have been last summer at Jackson's Point. Mister Ross had bought them a cottage there in 1900. It had tall green sides, plank and batten, and its deep shady porches were hung with hammocks and screened with bamboo blinds you could raise and lower on strings. Meg had been brought from some cousins down the road and ridden round and round the yard while Rowena begged to be lifted up and given a ride. . . .

Robert closed his eyes. The sound of the coyote lapping at the water crossed the distance between them and the sound seemed to satisfy his own thirst. He took a deep breath and sat like that, on his haunches, with his hands dangling down—fingertips brushing the raw blades of grass. The sun was shining on his face. He could feel that it was gold and red—just as he could feel that the grass was green. His face was a mirror to the sun.

When the coyote had drunk its fill it turned from the water and suddenly sat down, scratching violently behind its ear. Then it sat, panting and looking around the valley just like a thoroughly satisfied owner. It threw its nose to the air and snapped at some passing insect. It scratched its ear again but this time with the supreme indolence of a dog before a fire. It carefully tasted the tips of its blunted claws and licked them clean before it rose and trotted off through the trees. It had rested ten minutes.

Robert lost sight of it and was beginning to think perhaps its den was in the bluff when he saw it again, climbing the opposite bank of the valley. As it came to the edge it had to hoist itself over the top. This caused a bit of a scramble and the air filled up with dust. The coyote shook itself—turned around and Robert thought it was going to come back for some reason—that perhaps it had made a mistake traversing the whole of the valley and now must return the way it had come. But instead—it stood on the opposite bank, threw back its head and howled. Then it looked directly at him—right at Robert, with its tail slightly lowered—and barked. Then the tail began to wag. The coyote had known he was there the whole time: maybe the whole of their run across the prairie. Now it was telling Robert the valley was vacant: safe—and that Robert could proceed to the water's edge to drink. It barked three times—a precise announcement it was leaving. Then it turned around and trotted off towards the sun.

Robert was late that night for lights out. His punishment was that he was confined to barracks for two weeks. In the evenings, he sat on the roof and stared and stared and stared across the prairie—wishing that someone would howl.

13: It was because of horses that Robert met Eugene Taffler. They met on the prairie.

Robert had been assigned to a detail, earlier that day, whose job it had been to bring in some wild horses that had come down from Calgary. They were mustangs and later that week—destined as mounts for officers in France—they were to be broken one by one. They were magnificent horses with tremendous stamina—but they also had a lot of independent spirit. Getting them back to the Depot from the station was a job for cowboys, not for men whose only previous experience of riding had been around the circle of Queen's Park Crescent. They took a wild and circuitous route—miles out into the prairie—and the exercise that had begun at 9:00 a.m. was not concluded till sometime after 4:00 p.m.

When all the horses had been corraled, it was discovered two of them were missing. Robert, being well acquainted now with the prairie (this was August), volunteered to ride out and see if he could find them. A boy who had gone to St Andrew's with Robert—whose name was Clifford Purchas—volunteered to go out with him. After supper, they ventured in the direction of the barn Robert had seen from the roof which was about a mile distant.

As they rode, Robert and Clifford sang old hymns they'd learned at school. They sang at the tops of their lungs and they sang the old hymns because they were the only songs they mutually knew. Clifford also knew an obscene version of "Oh, Susannah!" which he sang in a high, clear tenor with exactly the same pitch of intensity he'd just applied to the Old Hundredth. When the song had reached its carnal peak—Robert suddenly said: "be quiet!" and reined in his horse.

"What is it?" Clifford asked.

"That's what I want to know," said Robert and nodded to one side where a figure could be seen throwing stones at a row of bottles lined up on a board. This person was about a hundred yards distant and was stripped to the waist, with his braces hanging down. A saddled horse was grazing about ten feet away from him and a dog was seated, with its ears erect, watching him. Every stone the man threw hit a bottle. He didn't miss once.

As Robert and Clifford sat there watching, the dog must have caught their scent, for it turned around and began to bark.

The man with the stones in his hand gave a friendly wave and called out: "hallo!" Then he threw another stone and broke another bottle.

Robert said: "who is it?"

Clifford said: "that's Eugene Taffler, you idiot."

Robert said: "oh." Subdued. Taffler was a hero. He'd already been to France—wounded and returned to Canada. Now he was fully recovered and sent West to look over the horse flesh prior to being re-posted overseas. He had also been a Varsity all-round athlete, though this was before Robert's time and therefore Taffler's face was not familiar to him. His name, however, was credential enough.

"Are we going over?" Clifford asked.

"I s'pose so," said Robert. He didn't want to go over. Even the thought of Taffler intimidated him. Still, it was impossible not to go, since Taffler was a Captain and therefore senior to Clifford and himself.

They rode over slowly.

"You're out looking for those mustangs, aren't you," Taffler said. He was over six feet tall and his face and torso were shrouded in dust. His mouth, his eyes and his nipples looked as if someone had been sculpting him and had left their thumbprints behind.

Robert said: "yes, sir. We lost them in this area this morning."

Taffler juggled the stones in his hand. Aureoles of dust appeared.

"I could come with you, if you think I'd be useful," he offered.

"No thankyou, Captain," Robert said, "We're sorry to have disturbed you."

"I suppose you wonder what in hell I'm doing, eh?" Taffler gave them a smile. "Wellllll . . ." he drawled and squinted at the bottles—took aim and threw a stone. It arrived and the bottle was demolished, "That's what I'm doing," he said. "Killing bottles."

"Oh," said Robert.

"I have to keep my arm in, you see."

"Yes, sir!" said Clifford with enthusiasm. "I've seen you give those varsity passes. What a pity."

"A pity, Mister . . . ?"

"Purchas, sir."

"A pity, Mister Purchas? Why's that?" He took aim and fired again.

Bam!

"Oh, I don't know, sir. Maybe just that we aren't all playing football, I guess."

Taffler looked off towards the sun.

"Yes," he said. "It's a pity." Then he turned and looked at the horsemen. "The distance," he said, "between our lines and theirs is often no more than a hundred yards. Did you know that?"

"No, sir."

"One hundred yards," said Taffler. He gestured at the remaining bottle. It was green and had a tall, thin neck. "All you get in this war," he said, "is one little David against another." Then he threw—and broke the tall, thin neck clean off. "Like that. Just a bunch of stone throwers."

Robert wondered if the bitterness was only the twist in his throat as he threw the stone—or was it really that Taffler wanted the war to pit him against Goliath?

Taffler reached down and picked up his shirt.

"You're sure I can't help?"

"Yessir. Thankyou, sir."

"Good." He smiled again. "There's still an hour till sundown. The dog and I can go and kill some rattlesnakes."

This was the end of their conversation and since Taffler was out of uniform they were not obliged to salute him, so they simply turned around and rode away. Robert forced his horse ahead of Clifford's at a gallop—Clifford crying after him: "alley! alley! alley!" just as if Robert had sighted a fox. But Robert galloped so far ahead that in minutes he was riding alone. Then, looking back, he saw that Clifford had given up pursuit and was ambling along at a trot—probably singing "Home on the Range." It was only then that Robert slowed to a walk. Taffler was just a dot on the horizon. Dots were anonymous. Don't ask questions. Distance was safety. Space was asylum.

Later that evening they rode home through sunset leading behind them two captured mustangs. The sky held both the sun and the moon. Far, faraway the coyotes howled. Robert kept on riding—leading. Clifford wondered out loud if Taffler could kill a coyote with a stone. The sky was green. Robert did not reply. He was thinking that perhaps he'd found the model he could emulate—a man to whom killing wasn't killing at all but only throwing. Bam! A bottle. A man to whom war wasn't good enough unless it was bigger than he was. Bam! A David. A man who made his peace with stones.

The sun began to sink. It was enormous. Clifford wanted to stop and watch. Robert said no. He was afraid to turn around and look, though he didn't know why. It just seemed dangerous. So they went on riding. Clifford sang. *"Bring me, oh bring me a cup of cold water, and cool my temple, the cowboy said; but when they returned with the cup of cold water, the spirit had left and the cowboy was dead. . . ."* Slats of orange were lifted all along the horizon. Four horses. Two horsemen.

14: The summer had been dry. When autumn came, the situation was reversed. It rained unceasingly. All over North America and Europe the rain poured down from late September through to the end of October. In November, it began to snow. It even snowed in England, where it hadn't snowed in years.

All through the prairie autumn Robert's parents showered him—almost perversely—with scarves and socks and mittens, most of which Robert gave away. They also sent him food. To them, it seemed he'd stepped outside the bounds of civilization—where people didn't wear clothes or eat cooked meat. Much that was useful, however, also arrived: the necessary accoutrement the army did not provide—such as liquid compasses and riding boots and blue-tinted field glasses. Robert also wrote to his father, saying he would like an automatic pistol. This letter produced some panic.

"DON'T THEY EVEN ARM YOU?" his father telegraphed. "ONLY WITH ARTILLERY" Robert replied.

Lest Robert's having to ask for his own side arms make no sense to those of you who weren't around or haven't read this part of history, it should be pointed out that this was a "people's army"—not an army of professionals. Officers provided their own uniforms and sometimes even their own horses if they so desired. Citizens with means raised their own regimental companies and financed their outfittings. Commissions could still be bought and even the private soldier got his socks from home. At any rate—many telegrams and letters were passed back and forth about this pistol. Would it be a Webley or a Colt—a Browning or a Savage? Its fate, like the fate of Leopold Bloom's bar of soap, became a minor Odyssey.

One last incident remains to be told of Robert's sojourn on the prairie. This is about the whores of Lousetown.

15: Lousetown was a hamlet twelve miles from Lethbridge—or "twelve miles high" as someone said. It would not be fair to reveal its true name because it has since become a respectable farming centre. In the old days, however, it was just a collection of houses—seven of them—sitting in the middle of nowhere. The road was hardly more than a pair of ruts. The houses were made of wood and have since been burned. The only building shared in common with the present was a General Store then run by a man called Oscar Dreyfus. But Dreyfus was a name that had fallen into bad repute, so the sign read OSCAR'S DRYGOODS. There were even people who called him that. "Hallo, Mister Drygoods!" they would call out, laughing as they went in. "How's

Mrs Drygoods?" *Mrs Drygoods* was the madam of the house next door. Her name was Maria—but she firmly adhered to the Dreyfus. Maria Dreyfus could read—and she had read *"J'Accuse!"* Her name was something of which she was very proud. But "Drygoods" stuck with everybody else and since beyond Maria's was the garbage dump, you had what came to be known as DRYGOODS, WET GOODS and SPOILED GOODS all in a row. *Wet Goods* was the favourite house in town.

Robert had to be coerced into going against his better judgement. But the "coercion" was simple. He was shamed into going. If you didn't go, you were peculiar. It was that simple. The barracks and the boarding school leave little room for the individual when it comes to sex. Either you "do" or you "don't" and if you "don't" you face a kind of censure most men would rather avoid.

As for its being against his better judgement—Robert was certain he would fail.

They went on a Friday night in a Chevrolet. It rained and the high, thin tires of the car kept bogging down in the ruts. As a consequence, when they arrived they were spattered with mud from cap to boot: Clifford Purchas, Roddy Taylor-Bennett, Robert and a man called Gas who seemed to be a civilian. All the way there, Mister Gas and Clifford Purchas sang while Roddy Taylor-Bennett drank from a bottle of sherry. The Chevrolet's interior stank of cigarettes and Florida Water cologne. Clifford dubbed it their "whorehouse on wheels."

Wet Goods' windows were agleam with blue lights—(blue lights for Officers—red lights for the men. Once, some card had placed a yellow light for quarantine in the window of a house across the street where body lice ran rampant.) Robert got out first. He was hatless. The rain felt good. Roddy Taylor-Bennett handed out the bottle. "Finish it," he said. Robert thought for once he would like to be drunk and tilted the bottle skyward, draining it dry. He had never been drunk before—and the smell of the bottle reminded him of his mother's room at home.

The road through Lousetown faded into grass beyond the garbage dump. It was not the sort of street that people hung about in, even in the best of weather. Now there was only a collection of dogs to greet them. Dogs—and a horse.

This horse was tethered to a hitching post in front of *Wet Goods*. It was standing with its head down. As Robert looked—he discerned there was a shape in the mud below its belly. When he and the others stepped up onto the boards of the sidewalk, Robert kept on looking at this shape and wondered what it was and why that juxtaposition of the horse and the shape disturbed him. Then—as he searched for a place to deposit the empty bottle—he twigged. Taffler. And the shape was Taffler's dog. Robert knew where to leave the bottle. He left it with a stone on top, by the hitching post.

16: On entering *Wet Goods*, you were greeted by a large, male mute who was said to be Swedish. His hair was of the white-blond shade most often associated with albinos. His eyes were the colour of steel and he had killed three men. A negro woman took away your coats and called you "Cap'n" no matter what your rank. Then you were left to stand in the hallway, not quite sure which way to turn.

There was a stairway with a potted fern on the landing. Directly opposite the door, there was a wall that was covered with paintings of Odalisques and mirrors, so the first thing you saw was yourself, intermingled with a lot of pink arms and pale breasts. Sweet rose perfumes mitigated the smell of horse and dog manure that came in on your boots.

Robert waited with his hands behind his back. It was not as he'd expected. He'd thought they would enter and be greeted by a horde of naked women wafted on clouds of opium. It was not like that at all. It was really quite sedate. In a moment, Maria Dreyfus came into the hallway from a room that had been hidden by a pair of sliding doors. Maria was German. She was small—with bright copper hair, frizzy as a Medusa's and she wore a black dress. She made no more apology for being a German than she did for being a Jew. She put out her hand and said: "good effning." Nobody laughed at the way she spoke. Her presence and her bearing forbade it. She ushered them into the room beyond the doors and the doors slid closed behind them.

In the room, there were seven girls and two other men. The men were cowboys, presumably, or railroad men or farmers' sons. At any rate, they were not in the army. Robert could not tell whether they were "finished" or "beginning." He had no idea of procedure. Neither, as it turned out, had any of the others he'd come with, with the possible exception of Mister Gas, who seemed to be known to one of the women.

The women—(or girls: they were really both)—at first appeared to be dressed like actresses in a play. The colours they wore were high-toned and garishly mixed: chartreuse and black—orange and blue. It was not until his eyes had adapted to the golden glow of the lamps that Robert realized he could see right through the dresses and the shadows weren't shadows but the shadings of hair and of nipples rouged with henna.

Whiskey bottles sat on a silver tray. Mister Gas went up and poured himself a drink. Robert did likewise. Every man in the room went over and stood by the whiskey bottles. The women sat discreetly waiting. They were smiling. Finally, Maria Dreyfus saw there was an impasse and went around the room booming at the girls: "minkle! Minkle! Shtand und minkle!" She placed a disc on the gramophone and started it spinning.

A girl with orange-red hair that was piled on top of her head came across the room at Robert. Her shoulders were naked bones and her eyelids were painted black. She was wearing a violet dress that was open down the front and tied with a sash and she seemed to be a walking pelvis.

"You wanna trot?" she said to Robert, breathing cloves in his face.

"Trot?" Robert asked.

"Dance."

"I don't think I know how to do that," said Robert. He didn't trust women with red hair. Heather Lawson had red hair.

"All right," said the girl with the cloves in her mouth. "Then I'll show ya." She said her name was Ella.

She put both her arms around his neck and pressed her pelvis hard against his groin. Robert was immobilized.

"Move," she said and pushed.

Robert began to stumble around to the music—"nigger music" as it was called in those days—full of shouts and thumping pianos and a golden wailing cornet. The dancers pressed around and around the room and the heat from the stove in the corner and the airlessness and the raw, high taste of the whiskey soon began to have an effect that was dizzying and Robert had never felt so far away from the floor before in his life. The dancing—pelvis to pelvis—had a kind of crazy, marching formality to it—everyone locked in military pairs—round and round and round—straight-backed and stiff-legged. Round and around and around, till Clifford Purchas fell down drunk on the rug. No one paid the least attention. Everyone went on dancing. Clifford lay on his back—with his eyes wide open—gazing upward, ecstatic. "I can see it," he said as the women stepped above his face. "Lordy, Lordy! I can see it! Look at that!"

Finally, Maria Dreyfus thought he'd lain there long enough. She clapped her hands for the mute and Clifford was lifted giggling from the floor and carried up the stairs, hanging down the Swede's wide back with his fingers dabbling in the skirts of the woman who followed him. Everyone applauded.

The music ended.

Robert was stranded in the centre of the room with Ella. Mister Gas had made his selection and nodded at Maria. Maria nodded back and she pinched his arm as he passed with the girl of his choice. "Enjoy. Enjoy," she said. Then, turning to the rest of the room, she smiled. People were going upstairs. Everyone was happy. Roddy Taylor-Bennett was next—taking a tall, dark girl with holes in the heels of her stockings.

Robert looked at Ella. Ella smiled.

The cowboys sat down—one with a girl on his lap. Robert watched as the cowboy slid his hand inside her dress to fondle her breasts. In fact he could see her breasts—and the nipples starting to harden under the calloused fingers.

Robert became alarmed. Even frightened. He thought they were going to "do it"—sitting right there in the chair with the girl's legs dangling over the cowboy's thighs and everyone watching. He looked at Maria

Dreyfus to see if she would stop them but Maria was pouring herself a drink and her back was to the room. Part of Robert's panic was his fear of what his own hands would do. It seemed they were magnets, drawn to his groin, and he had to fight to stop them from moving.

Ella was watching him.

Robert swallowed. "Have you got another clove?" he asked.

"Sure," she said and handed him one.

They went upstairs.

17: Robert sat on the edge of the bed with his hands folded on his knees. Ella was looking in the mirror, wondering what to do with this strange young man. He sat so still and he wouldn't look at her.

"Isn't there nothing special you'd like?" she said. "I mean—here we are and everything." She turned around and leaned against the washstand, playing with her sash, threatening to reveal herself.

Robert didn't know what to say. What was special?

"Look," said Ella. "This is what I'm *paid* for. To make ya happy. O.K?"

But how? Robert wanted to ask—except he didn't know how to put that into words. Nothing he'd read had covered this situation. Whores, of course, had been discussed at school but no one actually ever said *this is what you do*. They'd made it all up. But what they'd made up was not like this. At all. They'd flown from trapezes and made love in bath tubs and ravished several women tied to the bed posts, but no one had ever sat in a room with lilac wallpaper and been asked if there was "nothing special you'd like."

"Don't ya wanta touch me?" said Ella.

Yes; Robert thought. And no. He had sort of a problem he couldn't discuss.

"You're the most serious person I ever met," said Ella. "In my whole life I never met a man who didn't *say* nothin'. 'Cept acourse the Swede. But his tongue was cut out by In'ians." She sat down beside him and put her hand on the back of his neck. She was smiling. "Your tongue in there?" she said and ran her finger over his lips. "You're a nice hot lookin' boy," she said; "an' we shouldn't just be sittin' here. Why don't you let me . . . ?" And she put her hand inside his pants. Right inside—past his drawers. No one else had ever touched him there before. Heather Lawson's hand had rested on his thigh one night—and when he'd moved, to get her fingers closer to the mark, she'd thought he meant to move her away and withdrew her fingers and hadn't made that gesture again. It was not something Robert knew how to ask for. Now, the situation was worse.

"Oh," said Ella. But she was kind about it. She went on smiling—and kissed him at the corner of his lips. When she withdrew her hand, she kept it in a fist and crossed to the washstand. Then she picked up a towel and told him to stand up.

"You take them off," she said, nodding at his trousers; "an' I'll clean you up."

Robert had ejaculated coming up the stairs. His body hadn't waited for his mind. It did things on its own.

Robert lay back with his arm across his eyes. Ella performed her task with efficiency and tact. Nothing was said about what had happened. Even when Robert blushed, she had looked away in order to smile.

"There," she said and threw the towel across the

room. Then she clambered onto the bed and sat with her knees drawn up and watched him. "It'd be nicer to look at your face than it is to look at your arm," she smiled. Robert did not respond. "Hey," she said. She reached out and gave his arm a push. It fell aside. Robert stared at the ceiling. Ella sat back and lighted a cigarette. "You smoke?" Robert shook his head. "Well —at least we know you're alive!" She laughed.

Robert wanted to cover himself but he didn't know how to do that without making it look as if that was what he was doing. He thought of rolling over—but that would expose his backside.

"You oughtn't to be ashamed, you know," said Ella. "There's lotsa fellows do what you done. Specially the first time. An'—hell—I wish I could even begin to tell ya how many fellows can't do nothin'."

Robert sat up. He pulled the sheets across his lap.

"Look," said Ella; "we got all night: give yourself a little rest an' then—"

Robert stared at the floor.

"Jesus!" she said. "If you don't take the cake!" Now she was angry. "Dontcha un'erstand—if you don't do me I don't get paid!"

Finally, Robert looked at her.

"How would anyone know . . . ?" he asked.

"She'll know from the way you walk down them stairs," said Ella. "Guys that done it got a way o' walkin'. An' guys that haven't done it got a way o' walkin', too. She'll know. She c'n tell."

"But what difference does it make?" Robert asked.

"We ain't workin' if we don't do it, she says. Don't ask me. It's just her rule. Everybody's s'posed to *enjoy themselfs*." She imitated Maria. *"Minkle! Minkle! Ever'body gotta minkle 'n' screw!"* Ella laughed at herself. Then she got serious again. "She says if you go away unlaid, her house'll get a bad reputation. No one's s'posed to go away unlaid. That's her rule."

Robert heard a thump in the next room.

Then there were several other thumps and the sound of someone being slapped. Robert was sorry you could hear through the walls. He thought: now someone knows about me.

Ella got off the bed and tip-toed to the wall. Robert thought she was going to listen—but, instead, she leaned in close and placed her eye to one of the lilacs. She stood this way for several seconds and then she waved at him to join her.

"What are you doing?" he said. He thought she'd gone peculiar, poking her face at the wall and staring at the lilacs, waving at him like that.

"Shhh!" said Ella. "Hush and come here."

Robert shuffled across the floor—wrapped in the sheet.

"Lookit," she said, when he arrived beside her. She took him by the back of the neck and pushed him forward. The lilacs blurred, and he wondered what it was she meant to do with him and what sort of perversion this was and then he saw that one of the lilacs wasn't a lilac at all but a camouflaged hole. He could see right through to the room next door.

Ella's hand remained on the back of his neck so he couldn't step aside, even if he'd wanted to. But what he saw so confused him that he stood there on his own volition—desperately trying to comprehend. There were certainly two naked people—but all he could see at first was backs and arms and legs. Whoever it was who was there was standing in the middle of the floor hitting whoever else was there—striking out with all their force. Robert turned aside and leaned with his back against the wall. He'd never even dreamed of such a thing—of being hit and wanting to be hit. Beaten. Or of striking someone else because they'd asked you to. At school they'd done strange things but nothing as strange as this.

Ella took his place at the spy hole and after a few more seconds—she was giggling.

How could it possibly be funny?

Ella was like a child. She pulled him back and made him look again, laying her finger on his lips for silence.

Robert stared—one-eyed and breathless.

The pummelling had stopped and, at first, he could not locate the people in the room. Then he heard them. Breathing. They were breathing in tandem—just like two people running side by side. But where? He shifted his position. The bed could just be seen. Since Robert could only use one eye, everything was flat and undimensional. The bed appeared to be stuck against the wall like a picture. And on it there were two undimensional people—one as pale as the other was dark. One was lying on his back with his back arched off the mattress while the other sat astride his groin exactly like a rider. The one who played the horse was bucking—lifting his torso high off the bed, lifting the weight of the rider with his shoulders and his knees—and bucking, just like the mustangs Robert and the others had broken in the summer. The rider was using a long silk scarf as reins and the horse was biting into the other end with his teeth. The only sound was the sound of breathing and of bedsprings. The rider held the reins in one hand and, using a soldier's stiff-peaked cap, beat the horse on the thighs—one side and then the other. And the two—both horse and rider—were staring into one another's eyes with an intensity unlike any other Robert had ever seen in a human face. Panic.

Robert's heart was beating so fast he thought it

would explode. Even when he looked away and Ella took his place again he went on hearing and seeing everything he'd heard and seen in his mind and his mind began to stammer the way it always did whenever it was challenged by something it could not accept. He walked across the room and sat on the bed. He picked up a boot and held it in his hand. Its weight alarmed him and the texture of its leather skin appalled him with its human feel. He threw the boot across the room and shattered the mirror.

Then he threw the other boot and broke the water jug.

Ella ran and crouched in the corner—folding her arms across her head, afraid.

Robert didn't move.

Tick-tick-tick went the water.

Tick—tick—tick.

The man being ridden was Taffler. The rider was the Swede.

Goliath.

18: Robert remained at Lethbridge the whole of that autumn till late in November when he was sent back to Kingston, Ontario for further studies in military law and trajectory mathematics. Taffler had long since gone and the rumour was he'd been returned to France, although his picture appeared in the *Canadian Illustrated*—showing him in London with Lady Barbara d'Orsey: HERO AND DAUGHTER OF MARQUIS!

Passing through Regina, Robert saw a band of Indians—twelve or fourteen of them—standing by the railroad track. They all wore blankets, held against the winter wind. This was very early in the morning. All the soldiers pressed against the windows looking out. One of the Indians sat on a horse. The horse's head was bowed. Even though the wind blew—even though the snow was lifted from the ground and blown around their feet, the Indians did not make any motion to depart. They stood and stared at all the faces—ghosts through the frosted glass. Their eyes were pitchy black. Robert wanted everyone to raise an arm in greeting. Why should the Indians not be greeted standing by the railroad track? But nobody moved. Everyone was frozen in their places—staring till the train removed them—slowly tearing them apart like paper torn in half. All across the prairie, down through Winnipeg into the forests, pushing North of Superior past the Sleeping Giant, stuttering through the Sault and down, down, down the arms of rock and the broken, frozen fingers of nameless rivers, heralded by steam and whirling snow, the train returned him to his heritage of farms and cottages and cattle caught in fields by fences. Then he could smell the city of his birth—even though it lay about him in the dark—and he stood and he stared as he passed the fires of his father's factories, every furnace blasting red in the night. What had become of all the spires and the formal, comforting shapes of commerce he remembered—banks and shops and business palaces with flags? Where were the streets with houses ranged behind their lawns under the gentle awnings of the elms? What had happened here in so short time that he could not recall his absence? What were all these fires—and where did his father and his mother sleep beneath the pall of smoke reflecting orange and red and yellow flames? Where, in this dark, was the world he'd known and where was he being taken to so fast there wasn't even time to stop?

Transcript: Marian Turner—2:

"What you people who weren't yet born can never know is what it meant to sleep in cities under silent falls of snow when all night long the only sounds you heard were dogs that barked at trains that passed so far away they took a short cut through your dreams and no one even woke. It was the war that changed all that. It was. After the Great War for Civilization—sleep was different everywhere. . . ."

19: Robert and his brother officers were not in Kingston long. Every aspect of the war had worsened. Gallipoli had proved to be disaster. The Allies would have to withdraw. The Germans and the Austrians had reached deep into Russia—three hundred miles to the Pripet Marshes. Poland had fallen. Serbia was about to fall. All the Allies could think to do was to change their leaders in the field. Haig replaced French—the Tsar replaced his cousin, the Grand Duke Nicholas—Joffre was thrown the whole of the French Command in a gesture of desperate consolidation. (General French retired to his bed and wrote his King that General Haig was "mad.") All the Field Marshals seemed to be able to do was bicker and politick in behalf of their own reputations. Thousands were dying in battles over yards of mud. From Canada the word went out that thousands more were ready. It was at this precise moment that Robert received his promotion to Second Lieutenant. He was now a fully commissioned officer and ripe for the wars. On December 18th, 1915 the 39th Battery, C.E.F.—which Robert had joined in Kingston—was embarked on the *S.S. Massanabie* in St John Harbour. Three days before, with a bottle of wine provided by Clifford Purchas, he celebrated his birthday. They did this at midnight—singing songs in the latrine, long after lights out. Robert even smoked a cigarette. He was nineteen years old.

On August the fourth of 1914, Kaiser Wilhelm had stood on the *Unter den Linden* beneath the protection of a wide marquee. His withered arm was attached, as always, by a hook to his sabre. He was relaxed and smiling. The sky was full of birds and small white clouds. The Kaiser made a gesture with his good right arm and the gesture embraced the rows and rows of lovely shade. Then he said to his departing troops: "you will be home before the leaves have fallen from these trees!"

And now, the leaves had fallen twice. It was not for nothing he'd stood beneath the wide marquee that summer day. It would fill and fall on everyone.

20: Longboat, Robert's hero, was an Indian. He ran the marathon. He won things. Then he smiled and was silent. Robert smiled and was silent, too. He'd go upstairs into the attic, when he was ten, and take off his clothes in front of an old, dark mirror and wish that he was red. Or black. Or yellow. Any colour but pink. Smiling and silence didn't seem to go with pink. One night, later on when Robert was twelve—he decided he would run the marathon himself. Twenty-six times around the block—down through the ravine and back along the sidewalk—running in his bare feet. He did this after supper one night—while his father watched from the porch and counted off the laps. Twenty-six times. On top of liver and bacon with scallopped tomatoes. This was unwise. Mrs Ross and Eena the maid both said so. "He will die," they said. "Twenty-six times on top of supper! Surely he is mad!" But Tom Ross said: "no—let him. This is what he wants to do." In the end—by the 24th lap—the porch was crowded with all the Rosses—Bimbo the dog—Eena the maid and Charles the gardener—*cheering*. People even came out onto their lawns along the street and waved and called out "Keep on going!"—"Don't give up!"—and "That's the spirit, Robert!!!"

Then Robert fainted. Just at the end of the 25th lap. Fainted and was down with jaundice.

His father got him through it.

He came up every evening after work and sat in Robert's darkened room and talked to him and told him stories. None of the stories had to do with running. These were tales of voyages and ships and how to ride a horse. This was the binding of the father to the son. When the ordeal was over—Tom Ross took his boy upstairs and watched while Robert stood in front of the old dark mirror, slipping out of his pajamas and seeing that his skin was different now (a sort of ochre yellow). Robert smiled and was silent. He went downstairs in his dark skin and stayed that way for another day.

Tom Ross understood, it seemed. He too smiled and was silent. When Mrs Ross asked him what he was thinking of, he shrugged. But he was thinking of the time he'd climbed the steeple of a church when *he* was ten—and had seen, for the very first time, the world spread out around him like a gift.

* * *

Robert Raymond Ross—Second Lieutenant, C.F.A.

He is wearing his uniform. Nothing is yet broken down. Every stitch is stiff as starch. The boots are new —the latest gift from his father. He carries a riding crop made of Algerian leather. The grip is finely braided and Robert holds it lightly in his right hand— pointing it towards the ground. He is posed in mind and body. Only his left hand disobeys his will. Its fingers curl to make a fist.

Dead men are serious—that's what this photograph is striving to say. Survival is precluded. Death is romantic—got from silent images. I lived—was young— and died. But not real death, of course, because I'm standing here alive with all these lights that shine so brightly in my eyes. Oh—I can tell you, sort of, what it might be like to die. *The Death of General Wolfe.* Someone will hold my hand and I won't really suffer pain because I've suffered that already and survived. In paintings—and in photographs—there's never any blood. At most, the hero sighs his way to death while linen handkerchiefs are held against his wounds. His wounds are poems. *I'll faint away in glory hearing music and my name. Someone will close my eyes and I'll be wrapped around in flags while drums and trumpets-bagpipes march me home through snow. . . .* Afterwards, my mother will escort her friends across the rugs and parquet floors to see this photograph of me and everyone will weep and walk on tip-toe. Medals—(there are none just yet, as you can see)—will sit beside this frame in little boxes made of leather lined with satin. I will have the Military Cross. *He died for King and Country*—fighting the war to end all wars.

5 X 9 and framed in silver.

* * *

21: They went on board at ten o'clock and now it was nearly two. Robert was in a stateroom with Clifford Purchas, Captain Ord and a young lad called Harris from Sydney, Nova Scotia. The *S.S. Massanabie* was in convoy with other ships but just how many, no one was certain. Some were in the harbour—more were beyond the furthest point of land, unseen. There were rumours of a storm but there was nothing now except a low, grey sky and a damp demoralizing cold.

At two, there was commotion. Robert made his way on deck. Everyone was greatly excited. Horses were being brought on board. This was unexpected. No one had been told.

Each horse was lifted in a harness by a gigantic crane and lowered into the hold like cargo. Robert had never seen such a sight. A hundred and forty horses were brought aboard this way. High in the air, each horse lifted its head and cried aloud. Just once. And this was the only sound they made. Once they were all secured, the hatches were closed and the *S.S. Massanabie* pulled away from the dock and sat for an hour or more in the middle of the harbour. Now they must wait for the tide.

Someone came around and said the last tender would be leaving in a while and anyone with messages or letters had best get them ready. Robert wrote to his father and expressed his surprise at having seen him in Montreal. As the troop train sat in the yards, Robert had looked from the windows and seen the RAYMOND/ROSS private railway car sitting three or four tracks away at a siding partly obscured by an engine with a snow plough. It didn't seem possible. How had his father known he would be there? And why—though he didn't ask this in his letter—if his father had been able to come, hadn't Mrs Ross accompanied him? Anyway, the sight of his father had lifted his spirits immeasurably. And the feel of his father's hand on his arm had brought him back into a world he'd thought he'd lost. Even so, he had to write that the revolver his father had brought him—and come all the way to Montreal to deliver in person—was not the kind he wanted. Mister Ross had handed him a polished wooden box and cautioned him not to open it till the train had started moving. Now Robert wrote: "I guess the only thing to do is send it back and get the Rice-Lewis people where you bought it to refund the money."

Inside the box, there was a Colt six-shooter. Robert had wanted an automatic. "I hasten to add, it's not your fault," he wrote. "The last time I telegraphed I should have been certain they put down .455 and I guess they put down .45. I could put it in a parcel now, except I mustn't be without sidearms as an officer. I'll keep it till we get to England and have it returned from there. Maybe Mister Hawkins could forward it—slip it into the company packet or something. The fact is, some of the other officers were all set to take along six-shooters too but someone who knows about these things says an automatic is imperative once you get in the trenches. Since all this involves my safety, I'm sure you'll agree it's the right thing to do."

Clifford Purchas said that Robert should send his "love" to Peggy. Robert nodded as though he might—but he didn't. He and Clifford had been on the outs since Clifford had borrowed some money and not returned it. Oddly, too, he didn't feel like sending love to anyone. It seemed unmanly. What he did do was enclose a photograph (official) and say to his father: "this will show you that my draft makes a brawling, husky lot of men. Not quite gunners or drivers yet—just as I can't quite feel that I'm a soldier myself. Every time you think you're ready, someone says you're not. This is the way it's been since the beginning. Every time you get in shape, they either take away your men or send you off to some new place where everyone is raw. These men in the picture are mostly out of lumber camps and factories. You, of course, would like them. This battery hasn't been formed too long, so at the moment I've got a bit of a discipline problem. (Ha! Ha!) The Irishman I told you at the station had deserted is the tallest sergeant on the left. He stole a horse and never came back. Seems some people will do anything just to get a bit of the old attention! Well—I have to leave you now. Whistles are blowing and bells are ringing everywhere. Everyone on board is cheering, even in spite of the fact we're leaving in the dark and there's no one on shore to hear us. GOODBYE! Way, way out on the point some fires are blazing. I've written these last few words by lantern light. Green for starboard looking towards the sea. I hope you all can read this—because I can't. So—adios! as the bandits say. Robert Ross. Your son."

22: The 19th of December, 1915 was a Sunday. This was the day after Robert—(and, indeed, a whole Canadian contingent)—sailed for England. The Ross family went to church that morning, walking through the snow. Miss Davenport went with them. She was more and more a constant companion to Mrs Ross—who was less and less a companion to her husband and her children. The walk through the snow wound them down Park Road and up through the gulley of wild ravine to the other side past Collier Street to Bloor. They emerged about a block from their destination—(St Paul's)—where a piper was standing on the steps piping the worshippers in to the service. His presence meant that some regiment or other was on church parade that morning and the pews would be crowded with soldiers. Mrs Ross was sorry for this. It meant the tone of the sermon would be militant and more than likely bloodthirsty.

Mr Baldwin Mull—a neighbour somewhat dreaded for his temper and his habit of accumulating houses—preceded them along the sidewalk in his flowing beard and a tall black hat. Stuart made a snowball, taking off his mitts to warm it in his palm just long enough to let it form an outer coating of ice. As they neared the church, Mrs Ross became increasingly irritated by the number of acquaintances gathered on the sidewalks and the steps. Miss Davenport wanted to take her arm, but Mrs Ross refused. "If I fall down—I fall down," she said. Mister Ross heard this, but kept on walking. He and Peggy were busy nodding and smiling. Mister Ross kept raising his hat. Peggy always wore white gloves to church and she rested a white-gloved hand on her father's sleeve. The Rosses were dressed, quite naturally, in black and Mrs Ross wore a veil that hid her expression but not her features. The Bennetts and the Lawsons, the Lymans and the Bradshaws, the Aylesworths and the Wylies were all there. And the Raymonds. (The Raymonds were Mrs Ross's cousins and sisters.) She hated them all. She hadn't before—when she was growing up. But now she did. The only decent person she knew was Davenport. Davenport gave away chocolate bars to soldiers leaning out of trains. When Mrs Ross accompanied her and stood on the station platform it gave her the feeling she was mitigating bullets.

Standing on the steps, but not quite with her husband, Mrs Ross eyed the congregation of men and women with whom she had been a child. They had all

—she kept thinking—been *children* together. Why were they standing here in this snow, in these black, black clothes and blowing veils, listening to the wailing pipes and nodding at one another—shaking one another's hands as if to congratulate themselves that all their sons had gone away to die? Half the people here—or more—had sons like hers who were on those ships that had left St John the day before.

Stuart's snowball was melting in his mitts. Mrs Ross wanted to ask him why he didn't throw it. There were half a dozen people she would like him to throw it at—but of course that was madness. Slowly, they all went in. A company of Toronto Scottish arrived and filed into their seats, taking up one whole section of the church. The choir came next and everyone stood. Something was sung. They litanized. They sat down—they stood up—they sang—they sat down—they knelt. *God this and God that and Amen.*

Mrs Ross sat back.

Today, they would be spoken at by the Bishop. He spoke about those in peril at sea. He spoke about landfall. He spoke about flags and holy wars and Empire. He even had the gall to speak about Christmas. This was too much for Mrs Ross. She stood up. Standing, she leaned down over Davenport's magenta hat and said: "I need you. Come." She pressed past Dorothy Aylesworth's knees and old Mrs Aylesworth's shins and Mr Aylesworth's gold-headed cane and made it to the aisle without falling down. Davenport followed and they made their way to the doors—Mrs Ross walking on her heels to be sure that everyone heard her and knew that she was passing. The Bishop paused, but did not give up the struggle. . . .

Out on the street again, Mrs Ross sagged to the steps and sat in the snow.

"But—we can't sit here," said Miss Davenport.

"I can," said Mrs Ross and did.

She even lighted a cigarette. Why should it matter? The only people passing were children—and they were all running after motorcars, slipping and sliding on the ice.

Mister Ross, Peggy and Stuart remained inside. Peggy had almost followed, but her father had restrained her. He was afraid for his wife but he knew it was neither himself nor her children that she needed. What she needed was an empty cathedral in which to rail at God.

Davenport sat on her squirrel stole. Her hands were already cold. Mrs Ross reached inside her sable muff and drew out a silver flask. She drank and offered it to Davenport—but Davenport was afraid of censure, sitting so near the street, and she refused.

Mrs Ross adjusted her veil but did put the flask away. "I was afraid I was going to scream," she said. She gestured back at the church with its sermon in progress. "I do not understand. I don't. I won't. I can't. Why is this happening to us Davenport? What does it mean—*to kill your children*? Kill them and then . . . go in there and sing about it! What does it mean?!" She wept—but angrily. A child in a bright red tam-o'-shanter stood at the bottom step and stared. Mrs Ross looked away. "All those soldiers, sitting in there and smiling at their parents. Thank God and Jesus Robert didn't smile at me before he left—I couldn't have borne it." She put her hand on her forehead. The child was watching her intently and Mrs Ross in spite of the haze of brandy and the keen lightheadedness of her passion realized that the child was frightened to see her there—a grown-up lady, sitting on the steps in the snow with her furs thrown aside as if they were dead flowers. She realized she had to stand or else the child would think that she was mad—and the world had quite enough adults gone crazy as it was. She put her hand out for Davenport. Davenport took it.

Mrs Ross stood.

The child seemed pleased. In standing, reason was restored. She smiled.

Mrs Ross looked down—throwing her furs across her shoulder—masking the flask and putting it back inside the muff. She treated the cigarette like something she'd found and looked at it much as to say: whatever made me think that this was mine?—and threw it away. "Where are your parents?" she said to the child.

"At home."

"But—should you be on the street alone?" said Mrs Ross.

"We only live down there," said the child. "And I'm allowed to come and watch the people going in and out on Sundays."

"Oh," said Mrs Ross. "Well—we're going in. Will you come us?"

The child gave a look at Miss Davenport. The magenta hat was a little bit frightening since it had wings on either side—but the lady who'd been sitting in the snow had a veil and the little girl liked veils. They blew around your face like smoke. She nodded. Mrs Ross put out her hand.

The three of them went in and stood at the back and just as they did, the whole congregation stood up and began to sing.

"All people that on earth do dwell,
Sing to the Lord with cheerful voice.

Him serve with mirth, his praise forth tell.
Come ye before him and rejoice."

The band that had come with the soldiers played. The organ roared and bellowed. All the people sang.

"Know that the Lord is God indeed;
Without our aid he did us make . . ."

Mrs Ross tightened her grip on the child's hand to keep herself from singing, but in spite of that, the hymn rolled on.

"We are his flock, he doth us feed,
And for his sheep he doth us take."

Somewhere during the last verse, a trumpet began to play. The silver notes wound upward in a high and desperately beautiful descant—gilding the vaulted ceilings—raising everyone's eyes, and even Mrs Ross looked up to see where they had gone.

"For why? The Lord our God is good.
His mercy is forever sure;
His truth at all times firmly stood,
And shall from age to age endure."

There was a long and echoing *amen.*

The child let go of Mrs Ross's hand.

Mrs Ross looked at the whole congregation and the Bishop far away in a haze of candlelight and the high, gold cross beyond. And all she could think was: *I was married here.*

Down on the floor, the snow from everyone's feet

had melted. Mrs Ross was forced to smile. Snowballs can't be made from water.

23: Robert had always loved the sea. Calmer waters on earlier voyages had given him a false impression: the sea was deep—but temperate. It rolled you to your destination on the long green sweep of glassy swells. Any storms that troubled it got there by way of Joseph Conrad and the *Boys' Own Annual.*

Now, it was different. The storm that raged was real and it wreaked havoc in every quarter of the ship. The men—whose discipline was tenuous to begin with—were cramped into spaces meant to hold a quarter of their number. They fought and argued from one side of the ocean to the other. The food was always stew—and very often stew with curry in it to mask its true flavour. It was served in deep white bowls that showed off its garish yellow colour. The sittings were arranged by companies. Two hundred and forty men sat down together, feeding from plank-top tables that had foolishly been set on trestles. Once a day, the trestles would collapse—either kicked by someone's boots or sabotaged by the lurching of the *S.S. Massanabie* as she rose and fell and often seemed to careen through the storm. At nearly every meal the bowls and the cutlery—the pots of steaming tea and coffee and the great tin jugs of milk and water crashed and spun across the decks. Most of the jaundiced stew—one way and another—ended up on the floor.

Few of the men had ever been to sea and although they were tolerably used to the crowding of their barracks, nothing had prepared them for the airless jamming of their quarters underdecks. The makeshift latrines and showers were virtually open forums where privacy was unheard of. Men unable to find a space at the trough-like urinals simply turned aside and aimed at the bulkheads. Portholes were closed and locked against the cold. The air was blue with smoke and this plus the tremendous heat from the boilers drew off the oxygen. Everyone suffered from headaches and men who'd lived outdoors all their lives passed out because they couldn't breathe.

Bunks, perforce, had been constructed in tiers of four and six and even eight. Sleep—as opposed to loss of consciousness—was almost an impossibility. If you wanted to lie on your other side, you had to slither onto the floor—turn around—and climb back into your bunk facing in the opposite direction. Everything was in motion and the giant arms of the pistons drove the ship to a grinding tune that never ceased. Other than during boat drill, there was no escape unless you were one of those who were put on picket duty with the horses. Nothing had been thought of to entertain the men and so there was a good deal of fighting, most of it having to do with cheating at cards and sexual bullying.

Up in the first class accommodations, the officers were somewhat better off. There was crowding here, too, but it could hardly be called discomfitting. Staterooms for single passengers now contained four—staterooms designed for two had eight, etc. Only the senior officers were allowed to maintain the privilege of having their batmen to wait on them. Bathrooms were shared by all excepting the battalion commander. Privacy was desperately won but not an impossibility as down below. At least the cabinet doors could be closed on the W.C.'s and the showers had partitions. In the ballroom there was a grand piano fixed to the floor and on one of the earlier evenings four blond men stood up and sang and thumped the entire score from *Pinafore*. This was not a popular thing to have chosen and by the time they reached the end, they were singing to themselves. For the rest of the voyage, the piano remained closed. For those who could tolerate food, there were formal sittings in the dining salons. The officers ate from tables that were covered with long white cloths. These, the messmen dampened with glasses of water and as a consequence the dishes stayed more or less in place. The food was a glorified version of the stew below. On occasion, it was dolloped with wine and came to the table as a *bourgignon*. But the taste of regurgitated wine is no better than the taste of regurgitated curry, so in the end the effect of the food was fairly democratic. Most of an officer's time was spent lying down or else being sent below to see what could be done to keep the men from mutiny. To this end, Robert was glad he'd kept the revolver.

Wearing a holster gave you the ritual edge in authority. Even in spite of their training and the weeks spent establishing their rank through punishing drills and endless parades, the officers were very young and most of them were slimly built compared to the veterans of lumber camps and railroad gangs. In the end, it was only their mutual obedience to some intrinsic tyranny that held the men and the officers in check—apart. Perhaps it was the airless limitations of the ship. Perhaps it was the storm. Whatever it was, the confrontations always came to the same conclusion. Someone would laugh.

Of Robert's cabinmates, the only inactive one was Captain Ord. The second day out, he put on a pair of blue pajamas with white stitched anchors on the pockets and retired to his bunk. He claimed the privilege of having lost his voice and spent the voyage sitting propped against his pillows drinking brandy from a silver cup and reading the works of G.A. Henty. "What on earth are you reading that stuff for?" Clifford asked him; "God—I haven't seen those books since I was *twelve*," he added. Ord said hoarsely that since he was going to do a boy's work he must read the "stuff of which boys are made" and smiled. Clifford didn't appreciate the humour. To him, the war was a deadly serious and heaven-sent chance to become a man. Every night before he went to sleep he stood at the bridge with Horatio—brought the news from Aix to Ghent and smiling, fell dead. He said: "you're damned right!" a lot and spent a good deal of his time in the bathroom, secretly tilting his hat and his grin at the mirror. He also sang his songs and made up many verses of his own. He would sit on his bunk and polish his boots and buttons, nattering at Ord—completely unaware that Ord had fallen asleep up above or that *With Clive in India* was about to fall on his head.

Harris, the young lad from Sydney, Nova Scotia, was pale and always wore his collar up and his lapels spread inward across his chest. He had a pair of leather gloves that Robert admired. They were soft and lined with hand-woven wool. But they were ruined. Harris had bitten holes in the tips of the index fingers. He was an only child who'd never been away from home. His mother died when he was three and he'd lived estranged from his father, a silent man who owned a shipping yard where fishing boats were made. Harris stood for long hours gazing out of the porthole wishing that he'd see a whale. "You haven't much chance of seeing a whale in weather like this," someone said; "they're all off down in the South Atlantic anyway." "Oh, I know all that," said Harris. "But you never can tell. . . ." In the mornings when they woke up, Harris would already be standing there, fully dressed and sometimes wearing a scarf. The scarf was a wistful shade of blue.

The only fresh air you got was during boat drill but this was hardly worth breathing since the temperature had dropped to twenty below. In the wind it was minus forty. The only thing they were told about the boats was not to fall out. There was no survival in the water. You died as soon as it reached your skin. Officers and men lined up by platoons. The officers faced the boats—but the men stood in rows facing inward—staring at the funnels. If they'd been allowed to turn around they might have started counting and discovered there were not even boats for half of them. The wind was a blessing. Most men closed their eyes against it.

Robert and Clifford tried taking walks around the decks for the first few days but they always ended up crouching behind a box of deck chairs or an air vent. On the fourth day out, Harris went with them and promptly came down with a cold. Almost at once the cold became bronchitis and the bronchitis led to pneumonia. His temperature soared and after a day-and-a-half he was taken down to the infirmary where he shared the attention of the medical officers with two of the men who had beaten one another senseless with the heels of their boots. One of them had stolen the other's chocolate bar. It was because of Harris's illness that Robert became involved with the horses.

Harris had been in charge of the section detail whose job it was to care for the horses in the hold. It so happened that Captain Ord was Harris's company commander. He just looked down from his bunk where, by now, he was *With Wolfe at Quebec*—and appointed Robert as Harris's successor. When Robert protested that his own company commander might have something to say about it, Ord gave one of his charming smiles and whispered that "all that" had been arranged. "But don't be alarmed," he added. "You'll have the help of Battery Sergeant Major Joyce and I dare say he's the ablest man we've got on board this ship—of *any* rank." "Thankyou, sir." "Not at all, Mister Ross. Not at all," said Ord. "I hope you enjoy yourself."

24: It was hardly an enjoyable task. Robert's first reaction when he saw the hold was one of horror. Then of anger. Before you saw the hold, you heard it. The place was alive with flies. Robert wondered how Harris could have failed to do anything about them—until he tried to do something about them himself. Very quickly he discovered that no one on the ship would co-operate. This included the ship's officers and crew as well as those with the C.E.F.

There was hardly any light and the scuppers were awash with sea bilge and urine. Manure was left where it fell for days on end. This is where the flies bred. Thousands of them. Here, there were rats as well and the men on duty were forced to sit on the steps or high on the bales of hay. They all wore handkerchiefs across their noses and stayed, it seemed, as far away from the horses as they could get. Many of these men were sick and should not have been on duty in the first place. Robert's first order was to replace their section with another and to put the B.S.M. in charge of creating proper manure piles. He also organized a bucket brigade for sluicing down the decks. He thought of killing the flies with cold but was refused permission to open the hatches. He also requested another section of men to act as alternates, meaning to change the shifts every two instead of every four hours, but the Battalion C.O. wouldn't hear of it. "Those damn beasts shouldn't even be on this ship!" he wheezed. He was a red-faced malcontent with pudgy hands and a bottle of gin. "And when we get to England—I mean to have my say about that. Transporting men and animals in the same vessel! Barbarous! *Barbarous*!" So saying, he signalled that another hand of bridge should be dealt. "And in the meantime, Mister Ross, the fewer men involved with those damned horses the better. I don't want my soldiers coming down with any barnyard diseases. . . ." And that was all the satisfaction Robert got.

He spent a good deal of time in the hold and—oddly—found it was a marvellous cure for seasickness. He became intrigued with this world of horses, rats and bilge that had been consigned to his care. It took on a life entirely its own—presided over by the booming B.S.M. and watched from its towers of hay by the pale and looming faces of the pickets in their masks. Robert soon became completely disengaged from the other life on the upper decks. He even went below off duty.

25: At last they came in sight of land. This was at 2:00 a.m. on Monday, December 27th—but the storm, that had somewhat abated, took on a new direction and the whole of that day the *S.S. Massanabie* rolled about helplessly outside of Plymouth harbour. The wind now blew in gales of up to 70 m.p.h. and in the midst of these it was decided all the men should be brought up top and onto the decks and into the lounges just in case. They also filled the corridors and passageways in double rows and stood leaning back with their stomachs sticking out or else slid down the walls and squatted with their knees apart. All were dressed in greatcoats over which they wore their life jackets. If two men turned sideways, the passageway was blocked. Light was forbidden. Some, in the ballroom, lighted matches from time to time and these flared up and showed somebody's face and died. Nobody spoke. The piano rumbled and muttered every time a door was opened and the wind blew through its wires. Panic was perversely averted by watching one of the other ships in the convoy almost being sunk as she tried to make it into harbour past the rocks. This scene was lit by the moon.

Robert returned from the hold to his cabin at 4:00 a.m. on the Tuesday, so exhausted he could not remove his gloves. He lay on his bunk bemused by the sight of Captain Ord's hand dangling down beside him like a spider on a thread. Half-an-hour later, Battery Sergeant Major came and knocked at the door.

"I'm sorry to say so, Mister Ross, but one of them horses of yours has gone and broke its leg."

Second-Lieutenant Ross would have to go back down to the hold of the ship because the horse would have to be shot and, of course, an officer had to do it. They were the only ones with guns.

26: The B.S.M. waited at attention while Robert went to the bathroom. The door had no lock and it banged and banged and banged all the time Robert was in there. His mind took up its rhythm: stop, stop—forward—stop. He had never squeezed a trigger against a living creature in the whole of his life.

He stood there with his trousers open—leaning in above the toilet with his hand against the bulkhead. Nothing happened. His bladder, like his mouth, dried up. Robert thought desperately for ways of avoiding what had to be done. *Why couldn't Battery Sergeant Major Joyce do this?* Hadn't he been in the army all his life? He was a marksman—famous within the Battalion. He must have killed a hundred times or more —men and rats and horses—whatever it was you killed in wars. Robert's brain began its stammering.

Joyce had fought in the Boer War and had been left for dead in the battle for Paardeburg Drift. His jaw had been shattered and because there'd been no doctor it had been improperly set. It angled towards one side and his voice whistled up his throat and came out through his nose. Right now, he asked Robert: "are you all right, sir?" "Yes," said Robert. "I just felt ill for a moment." He turned around and came out of the cabinet doing up his buttons. "I been ill myself on several such occasions," the B.S.M. said. "Dry-ill, you know—when nothing will come up." Robert could see him in the moonlight that came through the port-holes and reflected in the mirrors. He thought no one could have thought to say a more decent thing in that moment. "Thankyou," he said.

Robert drank a glass of water and the Sergeant Major said to him: "you put your hand up the back of my jacket, sir, and take hold of my suspenders. I'll lead the way. Them corridors is full of men asleep." And so they left the comforting sinks and toilets and proceeded through the darkened passageways and gangways under people's arms and over people's feet down to the bowels of the ship—with the B.S.M. shining his torch on the sleeper's faces and Robert behind him holding the elastic reins in one hand and his other hand haunting his holster.

27: The hold was filled with a moaning noise and many of its lamps had been extinguished by the violence of the storm. Baggage, stores and hay were lashed in gigantic piles and only the shapes of these could be seen in the faltering light. Seventy horses, somewhere in this dark, were trying to maintain their footing. (The other seventy were beyond the furthest bulkhead in another part of the hold.) They were all in makeshift stalls along the aisles between the cargo—roped off in sections like corrals—ten horses to a section—two sections to an aisle, back to back. Each of the horses was cinched to a single cable that ran the width of the ship, the cable being guyed at either end to hooks in the hull. Mangers were non-existent. The horses fed from hay thrown down between their hooves. Water came in leather buckets. All the exercise they got was in trying to stay upright.

Robert had been hoping to find several others there to help them, but there was only a single picket. The B.S.M. explained that even though Robert had said the full complement of orderlies was to remain below—as soon as he'd gone to his cabin, the Brigadier had sent down to say the horses were to fend for themselves and the men were all to come up. That was when the horse had fallen.

The sole remaining picket was a pale and frightened boy named Regis from Regina. He was very much afraid of the ocean. The only body of water he'd ever seen was the yellow, flat shallows in the valley of the Qu'Appelle. He could not have been more than sixteen years old, in spite of what he must have told the induction officer. He was presently sitting on the steps with the rats at his feet and the wails of the fallen horse in the shadows beyond him. Regis had been weeping and his face was streaked with dust.

As they stood on the steps, the *S.S. Massanabie* began to crash and shudder—*bang*! *bang*! *bang*! The captain was striving to hold her back from the rocks and had turned her too quickly out of the wind. Regis said: "we shall all be drownded, sir" and Robert said: "no we shan't"—amazed at the authority with which he said it because he thought himself that the ship was sinking. The rats had fallen silent and Robert knew this was a sinister sign. The boy seemed mollified by the sound of Robert's voice and he hardly spoke again throughout the whole incident.

They turned to find the fallen horse.

It was down on its stomach—trying to rise against the motion of the ship—the broken leg stretched out behind it, so badly smashed that it showed the bone. Robert tried not to see this.

The horse's gaze was turned in their direction—white with alarm in the lantern light. It whinnied and tried to rise again but its efforts were completely useless. Its hooves could gain no purchase on the metal plates.

Robert could barely move in his panic but he knew that he had to show his nerve and his ability as an officer. Somewhere, afterwards, someone in an adjutant's office would write all of this down in a book. "Lieutenant Ross did this and that and the other. He showed decisiveness—(or he didn't). He gained complete control of the situation—(or none). He has proved his effectiveness—(or not)—as an officer. God Save the King."

"Sir—may I suggest before you fire—" the Sergeant Major said: "we'd best do all we can to separate the other horses from the sound of that gun."

Robert realized this was correct and he waited with his back turned while the boy and the B.S.M. removed the other horses from the section and cinched them to the wire in the next aisle.

When this was done, the B.S.M. said: "sir—we're ready for you, now" and he stepped to Robert's left-hand side as Robert drew the revolver. Something insidious remarked in Robert's mind as he did this how crazy it was to shoot a horse with a Colt. He stood with his legs apart, braced against the impulse to turn around and run away. The B.S.M. was watching him—squinting out of the dark, just like something mad staring down from a tree. Robert suddenly realized he didn't know where to fire at the horse and was about to ask when he remembered that somewhere in *Chums*—as a boy—he'd seen a picture of a cowboy shooting his horse behind the ear. The image rose in his mind—black and white and clumsily drawn—a child's world picture of exactly what to do.

Robert approached the horse with the hammer drawn back and held in place by his thumb. He stood above the horse's neck and the horse looked back at him, lifting its head and rolling its eyes in Robert's direction.

"I shouldn't straddle it, sir, like that," said the B.S.M., "in case it throws itself."

Robert stepped aside and stood more or less at attention.

He took his aim. His arm wavered. His eyes burned with sweat. Why didn't someone come and jump on his back and make him stop?

He fired.

A chair fell over in his mind.

He closed his eyes and opened them.

The air in front of him was filled with little fires but the horse was not dead. It had thrown itself forward, lurching towards the Sergeant Major, who calmly stepped aside with his hands behind his back. Regis ran to grab at the halters of the section behind them where all the horses started to pound the decks with their hooves.

The horse was trying to stand. Robert threw down his hat. Jesus; for Christ's sake—die. "I need more light," he said. He was shaking; his voice full of anger. The Sergeant Major turned the beam of his torch on the horse at his feet. *Snakes. Snakes. Rattlesnakes.* Its mane was a tangle of rattlesnakes. The horse was beating its head against the plates. Some sort of noise was emerging from its teeth. The B.S.M. said to Robert: "just be very quick about it, sir. Just be very cool and quick." Robert forced his eyes to open: aimed—and fired again. This time the horse was hit on the withers. Robert sank to his knees. He could hear himself breathing. He held the gun in both hands. He pressed it hard behind the horse's ear and swore at the horse: "God damn it, damn it, damn it—stop." His knees were wet and he drew himself into a ball and pushed with all his strength. He began to squeeze the trigger and he squeezed it again and again and again—so many times that when the Sergeant Major pulled him away the gun went right on clicking in his hands.

And then all hell broke loose. Robert stood in the centre of the roped off corral with the dead horse quivering beside him and all the other horses rearing back and pulling against their cables so that Regis was nearly trampled. But the B.S.M. ran through and got the boy away. Robert was left alone with the pounding and the sound of it went around and around the hull like an endless ringing down an iron rail while the horses rose and fell like rocking horses in a crazy nursery till Robert kicked his hat through the straw and walked away with the gun dangling down from his finger.

While the Sergeant Major clambered up to commandeer some men to come down and help, Robert and Regis stood beneath the iron steps in the dark. "Shall I light us a lantern, sir?" said Regis. "No," said Robert. "Not for a moment, anyway." He didn't want to see the other man's eyes just yet—though he didn't know why. For a long, embarrassed moment there was silence which Robert finally broke by saying "if this damn ship would sell us one I'd buy us both a drink." But Regis answered him: "no thankyou, sir. I promised my mother I wouldn't."

28: Shortly after dawn the storm abated and the sun came up in a cloudless sky. About 8:00 a.m.—(this was on the Tuesday)—the captain made his final bid for the harbour. The next two hours were the worst of the whole voyage if only because the rocks could now be seen and the waves, even though the wind had died, were still over twenty feet high. The ship's First Officer told the Battalion C.O. this was the closest call he'd ever had in thirty years at sea. They missed the rocks by only forty feet and all at once there was a calm and a great resounding cheer went up.

Just as they were going through the gap, Robert and Regis started up the steps. The ship gave one great lurch and Robert fell. Regis started back down but Robert got to his feet and said he was fine. He thought he was. He hadn't felt a thing.

Since there were other ships as well, the *S.S. Massanabie* sat at anchor for several hours before the tenders came to unload the troops. Robert went to his cabin where Captain Ord was packing away his books.

He had got all the way to being *With Wellington at Waterloo* and he offered Robert a silver cup of brandy. "That's where we're going, you know. I mean—it's sort of the same thing. Ypres is only sixty miles from Waterloo. Makes you feel better, doesn't it. . . ." *Why*? Robert wanted to ask—but he didn't. His legs were sore. He pulled down his trousers to examine them. "Good God," said Ord, "what happened to you?" Robert explained about the fall. His legs were black and his feet had begun to swell. He was afraid he would not be able to get his boots back on for days if he took them off. But Captain Ord was adamant: he relieved Robert of all his duties and sent him packing to the infirmary. Ord was alarmed. He had never seen such bruises—but he didn't say so to Robert. At any rate, it was because of this that Robert and Harris were disembarked together and in this way began their curious friendship that ended in ashes. They were taken off the *S.S. Massanabie* in stretchers and lowered into the tender much as the horses had been brought aboard—"in a kind of harness."

Looking back towards the ship from the quay where their stretchers had been laid side by side, Robert propped himself up on his elbow and then, when he realized what it was he was seeing he pulled himself up against the parapet. All the horses—who knows how?—were in the water and swimming desperately towards the land.

"What is it?" Harris asked.

"Come and see," said Robert.

He wrapped himself and Harris in blankets and they sat on the parapet, just like football fans, waving their arms and cheering the horses ashore.

They came ashore where the fishermen's boats had

been hauled out for winter and a section of soldiers was waiting for them with brightly coloured flags. The soldiers whirled the flags above their heads like cowboys at a round-up—driving the horses off towards the nearest street. There were also a number of townsfolk gathered to watch all this—some on cobblestones—some in windows—some who came running out of houses and pubs and shops—all of them calling: "horses! horses! horses!" Children dashed across the road to touch the horses' tails and ran away squealing and laughing—everybody holding up their hands and faces under the sheets of dazzling rain that shook and shimmered off the horses' backs in the sunlight.

When the horses had gone, Harris lay down again and turned on his side. But Robert waited—watching. He wanted something more, not knowing what it was. Then Clifford came and said that Robert must return to the stretcher so he and Harris could be carried onto the waiting train. Later, when Robert put the voyage down on paper for his parents, this is all he said: "here we are at last! It was an evil trip. I caught a cold and the doctor thought it might become bronchitis. There were storms. Someone put me in charge of the horses. England is black from end to end. We travelled through the dark for hours by train and not a single light was seen. I think perhaps you'd like this place where we are. It's in Kent. There's a grand country house with open fields on every side and an old, chalky town down below the cliffs. The war seems awfully far away. Even further off than when we were at home.

P.S. Do you think you could send the automatic soon? I want it very much. Battery Sergeant Major says if you could get a Webley .455 Mark I they're the best there is. They're wonderful to fire, he says, and they kill at fifty yards."

* * *

29: Mrs Ross's only brother—a boy called Monty Miles—had been killed while walking home on Shuter Street. This was many years before, when Mrs Ross was in the process of getting engaged and married to Tom. Monty Miles Raymond was everyone's favourite young man. All the girls loved him—all the boys wanted to be his friend. He wore brown suits and shoes with spats. He carried a walking stick. He whistled all the way to work and back. A wayward trolley left the tracks to strike him down. The mourning had gone on for years. "Do you remember Monty Miles . . . ?" and everyone would cry. Miss Davenport could still be brought to tears at the thought of how he'd strutted down the street with his cane across his shoulder. Now, the world was full of trolley cars and Mrs Ross could hear their brakes and see them jump the tracks in all her dreams. She began to wear dark glasses so her eyes could not be seen. Miss Davenport was moved from her rooms at 74 St George to the rooms at the top of 39 South Drive. Mister Ross was very solicitous. He would do anything for his wife—but his wife would have none of it. All she wanted was to sit in the corner of the room and watch the door for Robert's return.

When Robert had been posted overseas—just like that—Mister Ross called up everyone he knew to discover where he might meet the troop train. His idea was to let his wife have one last reassuring look at her son. And no child of his was going to be swept away without goodbye; he'd be damned if he'd allow that to happen. So he exerted the pressure of his Government contracts and at last the news came through. Mister Ross could see his son in Montreal. He and Mrs Ross got on board their private railway car and rode through the night.

She exhorted him to read to her. He read her *Huckleberry Finn.* When it was morning and the private car was on its siding in the Montreal freight yards, Mrs Ross put on her opal dress and tried to fix her hair. She dropped a lot of pins on the floor and couldn't see herself in the mirror. She decided to put on a large fur hat that would cover her head and hide the fact that she could not fix her hair the way she wanted to. Then she went into the salon and sat with her legs tucked beneath her in one of the pullman chairs and drank a third of a bottle of scotch. When Mister Ross came in and said it was time to go, Mrs Ross stood up—and fell down. "I can't" she said. Her legs had fallen asleep, Mister Ross was determined, nonetheless, that he should go—even if he had to go alone. He had brought Robert down a hamper of food as well as the Colt revolver in its wooden box. He wanted these gifts to pass from hand to hand. And so he went out and met his son—and afterwards, he stood on the platform—with the thought of Mrs Ross beside him, waving. But Mrs Ross just stood at the windows of the private car and was afraid to go outdoors. Her mind was full of trolley cars and she knew that if she tried to cross the tracks, then she and everyone would be struck down. Instead, she waved from behind the glass and she watched her boy depart and her husband standing in his black fur coat—it seemed for hours—with his arm in the air and the snow falling down around him. *"Come on back to the raf', Huck honey."* And this was what they called *the wars.*

30: Week after week, Robert wrote with unnerving formality to MR AND MRS THOMAS ROSS, 39 SOUTH DRIVE, TORONTO, CANADA and to MISS MARGARET ELIZA-

BETH ROSS and to MASTER STUART MONTGOMERY ROSS and he even sent field cards to BIMBO ROSS, his dog.

All these letters, neatly folded and tied, were laid in an oblong lacquered box beside the silent, booted icon of ROBERT ROSS, SECOND LIEUTENANT, C.F.A. in the silver frame on the black walnut table in the parlour. The box itself was lined with velvet—scarlet newly fading to maroon. The letters to MARGARET ELIZABETH ROSS, Peggy kept separate in a drawer upstairs—separate in their drawer and separate in their packet—laid aside from other packets, neatly folded and tied from Clifford Purchas—Roly Powell—Garnett Hughes and Clinton Brown from Harvard. Bimbo was always encouraged but always failed to sniff her master's scent on the overfingered cards she received of pale brown cardboard. Master Stuart made his letters into paper darts and launched them page by page from the roof of the house—watching them desend and fade into the green ravine below while he muttered *rat-a-tat-tat*! *Boom*! *Boom*! *Rat-a-tat-tat*! *Boom*! *Boom*! *Karoom*! Some he saved to trade at school for other artifacts of war sent home by other elder brothers like his own—but only the letters mailed from France were worthy of this exchange. They had to have the smell of fire.

PART TWO

1: There is no good picture of this except the one you can make in your mind. The road is lost at either end in rain. Robert's perception of it is limited by fog and smoke. On either side, the ditches are filled with fetid water. Everything is waterlogged. Even bits of grass won't float. In front of him the road is apparently empty. Behind him, there are forty horses—every fifth horse bearing a rider. Only one of these riders is visible. Far to the rear there are seven wagons drawn by mules and carrying ammunition. Robert is in charge of this convoy. It is February, 1916. He has been in France for a month and two days; since Monday, January 24th.

At the centre of the world is Ypres and all around the centre lie the flats of Flanders. To its rear—which is to say South West—is the only physical landmark worth mentioning: Kemmel Hill. This is three hundred and fifty feet high. Nothing in Belgium rises higher. To the east and to the north there is a ridge of land that anywhere else would not be the least exceptional. Here, the ridge was what you fought for. If you could gain its heights, you had the advantage. So far the Germans had maintained this advantage and almost two years of fighting had failed to dislodge them. The plain on which Ypres stands stretches like a broken arm through Europe from the Russian frontier to the border of

Spain. This is the one way west into France that does not encounter mountains. (Once, in Napoleon's time, it had been the only way east.) Because of its flatness this alleyway has been the scene of battles since the time of Caesar. All the great armies of modern history have passed this way and through this mud.

The mud. There are no good similes. Mud must be a Flemish word. Mud was invented here. Mudland might have been its name. The ground is the colour of steel. Over most of the plain there isn't a trace of topsoil: only sand and clay. The Belgians call them "clyttes," these fields, and the further you go towards the sea, the worse the clyttes become. In them, the water is reached by the plough at an average depth of eighteen inches. When it rains (which is almost constantly from early September through to March, except when it snows) the water rises at you out of the ground. It rises from your footprints—and an army marching over a field can cause a flood. In 1916, it was said that you "waded to the front." Men and horses sank from sight. They drowned in mud. Their graves, it seemed, just dug themselves and pulled them down.

All this mud and water was contaminated. Dung and debris and decaying bodies lay beneath its surface. When the rivers and canals could no longer be contained—over they spilled into clyttes already awash with rain.

Houses, trees and fields of flax once flourished here. Summers had been blue with flowers. Now it was a shallow sea of stinking grey from end to end. And this is where you fought the war.

12: Sometimes the roads were shelled. It depended how far forward you got. The trick was, at nightfall to lag behind your schedule and find some barn or blasted house to rest in. Nothing is worse than shellfire in the dark. Running was pointless at any rate, except to find some cover for your head—but here in the open any attempt to run in darkness led to drowning.

Robert's destination was a place called Wytsbrouk, now entirely emptied of its civilian population and occupied by the forward supply depot for the 18th, 19th and 20th batteries of the 5th Brigade. This was about a mile from the front.

They were coming from a town called Bailleul, which was known to the men as "the last place in civilization." There, you could actually sleep in a hotel—though you were rarely accorded the opportunity. Also at Bailleul there was a large, now emptied school for girls where the troops were often billeted. On the outskirts of town there was an asylum for the mad—(Van Gogh had been one of its patients)—and it was here the officers bathed in black iron tubs under high glass windows filtering sunlight down through a century of cobwebs and dust. This place was called *Asile Desolé*, which means desolated or devastated refuge. This was because it had been shelled in some previous war. Its proper name was *Asile d'alienés aux Bailleul et Ploegbeke.* All of the place names were either French or Flemish but the further you got towards Ypres, the more Flemish they became and the more unpronounceable to anyone whose mother tongue was English. Robert had had an encounter with the language problem only that morning when he was approached by a Flemish peasant who had lost his cows. More than likely he suspected Robert of having commandeered them for his soldiers so he was naturally excited. He spoke in Flemish. Robert first of all thought it was gibberish. The scene had taken place on the road in the rain and the man's incoherent words and waving arms made Robert think he'd possibly escaped from Desolé.

When his tale had been told and the farmer saw that Robert didn't comprehend, he began it again in French. Robert knew it was French because he recognized that *vaches* were cows. But that was all.

"Can't you speak English?" he asked politely.

This was the wrong thing to say. The man threw down his hat and began to shout.

"Enklesh! Enklesh! *Vous êtes anglais*? *Maudit anglais*!" he screamed.

Robert became alarmed. He backed his horse away, but the man pursued him. "*Maudit anglais*!" he kept shouting. He picked up his hat and threw it. "*Ce sont tout les assassins*!" he cried.

Robert did not understand a word of this but he imagined he was being accused of something he hadn't done. He thought if he could identify himself, it might explain his innocence. So he mustered the only coherent sentences he knew in a foreign language and shouted them back at the man: "*monsieur*!" he said. "*Je ne parle pas français*! *Je suis canadien*!"

The words rang out through the fog.

They did not seem to help.

The man just looked at Robert—sneered—and repeated: "*maudit anglais*." Then he picked up his hat and walked away.

Well, Robert thought; I tried.

3: Riding beside him was his batman, Bugler Willie Poole. Bugler was really an out-of-date rank and fairly meaningless but sometimes it was given to men whose age was suspect. In other wars they might have been drummer boys. Willie Poole was proud of his rank, however, because the fact was he actually played the bugle. "Why," Robert had asked, "didn't you apply to play in the band?" "Oh," said Willie, "if I was playing in the band I wouldn't be here." He was that uncomplicated. He carried his bugle on a string across his back. Unlike Regis, Poole was not under-age—but he looked it. He was in fact nineteen like Robert but he didn't yet shave and his voice still wavered, not completely broken. He was covered with freckles and his hair was the colour of sand. He'd been assigned to Robert two days after Robert's arrival—this previous officer having been killed when he'd stepped outside one evening "for a breath of air." The breath of air had blown his head off.

"Do you remember any barns or houses along this road where we could bivouac?" Robert asked.

"No, sir," said Poole. "But I could ride ahead and see."

"No," said Robert. "No one's riding ahead." He turned in his saddle. "I'm beginning to wonder if anyone's riding *behind*. Maybe we should stop and let the others catch us up."

They reined in their horses.

Poole said, "I have to get down, if that's all right."

Robert nodded.

Poole gave over his reins into Robert's hand and swung down onto the road. By the time he'd reached the edge of the ditch he'd already started to disappear. The air was foul with thick green fog. There was a smell that Robert could not decipher.

"What's that smell?" he said to Poole.

"Prob'ly chlorine," Poole replied. His back was to Robert—with his coat elbowed out like wings. Robert could hear him urinating into the ditch.

"You mean you think there's a gas attack going on up

front?" Robert had not yet had this experience. Poole had had it twice.

"No, sir. But the groun' is full of it here. There's some that says a handful of this clay could knock a person out."

"I believe it," said Robert. The smell was unnerving —as if some presence were lurking in the fog like a dragon in a story. Poole was quite correct; the ground was saturated with gas. Chlorine and phosgene were currently both in use. Mustard gas was still to come.

They were joined by the rider behind them with four horses. The horses were nervous and as soon as they were halted, they laid their ears back and started to skitter.

Robert did not get down himself, but he told the rider to dismount. He was nervous. He didn't know why. They waited.

Poole came back doing up his buttons. They stood there like that for fully five minutes—Robert on his horse, leaning forward to rest his stomach muscles, and the two men down in the road with the horses. The fog was full of noises. They were ill defined and had no perimeter. Distance had been swallowed whole.

"What if we've gone the wrong turning?" said Poole, whose innocence allowed him to make remarks like that —even to an officer.

Robert thought it was possible but didn't say so. He asked what the others thought the noises might be.

"Birds," said Poole. The other man remained silent.

"I'd be very surprised if any birds had survived in this plane," said Robert.

Just as he said so, something flew out of the ditch.

The horses shied and one of them snorted. Robert stood in his stirrups trying to see what it was that had flown. More and more of whatever it was flew up after it. A whole flock of something. Ducks? He couldn't tell. It was odd—how they'd sat so still and silent till that moment.

"What can be keeping those blasted others?" he said. "Orderly, maybe you'd best go back."

"Yessir."

"Poole and I will hold down here."

The man got into his saddle.

"Give him your bugle, Poole."

"Yessir." Poole handed over the bugle from his back.

"Now—use it," Robert said to the orderly. "Keep on counting to fifty and every fifty give us a blast. Let me hear one now, just to see you know what you're doing."

The man put the bugle to his lips and made a ragged noise with it. All at once the air was filled with shock waves of wings—sheet after sheet of them, rising off some marsh they could not see. The wind and the sound of their motion sent a shiver down Robert's back. Nothing could be seen except the shape of movement.

"All right. Go back," Robert said. "At a walk. And a blast at every fifty."

"Yessir."

The man turned his horse and was gone as he did so.

Robert muttered one to fifty. So did Poole.

There was a muffled shout from the trumpet.

"He's not very good at it," said Poole.

"Well—he hasn't had your practice," said Robert. "Give him a week or so. . ."

They were both trying to joke. But they couldn't. There must be something terribly wrong and they knew it but neither one knew how to put it into words. The birds, being gone, had taken some mysterious presence with them. There was an awful sense of void—as if the world had emptied.

Robert leaned forward. Even Poole was beginning to

disappear. He was cold. He had never been so cold. The fog was turning his greatcoat to mush. It was as if the rain had boiled and turned to steam—except that the steam was frigid. Robert tried to remember what it was like to bathe in hot water. He couldn't.

They waited.

The trumpet wailed and hooted further and further off in the green. The fog was full of light. Robert heard wings above them and around them. The birds were coming back. There was also the sound of lapping—of movement out in the field—and the sound reminded Robert of the early morning slap-slap-slap from the diving raft at Jackson's Point. Something floating in the water. All he could see was the shape of Poole and the heads and rumps of the horses—their lower parts obscured. The rain had stopped. An occasional chilly breeze blew through the fog—intimations of another world and other weather. These breezes carried the smells of smoke and ashes—bitter and acrid. The trumpet fell silent.

Poole led the horses back in Robert's direction. Warmth might be had by clustering. Neither man spoke. The horses didn't like being made to stand still. The wings had alarmed them.

"Name all the birds you can think of," said Robert.

"Storks," said Poole.

"I'm being serious," said Robert.

"So'm I," said Poole. "I'm sorry, sir; but I just can't think of any birds but storks. I'm too damn cold. . . ."

Starlings, Robert thought; they don't go away in winter. But these, whatever they are, are bigger than that. Ducks. They must be ducks. They're flying north and they need some place to rest so they've chosen these fields. That's what it is. They're resting.

The trumpet sounded. Close. Very close.

Poole was so startled he jumped.

"Ha . . . loooo!" Robert shouted. "Good," he said to Poole. "They're here." And then he shouted *ha . . . loooo*! again.

The trumpet replied.

Robert and the trumpet kept this up for six exchanges and after Robert's last haloo a voice came back from the fog.

"Don't move," it said.

"All right," said Robert. His voice thickened.

Poole stopped shivering. "What can be wrong?" he whispered.

"We'll soon find out," said Robert.

Each turned to watch where the voice had been. A man came floating through the fog. His collar was turned up. His hat was missing. This was not the man they had sent away. He was walking.

"Where's your horse?" Robert asked. "Who are you?"

"Me," said the voice.

"Who the hell is *me*?" Robert said.

"*Me*," said the man. "Levitt."

Levitt was a new junior officer who'd joined the convoy at Bailleul that morning. He'd just come over from England.

"Where's the other chap?" said Robert. "And why aren't you riding a horse? You shouldn't come up here without a horse." He was angry. Levitt was supposed to be officer at the rear. This meant there was now no one of rank with the wagons and two of the wagons carried rum.

"I'm sorry," said Levitt: "but I had to come forward. The other chap was soaked to the skin. He and his horse . . ."

"What happened?" said Robert, cutting him off.

"They went through the dike, sir."

"What dike?"

"*This* dike," said Levitt.

Robert blinked. Levitt stared through the fog. Robert looked over his shoulder. Birds.

Levitt said: "I can't tell how far, but somewhere back there you took the wrong turning and you've come out onto this dike and the dike is slowly collapsing." Robert now perceived that Levitt himself was soaked to the skin. "I didn't like the thought of sending one of the men," Levitt went on, "since there were all those horses and someone who knew what they were doing had to stay with them, so I came up myself. The corporal's in charge."

"Thankyou," said Robert. Levitt's sense of detail was practical, if nothing else. "All right," Robert said. "What's our situation?" He was trying not to shake—trying to sound like the C.O.—stiff and unmoved.

Levitt said there was a break in the dike and perhaps the break was a hundred to a hundred and fifty yards behind them. When the rider had gone through, the break was only about six feet across. When Levitt had come through it had widened to ten feet. By now, it might be fifteen or twenty.

Robert swallowed his alarm at having been so blind as to come out onto the dike in the first place. There would be lots of time to think about that. Now, the thing was how to get off. Three men and seven horses.

Levitt gave the bugle back to Poole and thanked him for it. "I was glad of it out there," he said; "because it occurred to me—if any Germans were listening they wouldn't fire at a man with a bugle!" He laughed nervously. "Anyone could be blowing a bugle."

Poole said: "you needn't worry about the Germans

here, sir. They're a long ways off yet. At least as much as two miles or more."

Levitt said: "oh." He seemed somehow demoralized by this news. Perhaps he thought you weren't in the war unless the enemy could shoot you. In this he was much like everyone else who'd just arrived. You weren't a real soldier unless you were in jeopardy.

4: Robert was in the vanguard. He stayed on the horse, knowing the horse's footing would be surer, more sensitive than his own. His father had taught him always to trust the horse's judgement above his own when it came to pathfinding.

The breeze had become a wind. The fog began to lift in places. The shape of the dike was perceptible—wide as a road; but the ditches weren't ditches at all. To the right there was a river, or canal and to the left there must be fields, though these were still unseen. The dike had in fact been often used as a road—and was rutted and torn by cartwheels.

One of the birds flew up and cut across Robert's path. The horse shied. Robert fought to control him. "There, there, there," he said. "Soo, soo, soo." The horse turned sideways—this side then the other. Any way but forward. Robert reined him in.

He crouched in the saddle: squinting. The horse would not go on.

"All right," Robert said aloud. "If you won't, then I must."

He got down and soothed the horse by rubbing its muzzle. Then he left it standing there and struck out into the fog alone. Poole gave a shout and Robert shouted back that they should stay by his horse until he'd found the break. Once, looking over his shoulder he saw them all gathered there—the horses and Poole and Levitt and then the curtain was pulled again and they were gone.

He paused and listened. Surely he would hear something. A river-sound or a waterfall.

Faraway there was a booming noise.

Guns.

5.9s.

They should have been behind him, but these were in front and slightly to the right. How had he got so turned around?

He tested the ground with his heel. Still only mud and slush—the slush like glass that was splintered and mashed. The fog had begun to thicken again. It was full of shapes that waved their arms. Then Robert did hear something. Water. A smooth, deep sound like a sluiceway. The sound was his undoing. He stepped towards it expectantly. Suddenly, his right foot went down. All the way down to the knee though the earth.

Dear Jesus—he was going to drown. He went in all the way to his waist.

He fell back onto his shoulders. All he had to hold with was his elbows. These he ground into the clay like brakes. The slide took him forward so his legs were as much in front of him as below. *Don't,* he kept thinking; *don't.*

His hands were useless to him. If he was going to use them he would have to relax his elbows and he would only slip further in. He lay with his head back. The mud pressed down on his thighs. His neck was raw against his collar. He choked.

Many people die without a sound—because their brains are shouting and it seems they've called for help and they haven't. Robert kept thinking—why doesn't someone come? But no one did. He'd told them not to. The only sound he made was the *o* in don't and this got locked in his throat.

He pushed. He tried to force his pelvis forward and up. The muscles in his stomach made a knot. If he could only lift the weight. The mud spread wider over his thighs. It began to make a sucking noise at the back of his legs. The fog came down like a muffler over his face. One way or another—he would suffocate and drown. He began to push again and to lift—thrusting his pelvis upward harder and harder—faster and faster against the mud. His hat fell off. The wind and the fog were dabbling in his hair. The back of his head went all the way down and into the slush. In and out in and out in and out. With his buttocks clenched and his knees. . . . He began to realize his knees were spreading wider and wider and his groin began to shudder. Warm. He was going to be saved. He was going to save himself. He sat up. His boots were still being held. But his thighs were free. He could see his knees. He began to pull at his legs with his hands. Nothing happened. Absolutely nothing. He leaned forward. He tried to pull at his breeches. His gloves were filled with mud and nothing would hold to them. He tore them off and locked his hands behind his right knee. Then he began to rock. His fingernails gouged his palms. He rocked from side to side and back to front. His leg began to move. Then he locked his hands beneath his left knee and rocked from back to front again. Both legs slid further out till only the ankles were held and his knees touched his chin. He fell back all the way and lay on his side. He reached above his head and shoved his hands down hard through the mud until he could curl his fingers deep in the earth. He pulled himself forward with his legs like twisted ropes and then he gave a violent, sudden spasm and flopped face down in the slush. He was free. In a foot of water.

He could hear himself breathing. Whimpering. He closed his eyes. I don't want to drown, he thought. *Please don't drown.* He pushed himself up with his head hanging down.

His breathing died away.

He knelt with both hands fisted on his knees. He listened. Something was near him. He could feel it.

He opened his eyes and turned his head to one side.

Through the fog he saw a man like himself—in uniform and greatcoat—lying down on his side. His back was to Robert. He was moving—or trying to move. Certainly something about him was in motion. *Slap—slap—slap:* like the raft at Jackson's Point.

Robert rubbed his eyes.

At once they began to smart and in seconds they were burning. The chlorine in the mud. Robert was blinded. He began to feel in his pockets for a handkerchief. There were noises he could not identify. Movement. What? What was it? Had the man got up?

Robert desperately tried to see but his eyes wouldn't open. They were flooded with burning tears and his lids wouldn't lift. He caught a fleeting glimpse of something moving in the air.

A hand fell on his shoulder.

Robert yelled and grabbed at it. Bones and claws. It drew away. Robert shuddered. Birds.

Poole called: "sir? Lieutenant Ross?"

Robert said: "it's all right." Then he realized he hadn't even raised his voice, so he called out: "it's all right. You can come forward now." He tied the handkerchief around his eyes and sat back—waiting. Crows. They'd been crows all along—with wings as long as arms.

When Poole and Levitt reached him with the horses, Poole got Robert to his feet and said to him: "there's a man just there. He's dead I think."

Poole said: "yes, sir."

"Can we help?" said Robert. "Should he be buried?"

"No," said Poole. "We'd best keep going." He took Robert's arm.

From the gap, when Robert's eyes had cleared, he cast a single look back to where the man had been. He saw that the whole field was filled with floating shapes. The only sounds were the sounds of feeding and of wings. And of rafts.

5: Robert went first—on horseback.

The gap in the dike had widened to almost thirty feet. The river washed through but by now the water levels were almost equal on both sides so the pull of the current was not too strong. Still, the horse had to swim for it. The breach was over nine feet deep. Robert took his boots out of the stirrups. He lay along the horse's neck and held onto its mane with one hand. In his other hand he held the lead line to three horses who came through the river behind him. He could feel the surge of the water against his legs as the horse's flank was turned by the current—but cold as it was, Robert was glad of it. The water was washing him free of the mud.

On the far side he could see that the men and the wagons and the rest of the convoy were drawn up near fires and he just kept thinking: warm, I'm going to be warm. The hardest part was not to swim himself—but to let the horse do the swimming. It was an odd sensation, being drawn through the water, almost submerged with his clothes flowing back and his knees pressed hard against the horse and the stirrups banging against his ankles. Pegasus. When he got to the other bank, Robert fell off the horse and the horse went suddenly up the incline without him. He was glad he'd had the sense to take his feet from the stirrups. Otherwise—he'd have been dragged. Several pairs of hands reached down and drew him to the top. The next thing he knew, he was naked and wrapped in a blanket and seated by a fire.

"Break out the rum," he said.

Poole, who was also naked and wrapped in a blanket, played a tune on the bugle and everybody sang: "*we're here because we're here.*" They stayed all night in the middle of the road and sometime after they slept it snowed. In the morning, Robert did not look back towards the field where he'd nearly been drowned. The long meandering line of horses and wagons stretched ahead of him, black and sharp against the snow. When he gave the command to move, he rode up past them all with his eyes on the muddy road. Above them, the sky was breached by a wavering arm of wings. The crows were following.

6: The front, after all, was rather commonplace. Two long parallel lines of trenches, each with its separate network of communications "ditches"—a great many ruined farmhouses and some villages. The situation had been more or less stable for almost a year. The Second Battle of Ypres had taken place in April of 1915 and from that time forward till the end of the war the city would remain in Allied hands. It was here that most of the Canadian troops were deployed. Their objectives were the towns and villages, ridges and woods for roughly ten miles either side of them. That was the larger picture. In terms of individual men and companies, their worlds could be limited to quarter-miles. In Robert's case, the furthest extent of his world was the four miles back to Bailleul.

There were five junior officers attached to the ammunition column (Levitt being the newest) and they spent their time between convoy duty and working the batteries; two weeks with the batteries and a week on convoys. Presently, Robert and a man called Roots had charge of the convoys. (There was a Scotsman in the ranks who took great delight in this combination of names and he would roll out "Rrrrrroots 'n' Rrrrrross!" to everyone's amusement. "Rrrrrroots 'n' Rrrrross is rrrrrrriding" he would say. Or "Rrrrrroots is rrrrrright 'n' Rrrrross is wrrrrrong!") Each man had charge of a Section—seventy-five men and ninety-five horses. Every second morning one of them had to get up at 5:45 to take a ride out for exercise, though sometimes these rides were combined with work duty. Bricks and sandbags and hay and straw had to be moved about or wheels and parts taken up to the guns. Every morning they cleaned the stable. When there was a "show" on, there would be a time alert and the columns would form to transport the ammunition. The size of the order would depend on how long the guns were required to fire. If they were to fire, for instance, for two hours—you knew that was important. Half-an-hour's firing was a mere gesture: *nuisance firing* it was called.

Sometimes, the air would be full of aeroplanes. Then the anti-aircraft guns would open fire. These were called *Archies*—but Robert had nothing to do with them. He was fascinated, though, by the planes. Sometimes the Huns would pass right over the farm where the billets and the depot were and once or twice they dropped bombs, though they did no damage.

There was far more danger from shelling. But Robert thought it was absolutely wonderful, the way the little planes would sail through hundreds of rounds of anti-aircraft fire without being touched.

The day it snowed was the 21st of February. That was the same day the Germans opened their great offensive on the Meuse against Verdun, where their objective was to create a "zone of death." (They succeeded. By August half a million men were dead.) Two million shells were fired that first day at the rate of 100,000 rounds per hour. The bombardment lasted for twelve hours. That same day, word came down the line that the Huns were also making a gas attack at the Ypres Salient. The gas drifted down in Robert's direction—but this was a distance of five miles, south-west—so all they got was the taste of it on snowflakes.

7: The 21st was a Monday; Robert's week of convoy duty was over on the 26th. On the 27th—a high blue, cloudless Sunday—he and Levitt went to take over the guns at the 18th Battery. Specifically, Robert had charge of the mortars. This was Levitt's "maiden voyage" as they said. The light was so good they were able to see some very interesting sights behind the German lines from the Observation Post. Robert was proud to be able to show Levitt just how real the enemy was. It made being up there important, somehow, if you could look out and say: "do you see that man right there with the blue scarf round his neck. . .?" and then describe how you had seen him before on a previous occasion. It gave the war some meaning if you knew that the men who took your fire (and returned it) wore blue scarves or had grey mittens like your own.

There were only two subalterns per battery, so

Robert and Levitt were on their own as far as running things went. One section stayed in the trenches with the mortars for a week and was then relieved by the other section. They lived in dugouts.

The past week there had been almost continuous scrapping in their region, so when Robert and Levitt came down from the O.P. to made their way to quarters, they discovered there was practically nothing left of the trenches. Most of the troops they passed on their way had already been in for sixteen days and were absolutely peppered out. Several men were asleep on the fire steps —leaning back with their mouths open and their rifles stuck up between their legs.

They also passed a German who had lain out in No Man's Land for four days without food. He was staring at the sky—lying on a stretcher. There was a party, too, of about twenty-five or thirty German prisoners who had deserted and come over that morning. The problem was that most of the dugouts in this section of the trench had been destroyed—so there was nowhere to sit or lie down except in the mud. Almost everywhere the fire step remained, it was utilized by sleepers. Hardly anyone was moving. The Germans stood in a sullen row and turned their backs as Robert and Levitt passed.

Since there was practically nothing left of the parapet, Robert and Levitt had to walk the next hundred yards or so in full view of the enemy. Not a single shot was fired and Robert said: "we can thank our lucky stars the Germans must be just as badly off as our poor chaps—or worse, if they're deserting. Otherwise—we'd sniped every second step of the way. . . ." "Do you think we could walk a little faster?" said Levitt. "No," said Robert. "That's the quickest way to get shot. Wait a minute," he said. "Watch this."

Robert stopped walking and turned and waved at the German lines. Nothing happened. He waved again. Still nothing. He called out: "hallo there!" Still nothing. "Now," he said. "Watch this." He ran. At once there was a shot. Robert fell.

After a moment—he looked up out of the mud. "Come on," he said with a grin. "But take your time."

Levitt walked.

Miraculously—their dugout was there. So were both Devlin and Bonnycastle, the men they were relieving.

Levitt was introduced. He swung down the bag he'd been carrying on his back and it bumped dangerously near the door.

"Don't hit the door! Don't hit the door!" Devlin cried. "Great God—don't hit the door!" He was a tall, frail man with a drooping mustache and a slightly receding hairline, despite the fact he was only twenty-seven. He tended to carry his head thrown back, which gave him at first glance a superior look that might have indicated snobbishness or grandeur. But Devlin was possessed of neither of these traits. Anything but. He was gentle as a lamb and wanted to own a shop and sell antiques.

Levitt wondered what made the door so special that he shouldn't hit it. After all—a door should bear striking from time to time. But not this one. As soon as he looked he could see why it was precious. It contained a panel of stained glass.

"What an extraordinary piece of work," he said. "Where on earth did you get it?"

"I collect it," said Devlin. "I got this off a house in St Eloi."

He then showed Levitt three or four other pieces that he kept wrapped in burlap. These were fragments from a church and they depicted the Flight into Eygpt—(the head of the donkey and the head of the Virgin)—Christ Walking on the Water—(His feet and the hem of His gown)—and the Martyrdom of St Marinus, the Roman soldier who was denounced as a Christian and put to death by his fellows. This fragment showed his sword and helmet—laid at his bodied feet.

"All very interesting," said Levitt, with his hands behind his back. He turned to look again at the door.

The glass, in spite of the fact that it came from a house, as Devlin had said, nonetheless depicted a saint —or at least someone holy enough to warrant a halo. The figure—of a bearded man—was stripped to the waist and wore a leather apron. He was working at a forge and held a gigantic "butterfly" in a pair of tongs. The butterfly was rather grotesque and one had to assume that it was such. It was shown as having just been recovered from the flames, in a white hot state.

"Who's that?" Levitt asked.

"That's St Eloi himself," said Devlin. "You see— he's the patron saint of smiths and metalworkers and I find the whole piece rather attractive. Don't you?"

"Very much so," Levitt lied. He thought it was the ugliest piece of glass he'd ever seen. Looking around the dugout—which seemed an inordinately civilized place—he noted there was also a kneeling angel made of plaster and a pair of plaster sheep, no doubt from a crêche. "Are you religious?" he asked Devlin point blank.

"Not in the least," said Devlin. "The fact is, I'm devoted to fragility. Glass has a certain fineness and brittleness that a man with my bones appreciates." He laughed.

"What on earth is that?" Levitt asked—crouching in a corner to look at a small wire cage.

"That's Rodwell's toad," said Bonnycastle, "You mustn't touch it."

"I won't," said Levitt. "Who's Rodwell?"

Robert also wanted to know who Rodwell was. He'd never heard of him.

"He's a visitor," said Bonnycastle. "I think you'll like him. He was shelled out two days ago and came along and asked if he couldn't stay here since we had the four bunks and usually only two chaps. So we said yes. I hope that's all right with you."

Robert nodded. "Who's he with?" he asked.

"One of the Lahore batteries," said Bonnycastle. "They've been out here for ages. Almost since the beginning."

"And he keeps a toad, is that it?"

"Well—" Bonnycastle looked at Devlin. Devlin smiled. "He sort of keeps a lot of things. Maybe you'd like to look under the bunk just here. . . ."

Robert looked.

There was a whole row of cages.

Rowena.

Robert closed his eyes.

"What's in them?" he said. "I can't see."

"Birds. Rabbits. Hedgehogs. Toads and things. . . ."

"Why has he got them down there in the dark like that?"

"They're resting. They've all been injured. That's his sort of hospital, you see." Not one of the animals made a sound.

Robert stood up. "Well—Rodwell's not the only one who has surprises," he said. He crossed over to his knapsack and began to empty it onto the table. "Eggs . . . two dozen. Condensed milk . . . four tins. . . ."

"Eggs—two dozen!" Devlin crowed. "Eggs—two dozen! I don't believe it!"

". . . Cigarettes . . . five hundred," Robert continued. "Canned peaches—four tins . . . canned salmon—two tins. Candles . . . forty-eight . . . Nestlé's chocolate—*six bars*." He stood back in triumph.

"No wine?" said Bonnycastle.

Robert reached into the knapsack one last time: "Cognac—one litre!"

"Cognac—one litre," Devlin muttered. "Robert—Robert: bless your soul and heart. . . ." He seized the bottle and gazed on it lovingly. "Cognac . . . one litre."

"That's not all," said Robert. "Poole is bringing us a chicken stew."

"There now, Bonnie—chicken stew and peaches!" said Devlin. "Doesn't that cheer you up?" Bonnycastle had a small round mouth against which he often laid his fingers as if in deep thought. He was very easily depressed. A single drop of rain could depress him.

Devlin turned the dome of his countenance on Levitt.

"What's in *your* sack?" he asked.

"Yes," Bonnycastle echoed Devlin's evident expectancy. He poked at the sack with his wet fingers. "Uhm? Eh? Uhm . . . ?"

"Books," said Levitt.

"Oh," said Bonnycastle, "Books, eh? What a waste of knapsack."

Delvin threw his head back—only just missing the beams above it—and gave a loud, nasal laugh. "Go on, Bonnie! Don't be too hard on him. After all—everyone likes a good read from time to time. What have you brought us, Levitt?"

"Clausewitz on War."

Bonnycastle and Devlin and Robert stared at him in disbelief.

Levitt picked up the sack protectively. "Well," he said: "someone has to know what he's doing."

8: The dugout, in fact, was rather grand as dugouts go. Levitt's assessment of its being civilized was proper. There were four bunks—four stools and a chair and a large handmade table. Candles and lamps were set in holders nailed to the support beams and a large central lamp swung from a chain over the table. There was a stove at the rear with a coffee pot made of enamelled tin and there was a knotted rug on the floor. Levitt's books now graced the shelf above his bed and the kneeling angel was set in a semi-circle of candles. Down in their cages, the animals stirred—ruffling their fur and feathers. The toad's eyes glistened in the lamplight. Rodwell, it turned out, was fat and dour as a portrait of Doctor Johnson and Robert feared he would be a bad-tempered man, since he seemed to continually scowl and squint. But it was evident that Bonnycastle and Devlin were devoted to him in some way. Throughout the first part of the meal he didn't have a great deal to say—other than thanks for what was put before him. Of this, he was appreciative and he praised the chicken stew, which made Willie Poole feel proud, since the pleasure of strangers is always the most rewarding experience to someone who cooks.

There were six of them for the "banquet" and there being only the four stools and a chair, Poole sat on the steps and ate looking at the winter sky. The door, it turned out, could not be closed. At night, they dropped a canvas tarp across the entrance to keep out the rain.

At any rate, you didn't want to be sealed in tight, since there was no way other than the door to get air.

Levitt, thinking to inject some interest into the conversation, made himself thoroughly unpopular by quoting Clausewitz as follows: "Clausewitz says the true basis of combat is man to man. He says for that reason an army of artillery is an absurdity. . . ."

Somebody coughed.

Bonnycastle said: "are you saying we're absurd?"

"No. I don't think so," said Levitt. "Just that man to man combat is the only true test of what we're doing here. No one's going to prove anything by firing off guns."

"I hope you don't live to regret that," said Devlin pleasantly.

"If the artillery's an absurdity, Levitt," said Bonnycastle, "what are you doing in the C.F.A.?"

"I wanted to join the cavalry, but the cavalry is sort of on the outs," said Levitt. "The only other place I could be with horses was in the Field Artillery."

"You like horses, eh?" said Rodwell.

"Yessir," said Levitt. (Rodwell was a Captain.)

"Well, then—" said Rodwell—smoothing the waters. "Any man whose love of horses is stronger than his fear of being an absurdity is all right with me." And he put out his hand. "How do you do?" he said.

Levitt stood up—shook Rodwell's hand and sat down.

There was a silence.

They ate peaches.

"Where did you find the hedgehog?" Robert asked.

"Under a hedge," said Rodwell.

Everybody laughed.

"I suppose that means you found the bird in the sky, sir," said Devlin.

"Would that I had, Mister Devlin," said Rodwell. "No, sir—I found him with the hedgehog. They were crouched there side by side when I got them and I got them by putting out my hand to secure the toad. We were all there together, you see. It was a popular hedge, just at that moment."

Robert smiled at the thought of Rodwell under a hedge.

"Are you a botanist, sir?" he asked.

"Well, no," said Rodwell. "Not in the professional sense. I'm an artist, you see."

"An artist?" said Devlin. "Mercy me. I'm sorry to say I don't think I know . . ."

Rodwell waved the apology aside with his hand. "Think nothing of it," he said. "I don't expect people to know my work. I'm an illustrator, you see. I illustrate children's books."

"Fairy tales?" said Levitt. He could barely keep the contempt from his voice.

"There's nothing wrong with fairy tales," said Rodwell. "Although, that doesn't happen to be my line. Sometimes, I wouldn't mind a good old fashioned beanstalk to get me out of all this mud. But no. What I do is quite realistic. I should draw that toad, for instance, just as he is without embellishment. In his own right, you know, he has a good deal of character."

"I thought it was improper, sir, to refer to animals as *he* and *she*," said Levitt.

"You're quite the pedant aren't you," Rodwell sighed. "Well—I suppose in the strictest sense—perhaps. It depends how well you know them. . . ." He smiled. "Toad, there—I think of him as *he*. We've endured a lot together."

"May I ask what rank he has?" said Devlin in good humour.

"You may," said Rodwell. "He's a Field Marshall."

"Well then, Levitt—we must call him 'sir' and have done with it," said Devlin and sat back.

After another moment, Bonnycastle said: "I do like a peach. I think a peach is probably the finest thing I can think of."

"You're drunk, dear," said Devlin.

"Bugler," said Bonnycastle. "Play us a song. The peaches have made me sad."

"I will indeed, sir," said Poole. He liked to play for an audience. He drew off his trumpet and made himself comfortable. "Anything you'd like?" he asked.

"Just don't play *Abide With Me,*" said Devlin.

9: Devlin and Bonnie went back through the dark with their scarves around their ears. It was a frigid night. The only lights were the stars. Nothing was afoot. On the far horizon to the south towards Verdun there was a sickly, yellow pall. Nothing else—not even the usual sniper fire.

Robert lay on his bunk half-asleep. Levitt sat at the table reading. When he read he put on spectacles that made him look old. He was a strange man, Robert decided. Eager to be of help—and resourceful in his way—he was also a cold man to whom, it seemed, nothing much existed outside of the mind. He had come back all that way alone with the trumpet to save Robert's life—and Poole's; but what he was doing was merely practical. It had nothing to do with courage or a lack of it. He was the sort of man who when asked *who was there*? said *me*. Who else might there be?

Robert looked along at Captain Rodwell. He too was strange. (We're all strange, Robert thought. Everyone is strange in a war I guess. *Ordinary* is a myth.) Rodwell was feeding the toad. They were two of a kind.

Robert rolled over. He wanted desperately to sleep but his eyes wouldn't close.

Levitt said: "Clausewitz says an excess of artillery leads to a passive character in war. He says artillery must seek out great natural obstacles of ground—*mountain positions*—in order that the topographical impediments may aid the defence and *protection* of our guns. He says in that way the enemy's forces must come themselves and *seek their own destruction.* That way, he says, the whole war can be carried out as a serious, formal minuet. . . ."

"That's nice," said Rodwell. "Everybody likes to dance."

Robert began to drift.

He was lying on a thick bed of chicken wire over which he'd spread his blankets. The wire was strung from the sides of the bunk and the longer you lay on it the deeper it sagged. Robert hooked his fingers through the mesh and held on. His elbows ached. And his wrists.

The sound of distant rifle fire clattered against the dark like a handful of pebbles thrown against a window pane. The pickets were letting one another know they were there—or perhaps a patrol had stumbled on someone alive in No Man's Land. Robert was more perturbed by the turning of Levitt's pages. He wished the tarp was open, no matter how cold it might be. The smoke from the brazier burned his eyes. He was fearful of the fumes from the coke. Men had died in their sleep down the line in a dugout with no ventilation. Coke had a dreadful smell. It wasn't anything like the comforting smell of coal that, for Robert, was the childhood smell of winter living rooms where great blue chunks of cannel-coal had burned all day—and of evenings barely recalled when someone held him in a knitted blanket almost asleep by a yellow flame.

The dugout was full of eyes: Robert's that would not close; Levitt's that stared at Clausewitz; Rodwell's squinting against the smoke and the animals' staring at the dark that only they could penetrate. Rodwell held the toad in its cage on his lap. The only one who slept was the bugler. If it hadn't been for the battle, Rodwell's toad would probably still be asleep in the mud like Poole, who was lying on a shelf cut into the earth. His pillow was a rubber boot he'd stuffed with socks. Robert's pillow was his haversack, with its buckles turned down and caught in the wire. He wished he'd thought of a rubber boot himself but it was too late now for that. He was as near to sleep as he'd get and he didn't want to jeopardize his chances of getting all the way, though he knew the chances were slim. Sleep was dangerous. The animal memory in you knew that. No matter what your mind said, your body didn't listen. Part of you always stayed awake. In Robert's case it was his hands and feet. His fingers, in spite of gloves, were bound to bleed before morning because they clung so tightly to the wire. His toes were curled like fists inside his boots—like a monkey's toes or the claws of a bird that are locked to a branch. Robert smiled. Perhaps his hair would sleep—but that would be all.

Poole's breathing was harsh and liquid. He'd probably caught a cold in the marshes. It reminded Robert of Harris—and that was the last thing he needed reminding of. All he wanted was a dream. Escape. But nobody dreams on a battle field. There isn't any sleep that long. Dreams and distance are the same. If he could run away . . . like Longboat. Put on his canvas shoes and the old frayed shirt and tie the cardigan around his waist and take off over the prairie. . . . But he kept running into Taffler. Throwing stones. And Harris.

10: The old country house in England that Robert had described for his parents was near a town in Kent called Shorncliffe. It was here the C.F.A. maintained its reserve brigades that supplied reinforcements to the Canadian Corps in France. Robert and Harris had only been there a week. Harris became so ill the doctors in the small infirmary couldn't cope and he was sent to London where he was installed at the Royal Free Hospital in Gray's Inn Road. Robert, at roughly the same time, received his embarkation leave and took it in London—mostly in behalf of Harris with whom he'd become close friends—but also because Mister Hawkins, the RAYMOND/ROSS representative in England, had procured a Webley automatic for Robert at his father's request and Robert wanted to have it. The dates are obscure here—but it must have been mid-January, 1916 since Robert's tour of duty began on the 24th of that month.

The buildings of the Royal Free Hospital had once been the barracks of the Light Horse Volunteers. That was at the time of Waterloo. Sometime in the 1840s they'd been converted to their present use. They were red and formal and damp. Robert went nearly every day to visit his friend. The afternoons were dark and foggy—lonely and full of hollow noise. The people in the streets all hurried along taking small nervous steps with their collars turned up and their hats pulled down. No one spoke, except to say "excuse me" or "watch where you're going!" It was like a tunnel through which you walked not knowing your destination. Everyone remained a stranger. At night—the Zeppelins came. There was a sense of silent menace.

Harris had no other visitors. No one had responded to the cablegrams sent back to Sydney, Nova Scotia. It was evidently true that Harris's estrangement from his father was final. There was not even thanks. Just silence.

Some afternoons, Harris couldn't open his eyes. Every ounce of energy was devoted to breathing. Robert sat in a chair and watched him. Harris's hair was damp with fever. His nurses and doctors shook their heads. They were glad that Robert had come. They told him bluntly no one should die alone.

The ward was filled with wounded. Some of these were on the way to recovery—others lay silent, wrapped in bandages and held together by splints. Many visitors came and went—some with bottles of stout and tins of cake and others with hampers of chicken sandwiches, devilled eggs and breast of grouse. Flowers were carried in of every kind—from single camelias to clusters of wilted daisies in the hands of children. Once, on a snowy afternoon, the corridors were cleared for the Princess Royal who came to visit a cousin wounded at Gallipoli. She carried a dozen yellow roses. Sometimes there was even an atmosphere of gaiety as the visitors spread their gifts and flowers like picnics over the covers. Robert sat in the midst of all this wearing his polished boots and his uniform with the spotless breeches and he crossed his feet beneath the chair and folded his hands and watched for hours while Harris fought for breath. The hours were made worthwhile whenever Harris woke and smiled and sometimes Robert had to look away because he was confused by what he felt.

The thing was—no one since Rowena had made Robert feel he wanted to be with them all the time. If what he felt could be reduced to an understanding—that was it. "I have to get over there and see him," Robert would think every morning when he woke up. He also wanted to be there if Harris spoke. Harris said the strangest things—lying on his pillows staring at the ceiling. Strange and provocative. Robert didn't know, sometimes, what to do with Harris's sentences; where to fit them in his mind, or how to use them. He only knew they went somewhere inside him and they didn't come back out.

"Where I swam, there was a shelf. I used to walk to the edge of the shelf and sit with my legs dangling down. I've no idea how deep it was. Sitting on the shelf at low tide, my head was just above the water. Then I'd slide. Like a seal. Out of the air and into the water. Out of my world into theirs. And I'd stay there hours. Or so it seemed. I'd think: *I never have to breathe again*. I've changed. It changes you. But the thing was—I could do it. Change—and be one of them. They aren't any friendlier—the fish, you know. But they accept you there. As if you might belong, if you wanted to. It's not like here. It's not like here at all."

Then he would sleep. And in his sleep his hands would move at his sides as if he dreamt of swimming—or of "breathing" in the other element.

One day—very early in the morning—Harris said to Robert: "once I got lost. In a school of mackerel. Silver. Blinding. Every time they turned, I was blinded by their scales. We swam into seaweed. Kelp. Long, slippery arms, like horses' tails. It caught round my neck and I thought I couldn't breathe—that I was going to drown and die. Until I began to swim again—and once I began to swim again I realized the kelp was coming with me. See? In that place—there—in *that* element—somehow I was safe—even from choking. The kelp just slid away—let go of its root and came with me. But once I'd landed on the shore, it knotted and dragged and I couldn't get it off. It wasn't till then that I nearly died. In the air. With this thing around my neck. In the *air*. . . ."

Then he'd look at Robert—once he'd spoken. Never while he spoke. He was really only talking to himself, Robert guessed, before he slept.

One afternoon Robert came late because he'd been to a matinee at the theatre. His mind was full of music and it was hard to sit there on his death watch and not tap his toes. Harris was more or less asleep, his breathing more and more forced. There was talk of an iron lung—but these were rare and at a premium. There was nothing to be done but listen. All at once, there was laughter down by the doors that led to the corridor and Eugene Taffler came in with a woman Robert recognized as Lady Barbara d'Orsey. It was she who'd been laughing but when she came around the corner, the laughter stopped. Her arms were filled with freesia. There was snow in her hair. Her lips were parted.

The effect of her sudden appearance was the same as always when you see someone materialize whose fame has kept them at a distance. You think how small they are and you wish they'd stand still. Her picture, like those of Cathleen Nesbitt and Lady Diana Manners, was "everywhere." Recently, more often than not, she was photographed with Taffler; dancing for charity—joking with the Prince of Wales—riding in the park. Taffler was looking more like a *Boy's Own Annual* hero than ever, dressed in his uniform with its green field tabs; carrying a swagger stick and groomed within an inch of his life. He'd just had his hair cut—a sure sign he was returning to the front. It was always the last thing you did. His head seemed enormous. His eyes and his mouth were like pictures of a mouth and eyes: static. His hands were naked. Robert blushed.

He stood up. It seemed the only thing to do. Taffler spotted him at once and came across the room, leaving Barbara d'Orsey behind him near the doors. All the time she waited, she stood with her furs against one cheek, gazing from the windows and showing no apparent interest in anything, though Robert noticed that her hands were shaking.

"It's Ross, isn't it?" Taffler said, taking Robert's hand in both his own. His pleasure seemed genuine. It probably was. Considering where they were it must have been heartening to see someone still unscathed and in such good health as Robert at that moment. (The bruises on Robert's legs had paled and he no longer limped or felt any pain.)

Robert stammered an explanation about Harris and after he'd done this, Taffler said he must come across the room and meet Lady Barbara. Robert didn't want to intrude. Taffler insisted. He put his hand on Robert's elbow and guided him between the beds.

Nothing happened this first time they met. Barbara was distracted. Robert noticed the shape of her eyes and the way she watched him. She stared—not rudely—but with kindness. It was as if she willed him politely to go away. Robert soon took his cue and left them. For a moment, Barbara didn't move. She looked around the ward and then at Taffler much as to say: what am I supposed to do now? He indicated a figure in a bed at the farthest end of the room.

Watching from his chair beside Harris, Robert could

not help witnessing the scene that followed. Taffler and Barbara moved down the aisle with Taffler's hand on her elbow just as he'd used it to propel Robert earlier—Barbara tightening her grip on the flowers in her hand. In the bed where they stopped was a man entirely encased in bandages. He was quite unable to move. Robert had already been intrigued by his silence.

Barbara stood at the foot of the bed and looked at the man without speaking. The aroma from her flowers filled the ward. The profile she turned to Robert was unsmiling. She held the flowers the way that wreaths are held—as an emblem, not as a gift. Taffler went to the head of the bed and leaned down over the man to speak. Barbara took a deep breath and closed her eyes. Whatver it was that Taffler said, it went unheard by anyone except the man in the bandages. Robert could see he was straining to reply—but no words came: not even a whisper. Finally Taffler touched him on the shoulder as a signal they were going and, collecting Barbara, he left quite suddenly without turning back and without even nodding in Robert's direction. Barbara still held the flowers and her expression was as blank as that of someone drugged. When they'd gone Robert could feel the man in the bandages "screaming" and the sensation of this silent agony at the other end of the room was finally so strong that Robert had to go and get one of the nurses. When she came and had administered some morphine she thanked him for his quick response. She told him the man had been trapped in a fire and his vocal cords destroyed when he'd swallowed the flames. Robert asked who he was. The nurse said: "Captain Villiers." Then she said something strange that made Robert blush—though he didn't know why. Perhaps it was the nurse's vehemence

—and the way she lowered her voice. "Just don't ask me about that woman. I don't know how she dares to come here." *That woman* was Barbara d'Orsey.

11: This part of the narrative is told by Lady Juliet d'Orsey, whose memories of Robert Ross—for reasons that will become apparent—are the most vivid and personal we have. At the time of the events she describes, she was twelve years old. She is now in her seventies.

Juliet d'Orsey is the fourth of the Marquis and Marchioness of St Aubyn's five children. She is the lone survivor and has never married. She still resides in rooms at number 15, Wilton Place—the St Aubyn's London address since 1743. The lower floors of this house are currently occupied by the Ministry of Scientific Research. To reach Wilton Place, you get off at Hyde Park Corner and walk down Knightsbridge passing St George's Hospital and shortly afterwards a somewhat sinister sign proclaiming the *Royal Society for Prevention of Accidents.* Wilton Terrace is to the left, in sunshine.

You can feel the bureaucratic atmosphere of the Ministry as soon as you enter the hall. The place is infused with the threat of large numbers of people in hiding. Everyone is studiously dedicated to ignoring what you want. Backs are turned as soon as they perceive that you're a stranger and might ask questions. Secretaries wander up and down the stairways, with their hands against their foreheads, muttering "*where —where—where did I put it?*" Telephones jangle for hours on end, unanswered. Someone turns to you and says: "was that the 'phone?" When you ask for Juliet d'Orsey, they tell you they've never heard of her. One bright lady informs you "she was fired last week." Other doors mysteriously close as you approach. You're aware, through a window at the end of a hall, that a large black Daimler has drawn to the curb. A hatless little man gets out and stands on the sidewalk looking lost. Everyone stops and holds her breath: *the Minister has just arrived. Dear God—will he come inside*? At last you make your way by trial and error to the second-floor landing and a door marked LADY JULIET D'ORSEY—PLEASE RING TWICE. You feel like Aldren on the moon.

The door is opened by Lady Juliet's young companion who introduces herself as Charlotte Krauss. Miss Krauss is twenty-eight or so and wears a neat, tan dress. She tends to pocket her hands and stand on her heels. She is bright and attentive and discreet. She retires almost at once to make some tea. You have already been directed down a long cream-coloured hall hung with ancestors and lit by open doorways. At the far end there is a wide and charming drawing room full of tall blue chairs on an apricot carpet. A fireplace, crowded with blazing logs, dominates a whole wall. The windows, leading to balconies, look out directly at the portals of St Paul's, Knightsbridge—a Gothic miscarriage where a choir practice is presently in progress.

Lady Juliet has her back to you. "Just one moment," she says, without turning, and you wait with your brief-case and tape recorder in your hands in the middle of the rug. There are freesia on the mantelpiece in a plain white vase. Something in Latin being sung across the road comes to a conclusion and finally Lady Juliet turns to you and says: "I know you'll forgive me. I can't resist the Mass." She smiles and moves to the other end of the room by the fire, where she lights a cigarette and throws back her head in order to see you through the sunlight. "All I ask," she says, fitting the cigarette into a holder, "is that you don't call me Juli-*et*. I cannot abide Juli-*et*. It maddens me!"

"Yes, ma'am."

"Here, we say Joolyut. *Joolyut. Joolyut.* Say it for me."

"Joolyut."

"That's right. How-do-you-do?"

She has short, grizzled hair that has always been curly and fine, long quivering hands that are crippled with arthritis. She is tall and seems to be dangerously thin. She is one of those women who live on a starvation diet by their own free choice. Hers consists of spinach and melba toast, cigarettes and a lot of gin. The gin has no effect whatsoever on her speech or her clarity of mind. It is simply one of her foods. She sits with her hip against one side of the chair, leaning towards the other side, smoking one cigarette after another. She doesn't seem to be able to butt them very successfully. The ashtray smoulders the whole afternoon.

She is proud of Robert Ross. The only time that anger flashes is when she mentions his detractors. The name of Stuart Ross, for instance, causes her to stutter. "Still," she admits, when she's regained her composure, "a brother is a brother. I had them myself. There are enmities in families that have to be foreborne. But oh . . . when it turns to hate. I gather he refuses to speak to you."

"That's right."

"I don't understand. It's as if Robert did something evil."

"Some say he did."

"Some maniacs. Oh yes—I've heard that, too."

For a moment she looks from the window and listens, seeming to draw restraint from the Mass in progress.

"Exaudi orationem meam,
ad te omnis caro veniet."

Hear thou my prayer—unto thee shall all flesh come. . . .

"It's comforting, isn't it," she says.

But you wonder.

12: Transcript: Lady Juliet d'Orsey—1:

"They met—my sister and Robert Ross—because of that man Harris. And Jamie Villiers . . . . ." (*Captain James Villiers was the man in bandages Barbara and Taffler went to visit.*) "Jamie had always been a friend of ours. He was very close to my brother Clive. Clive's only sport was riding. Jamie was one of the finest point-to-pointers in the country. His greatest ambition was to ride the Grand National. This was unheard of—of course; not just because he was the son of a duke but because he was enormous. Enormous! Tall as a giraffe. And just as sweet. Dear Heart. He was a lovely man. Barbara was devoted to him. Weren't we all? But Barbara made a dreadful nuisance of herself. I should explain that all of Barbara's friends were men. Women—myself amongst them, alas—irritated and irked her. *They make me itch,* she said. She adored our brothers, who were closest to her in age. I was eight years younger. Temple was a mere babe. So Barbara grew up with Michael and Clive and all of their friends were her friends. It was always understood, in our family, that when somebody spoke of 'the girls' they referred to me and Temple—never to Barbara. For as long as I can remember she had a taste for heroes and athletes. She enjoyed the spectacle of winning—but more than that, she made a sort of cult of exclusivity: letting people in and out of her life. She was like a club. But she wasn't a *snob*. Anything but. It was just that a wall went up if you didn't intrigue her. I think that was it. You had to intrigue her or you didn't exist. There she is over there. It's not a bad picture. You can see the sceptical eyes and the strange perpetual smile. I'll tell you a secret about that smile. It wasn't a smile at all. It was a nervous dimple on her left side. True. I swear it. I was saying . . . . Jamie Villiers. Yes. This was before the war. I was only nine. Or eight or something. Barbara always tagged along when Clive and Jamie took the horses out. Clive and Jamie were both at Cambridge. Just. I think they hadn't even been up a year. Barbara hadn't an ounce of sophistication. She was very much like a man in that. I've never met—have you?—a truly sophisticated man. World-weary and discreet—of course. But never sophisticated. Barbara couldn't even see what she was interrupting. She could be such a dreadful *clod*, you know. Day after day she'd tag along till Clive had to *tell* her. Well—he had to *indicate* that she was mucking up a friendship. She came storming into the house—this was up at Stourbridge St Aubyn's—and flew around in an absolute rage. *I don't understand! I don't understand!* she kept saying. Finally, I had to tell her. *They're in love*, I said. Barbara said: *who with*? She really was rather stupid. I said: *don't you know anything about boys at all? They're in love with each other*. (LAUGHTER) Oh dear. Barbara hated me for that. And Clive. They had the most frightful argument. Mummy had to stop them. Mummy was enormously understanding. She'd had her own brothers and knew this thing would pass. But Barbara said that Clive had undermined Jamie's morals and she called them *Oscar* and *Bosie* and ultimately settled her affections elsewhere. On Ivan Cromwell-Jones, I think—or someone like that. But you see—that isn't just an amusing story. There's a point. Barbara's wrath. Her coldness in the presence of someone else's death. No one else was allowed to love—possess—or steal her heroes and her lovers. If you substitute the war for Clive in that story . . . well, I'm sure you get my point." (*At this juncture Charlotte Krauss arrived with the tea tray. You were invited to listen to the music and make a choice of sandwiches while the tea was poured. Miss Krauss—with no attempt to hide what she was doing—laced the bottom of Lady Juliet's cup with gin and placed the bottle on the table with the smouldering ashtray. Then she departed and the machine was switched back on.*) "Barbara went through a lot of men and didn't get back to Jamie Villiers till the summer of 1915. That was when he got his first decorations and came home a hero and Barbara snatched him away from Diana Menzies. You can see that Barbara was possessive, to say the least. Once she set her cap—that was that. It couldn't matter less who got hurt. She even tried to hold on to Clive and Michael. Her *brothers*! (LAUGHTER) Oh, I can tell you I'm certainly glad I wasn't a boy in our family! Or in love with a boy in our family. Later, when Clive was engaged to Honor Hampton, Barbara refused to give her blessing and made life hell for poor dear Honor—who of course never did marry Clive. He was killed on the First of July."

(*When men and women of Juliet d'Orsey's vintage*

refer to the "First of July" they inevitably mean the first of July, 1916. It was on that date the Somme offensive was begun. In the hours between 7:30 a.m and 7:30 p.m. 21,000 British soldiers were killed—35,000 were wounded and 600 taken prisoner by the Germans. This is perhaps as good a place as any to point out that Lord Clive Stourbridge, Juliet and Barbara's eldest brother, was one of the Cambridge poets whose best-known work—like that of Sassoon and Rupert Brooke—had its roots in the war. Other poets who were present on the First of July, besides Stourbridge and Sassoon, were Robert Graves and Wilfred Owen. Both Sassoon and Graves have written accounts of the battle.)

"The thing you want to know about is Barbara meeting Robert and how it was that Harris brought about their ultimate relationship. These are the circles—all drawing inward to the thing that Robert did. You know—I'm guessing at this—but I think that Robert was in love with Harris. Somewhat the same way Jamie had been in love with Clive. It may be pedestrain to say so—but the truth is often pedestrian and I think the fact is that extremely physical men like Robert and Jamie and Taffler are often extremely sensitive men as well. Not your local football players, mind you! They're more apt to be maudlin and sentimental. But the true athletes—the ones who seek beauty through perfection. I think they seek out poets and artists just as poets and artists seek them out. Maybe not always as lovers—though 'love' has so many ways of expressing itself outside of the physical. I certainly don't want to paint a picture of a lot of poets and athletes lusting after one another's bodies! But love—yes. Robert, though he never said so, loved Harris. It was clear in the way he dealt with his death and in the way he spoke of him afterwards to [illegible] war was part of it too. You cannot know these [illegible] You live when you live. No one else can ever live y[illegible]r life and no one else will ever know what you know. Then was then. Unique. And how does one explain? *You* had a war. Every generation has a war—except this one. But that's beside the point. The thing is not to make excuses for the way you behaved—not to take refuge in tragedy—but to clarify who you are through your response to when you lived. If you can't do that, then you haven't made your contribution to the future. Think of any great man or woman. How can you separate them from the years in which they lived? You can't. Their greatness lies in their response to that moment. Well—let's forget about greatness and get back to what I began to say. The war. Siegfried said a marvellous thing—" (*Sassoon*)— "He was taking his troops to the front and they were walking along a road that had been shelled and he saw a soldier lying dead by the road whose head had been smashed. It was an awful shock. The first dead man he'd seen, I think. And he sort of accepted it. But the acceptance made him mad and he said this marvellous thing: *I still maintain that an ordinary human being has a right to be horrified by a mangled body seen on an afternoon walk*. So what it was we were denied was to be ordinary. All our ordinary credos and expectations vanished. *Vanished*. There was so much death. No one can imagine. These were not *accidents*—or the quiet, expected deaths of the old. These were murders. By the thousands. All your friends were . . . murdered. (PAUSE) I know 'the bomb' is terrible. But if the bomb falls, we all die together. In the war you had to face it day after day—week after week—month after month—year after year. Every day another friend. And what I hate these days is the people who weren't there and they look back and say we became inured. Your heart froze over—yes. But to say we got *used* to it! God—that makes me so angry! No. Everything was sharp. Immediate. Men and women like Robert and Barbara—Harris and Taffler . . . you met and you saw so clearly and cut so sharply into one another's lives. So there wasn't any rubbish. You lived without the rubbish of intrigue and the long-drawn-out propriety of romance and you simply touched the other person with your life. Sometimes to the quick. Robert sat by Harris day after day and day after day Barbara and Taffler came to see Jamie. This is the hardest thing of all for me to admit about my sister. Her silence in Jamie's presence. Was it cruel? Of course it was. Not to let him hear her voice. Nothing was left of him, you know. Nothing but nerves and pain and his mind. No voice—no flesh. Nothing. Just his *self*. Later, as you'll see, this forms a sort of pattern . . . well—a very definite pattern. Barbara with her flowers. Her freesia. Emanations. There they are on the mantle. And she was like that cold white vase and never said a word. She stood and watched them dying like a stone. Ariadne and Dionysus. Well—it's not a bad analogy. Yes? Deserted by one god—she took up another. Every year, Dionysus was destroyed and every year he was born again from ashes. So Barbara went there every day and stood by Jamie's bed with Taffler and every day she saw Robert Ross. Probably only from the corner of her eye. But she was aware of him. She'd come back here—sometimes with Taffler—and sit by the fire with a glass of sherry in her hand and watch the flames and Taffler would tell about the other men in the ward—Robert and Harris among them. Mummy was the one who said we should invite Robert up to St Aubyn's. But that was not till later and that's when I met him myself and he told me all about Harris. After their arrival in England, Robert and Harris were in the infirmary at Shorncliffe together—Harris getting worse and worse and Robert recovering his legs. Harris did a lot of talking through the nights when neither man could sleep. He'd never been abroad. He was an only child and had a brilliant mind. Almost, if not, a poet. Certainly a storyteller. Lying in the dark he told Robert tales of forest fires and men out lost in ships in winter storms. Of summers climbing shale and watching birds. Of the high, hot valleys filled with clattering stones and rivers running underground. And whales. He told of having swum with schools of whales and claimed that underwater you could hear them sing. Robert was sceptical. Whales made no sound at all. Now, of course, we know that Harris was right. I even have a recording of whales myself. But Robert didn't believe it. Then. Harris said that sometimes the whales would beach themselves and then the fishermen would come in boats and slaughter them. Harris said he would sometimes lie offshore and let himself be carried in by tides that washed him up the sand—the sand was red and he told how he would float that way sometimes for hours, just to get the feel of landfall—sort of the way a million years ago or more we came ashore ourselves as fish or frogs or whatever it was we were—floating through slaughter. But Robert said: *we were always men.* He didn't believe all that stuff about fish and frogs. He said he believed that everything was what it was. *No*—said Harris—*Everyone who's born has come from the sea. Your mother's womb is just the sea in small. And birds come out of seas in eggs. Horses lie in the sea before they're born. The placenta is the sea. And your blood is the sea continued in your veins. We are the ocean*

—walking on the land." (THERE IS A PAUSE—THEN LADY JULIET SAYS) "I wish someone would tell them that, downstairs in the Ministry of Scientific Research!" (YOU CHANGE TAPES) "Robert asked Harris once if he wasn't afraid, swimming around with whales that way and floating on the tide. Drowning had always been a particular fear of Robert's. *No*, Harris said: *he wasn't afraid at all.* His mother had died when he was three. He'd grown up eating alone with his father at a twelve-foot table with a candle in the centre between them. Burning and silent. When he died, Robert took his gloves with the bitten fingers and the long blue scarf he'd wound around his neck." (*The Mass intrudes at this point—"Kyrie eleison. Christe eleison. Kyrie eleison." Then Lady Juliet concludes.*) "The last scene of this ties them all together: Robert —Harris—Barbara—Taffler—even Jamie, I suppose. You have to remember they'd seen each other every day for over a week. Harris's death occurred two days before Robert was scheduled to leave for France. He opened his eyes—smiled the way he always did when he woke—and waved. *Thankyou*, he said. And died. Like that. Robert went away and walked in the snow. He didn't know what to do. His leave was nearly up. He didn't want to abandon his friend to strangers. The army might have buried him—but that was grotesque; a body in a box beneath a flag he'd never had a chance to fight for—and by the time all that could be arranged, Robert would be gone. He'd tried to get a response near the end from Harris's father—cablegrams and letters. Nothing. He'd even requested his own father to send a cable from Toronto. Nothing. Then it was solved—through a dreadful mistake. When Robert returned to the Royal Free Hospital the day after Harris's death to ask their advice and to deal with

Harris's effects, he discovered to his horror that Harris had been cremated. The technical reasons for this are far too complicated to be of interest—having to do with procedures in the morgue and mistaken identity and a rather stupid orderly. Suffice it to say that when Robert arrived he was told of the mishap and offered the ashes as a *fait accompli.* They were in a square wooden box about the size of a very large cannister of tea and the box was wrapped in burlap. Robert sat in the foyer of the hospital with the box in his lap. He sat there for hours. He sat there so long that he was there when Barbara and Taffler arrived to visit Jamie. He explained what had happened. Barbara, as usual, was carrying flowers. This time they were roses. The problem was—what to do with the ashes. Robert couldn't carry them to France. And there wasn't any church where they'd accept them because no one would accept the ashes of a man who hadn't been a parishioner. Barbara said: *why don't you scatter them*? *Where*? Robert asked—and Taffler said *where would he like to be, do you think*? Robert thought about it. *The sea*, he said. But the sea was too far. Barbara decided on a compromise. They would take the ashes to Greenwich and scatter them on the river. The river is marvellous there and wide and the next best thing to the sea. So that is what they did. They hired a cab and drove all the way to Greenwich—Robert sitting on the jump seat with the ashes on his lap—Barbara sitting apart from Taffler with the roses cradled in her arm. Nobody spoke. They left the cab at King William's Walk. It snowed. They decided to throw the ashes from the end of the pier. Robert went first and Taffler followed. Barbara stood in the centre of the pier with the roses hanging down against her side. She could hardly see through the snow, she said. It was terribly cold and the wind blew down the river and all the mournful whistles sounded from the ships. The cab had gone. They were deserted. Only the three of them stood there. Just before he removed the lid from the container, Robert turned to Taffler and said to him: *this is not a military funeral. This is just a burial at sea. May we take off our caps*? Taffler, who had a seniority, said yes. He removed his cap and Robert did the same. The tide was in their favour and the flats across the river were melting in the rush of snow and water. Robert pried off the lid and placed his hand for a moment over the exposed ashes. They were grey. A sort of yellowish grey. Robert thought: I've never seen this done or read about its being done—not even in *Chums* or Joseph Conrad, so I don't know what to say. He made it up. *Go*, he said; *in peace. And sing with the whales*. That was all. Then he scattered some of the ashes with his fingers—flinging them as far as he could, but the wind would not let them settle on the water. Robert turned to Taffler. He remembered th stones on the prairie. And the long Varsity passes. *You've got a better arm than me*, he said. *Would you put him in the centre of the river*? Taffler nodded. Even in the snowstorm, he removed his jacket. He handed it to Barbara. She said it was like a ceremony. He also handed her his cap. Robert gave him the container. Taffler weighed the box and stared at the river, gauging the distance and measuring the wind. Then he leaned way back and wound the box behind his ear—just like a football and giving a great, inadvertent yell he threw it out so far it passed the centre and was gone from sight. Barbara said they stood and watched for a very long time, until the roses began to crumble. After, when Taffler had put his jacket on and he and Robert had struggled back into their greatcoats, the three of them walked away towards the Royal Naval College, Barbara trailing rose petals, and Barbara said to Robert: *you may not realize, Lieutenant Ross, that General Wolfe was born at Greenwich.* No. Robert hadn't realized. *Yes*, said Barbara. *Then he grew up and got your country for us.* Robert said: *no*, ma'am. I think we got it for him. *We*? Barbara asked. *Soldiers*, said Robert. It was the first time he'd truly thought of himself as *being* a soldier. Maybe it was because of the ashes on his fingers. That night, he boarded the troop train at Victoria Station and went down through the dark to Folkestone where he crossed in a storm to Boulogne and was in France."

This is where the first transcript of Juliet d'Orsey ends. But only because the choir across the road had begun to shout—and she "cannot resist the Mass."

"Please come again," she says.

And you will. For hers is the end of the story.

13: On the 27th of February, Robert had finally fallen asleep close to midnight. At exactly 4:00 a.m. on the morning of the 28th, the Germans set off a string of land mines ranged along the St Eloi Salient. One of these blew up the trenches five hundred yards directly in front of the stained glass dugout. The blowing of the mines was a signal for the artillery to start firing and the whole of the countryside seemed to jump into flames. This was the beginning of the second phase of a battle the Canadians had thought was already over. But it was to rage for five more days. In it 30,000 men would die and not an inch of ground would be won. It began with Robert lying under his bunk with a rabbit, a hedgehog and a bird. After the landmines had gone up and after the first long salvo had been fired by the guns, there was a very brief moment of silence.

In this silence, Rodwell was heard to say to Levitt: "some minuet."

PART THREE

Monday, February 28th
4:00 a.m.

When the mines went up the earth swayed. Forward. Back. Forward. Half-back. Then there was a sort of glottal stop—halfway to nowhere. The spaces that had been opened filled with smoke and things began to fall. Helmets, books, canned goods, gas masks and candles fell off the shelves. Then the shelves fell. Then the earth fell in clods.

Robert held to the wire until the swaying stopped. That was when he went under. He was lying on his stomach with the cages gathered into his arms before he realized where he was. For a moment he was deafened. All the sounds were muffled and interior—far away inside his head. The contents of a bag of flour and some talcum powder from a shaving kit were floating in the air. His eyes wouldn't close because his lids were caked with what amounted to paste. His mouth and his nostrils were clogged with earth. Blood ran down the back of his throat because it couldn't escape through his nose.

At first there was darkness, all the candles having been extinguished by the wave of concussion. Then, because the tarp had fallen at an angle, light began to filter through from the fires outside and Robert could see the shapes of the cages and the standing uprights of the bunk in front of him. The light was thick and foggy: yellow through the morning air.

It wasn't till Rodwell spoke that Robert realized he could hear. After that, the pounding of the guns was less a noise than a brutal sensation of being repeatedly hit. The blows came upward into his stomach and groin. Someone—or a sandbag—was lying on his back. He couldn't feel his legs. His feet were dead. He wondered where they were. As the pounding of the guns increased there was a howling, yawning noise that came from the other side of the dugout. Robert turned his head to see what was happening.

The roof was coming down.

The yawning noise was made by the spikes as they were drawn from the wooden supports. The roof was a single sheet of corrugated tin—piled with sandbags and earth. It didn't "fall." It tipped—slowly angling upward over Robert's side of the dugout and down towards the ground on the other side. As it did this, the earth and the sandbags slowly slid across the tin, making a sound like a long, deep wave retreating over a pebble beach. It seemed to go on forever. Robert waited—holding his breath—thinking they were going to be buried alive. But the heaving stopped at last and it appeared that whatever was going to collapse had done so. At least for the moment.

The bird shook its feathers.

The rabbit turned with its eyes shut tight and huddled in the corner of its cage facing Robert. The hedgehog lay on its side in a ball.

Robert said: "Captain Rodwell?"

"Yes?"

"Where are you?"

"I'm on top of you."

"Can you move?"

"No. The other bunk is lying on top of me and I think it's full of earth."

The wire was cutting into them both.

Levitt spoke from under the table.

"Do you think I should come out?" he asked.

"We aren't playing hide-and-seek," said Rodwell. "Please come out, by all means—if you're so inclined."

The flour and the dust had settled sufficiently for Robert now to be able to see the table and, under it, Levitt on his hands and knees. He crawled out—still clutching Clausewitz—and banged the book against the tails of his greatcoat and stamped his boots and slapped his arms, sending up clouds of talcum powder into the air. Lavender.

"Where is Poole?" said Robert—suddenly aware that nothing had been heard from the bugler.

"Who is Poole?" said Levitt.

"God damn it!" said Robert. "Poole, my batman! Where is he?"

"Please don't swear at me, Lieutenant Ross," said Levitt. "I really can't bear it."

Robert said: "will you see what you can do about getting Captain Rodwell off my back?"

"Yes," said Levitt; "but please don't swear at me."

Robert didn't reply.

Levitt—who in fact was suffering from shock—stood quite still for a moment looking about the half-collapsed dugout.

Robert said: "what are you waiting for?"

Levitt said: "I'm looking for somewhere to put down my book."

"Give it to me," said Rodwell sensibly. "Then you can pull this stuff away."

Robert watched Levitt's feet beside him as Levitt

started pulling things aside and throwing them over his shoulder. Rodwell said: "don't be so hasty. You're hurting me." Slowly, the weight began to lift from Robert's back and he realized his legs were still intact when the blood began to flow again and his toes began to burn with pins and needles. Then there was a sudden cry and a lurch and Rodwell's feet appeared beside Levitt's.

A wedge of chicken wire was sticking out of Rodwell's knee. He plucked it away and threw it aside. "Ouch," he said—and laughed.

They dragged Robert out by his arms and pulled him to his feet. As soon as they let go, Robert sank to his knees.

"Something broken?" Rodwell asked.

Robert said his legs were just asleep and sat on the earth for a moment rubbing his shins. Rodwell collected the cages one by one—inspecting the contents with his fingers, prodding and cooing, muttering "so—so—so" and then he placed the cages in a row near the step with the toad on top. All the animals had survived, although the hedgehog still had not unrolled himself.

Levitt was picking up books—dusting them off with his sleeve and making a pile of them on the top of the table. The roof—angled open—gave a view of an orange and rolling sky. Long, thick curls of smoke were blowing overhead as if there was a storm of fire.

Rodwell started lighting candles and setting them on top of the books—the only level surface in the dugout.

"Would you please not put them there?" said Levitt. "I'm doing my best to clean things up and get this place in order. You fellows just keep knocking everything down and putting things where they don't belong! Leave my books alone!" There was an edge of craziness in his voice that sounded dangerous. Rodwell said:

"certainly. Certainly. Anything to oblige," and took up the candles and stuck them in the earth where most of them promptly sizzled and went out.

Robert suddenly stood up.

Poole.

The ledge cut into the earth where he'd been lying had completely disappeared.

Robert began to pull aside debris. Rodwell helped.

"Stop it! Stop it!" said Levitt. "You're doing it again! You're messing everything up!"

Rodwell turned and struck him in the face.

Instantly, Levitt turned and ran from the dugout.

Rodwell said: "he'll be back in a moment. Pay no attention" and they went on digging.

The debris was a mixture of clay and bricks and bits of timber. Some of it was hot and some of it was icy cold. It stank of sulphur and chlorine. Wherever it was wet, their fingers only made furrows and nothing could be pulled away. All they got for their frantic digging was clay beneath their fingernails. Robert began to sweat. Rodwell found a spoon and a fork on the floor and they used these as claws. It was futile. Still—they didn't stop for a second. One by one, the remaining candles guttered and went out. The only light was reflected from the clouds of smoke beyond the angled roof. Robert felt someone come and kneel between them. Levitt returning. He too began to dig in silence. All that could be heard was the guns and the urgent breathing of the three men. Robert's forearms and shoulders began to seize up with cramps. He was certain Poole, by now, must have suffocated in the clay. He had no idea how long it had been since the mines went off, but it must have been hours. (In fact, it was twelve minutes.) Robert was just about to give up when the man between himself and Rodwell spoke. "Who are we digging for?" he asked.

Robert fell backwards.

It was Poole.

He'd gone outside to relieve himself and was caught between the dugout and the trench when the mines went up. Once the barrage had started, he didn't dare move.

Robert heard himself saying: "next time, stay in your place so we know where you are." He was angry with relief.

"Yessir," said Poole. But he was smiling when he said it.

4:25 a.m.

The previous evening Robert had taken Levitt down and introduced him to the men. There were seven of them in the trench with a lance corporal in command of two mortars. Seven more men and a sergeant were on rest in a bay where they'd made themselves a very comfortable dugout with a brazier. Robert had done no more than make the introduction—spoken briefly to the sergeant and the corporal and left them. This was normal procedure when there were no specific instructions and the front was quiet. Now, Robert stood outside the Stained Glass Dugout (for that is what they called it, in honour of Devlin's collection) and looked down to where the trench had been.

It was gone. In its place there was a hole.

All of this could be seen and not seen. Robert's eyes watered in the cold air. The smoke from the bursting shells collected light and dispersed it over the battlefield. Fires had been started wherever anything was dry enough to burn. The crater itself was spotted with fires

—some around the rim, others down its sides and in its depths. Men were woven with smoke like whirlwinds of dust. Everything moved slow-motion—even things that fell seemed to float. The shells, for the most part, were bursting in the air, just as if the stars were falling all together. There was a lot of noise but none if it seemed to be connected with what one saw. The driven, ceaseless pounding of the guns (from both sides now) had nothing to do with the bursting of the shells and the bursting of the shells had nothing to do with the thudding of the earth beneath one's feet. Everything was out of sync.

Robert slid and stumbled down towards the crater thinking that surely one of his men at least had survived. But the trench where they had been did not exist. He began to walk north-east, which is to say towards St Eloi where the whole town was blazing on the horizon, but after three hundred yards or so he gave that up. It was madness. The trench itself and all the communication trenches were clogged with dead and wounded and stretcher bearers trying to go the other way so Robert finally decided to make instead for the Battalion Signals Office thinking it might serve as a natural magnet to anyone of the men who might have survived. This meant turning back the way he'd come and striking off on an angle almost directly westward.

The dark was pitted with holes and he kept falling down. He fell down once and put his hand in someone's face. He apologized—even though he knew the man was dead. In another hole there was a rat that was alive but trapped because of the waterlogged condition of the earth that kept collapsing every time it tried to ascend the walls. Robert struck a match and caught he rat by the tail. It squealed as he lifted it over the edge and set it free. Robert wondered afterwards if setting the rat free had been a favour—but in the moment that he did it he was thinking: *here is someone still alive.* And the word *alive* was amazing.

The distance Robert had to go was just about a quarter of a mile—a distance he could have walked, under normal circumstances, in about seven minutes and run in one-and-a-half. This time it took him over an hour.

5:30 a.m.

Robert couldn't get through to his O.C. for orders. Most of the wires were down and the few in use were constantly being commandeered by Battery Commanders and other senior officers. The Signals Office, in a farmhouse, was as busy as a stock exchange in a falling market. Dawn had begun to break and men were being poured up the communication trenches from the rear. There was a horse-railway, too, leading back to Wytsbrouk and flat-car-loads of wounded were being drawn away by huge black horses or pushed along the track by walking wounded. The whir and rattle of the wheels was constant.

The Germans had started putting over 5.9s by now and sixty or seventy shells had landed while Robert waited to send his message. Luckily, their range was off and the shells were landing to the left of the farmhouse. One or two came fairly close and everyone dived for the floor with a clatter of falling tin hats and tea mugs. The shells could be heard in the air when they got about four seconds from you.

Standing up after one of the closer calls, a bright young man with popping eyes turned to Robert and gushed at him: "isn't it *marvellous*!" Robert nodded vaguely and walked away. Afterwards, he saw the young man going up to several others—including a Lieutenant Colonel—and saying the same thing: "isn't it marvellous! Isn't it absolutely marvellous!" Robert went out and stood with his back against the wall and smoked a cigarette.

6:10 a.m.

Robert got lucky. His company commander, Captain Leather, arrived from Wytsbrouk on one of the flat-cars, bringing with him a section of men, four trench mortars and a carrying party with a quantity of ammunition.

"There you are, Ross! Good for you!" said Leather, as he slid from the still moving car and crossed the barn yard. It was just as if the meeting had been arranged for weeks. Robert scanned the cars to see if he'd brought another subaltern with him, but he hadn't. Robert's stomach sank as he realized he was going to be put in charge of whatever scheme had brought Captain Leather forward. Leather beckoned him into the Signals Office and consulted a map. He wanted Robert to explain the situation. "Just so," he kept saying, as Robert pointed out where the mines had been blown and what he could guess about the state of the trenches he had visited in the dark. Leather even said: "just so" when Robert explained that he hadn't been able to locate his men and that he feared they had all been killed. Then Leather studied the map in silence for a moment and finally said: "here we go, then" and laid down the purpose of the new guns. Gun beds would have to be put in "here and here" and "there and there." *Here and here* was all right—but *there and there* was a death trap. Robert pointed out that the second set of positions was more than likely at the far edge of the crater nearest the German lines. Leather said: "just so" and seemed very pleased. Robert felt constrained to silence.

He wanted to advise Captain Leather of the state Levitt was in . . . he wanted to request another junior officer . . . he wanted to say the forward positions were crazy . . . he wanted to say that guns would sink in the mud. But he didn't say anything. He just went out with Leather into the cold and was introduced to a Corporal Bates who was in charge of the men. When this had been done, Leather took him aside and turned his back on Bates and said in a very pleasant way: "I think you should know that most of these men are trouble-makers, Ross. You know what the Mortar Squads can be like. We seem to get all the worst. But they should be all right once you get them into action. I'll be down the line as soon as I can—but I have to check on the other two batteries." "Thank-you, sir" said Robert—and saluted. He felt condemned. "Good for you," said Leather, who then gave a little wave of his hand at Bates and went inside for a cup of tea. Robert distinctly heard him being greeted. "Isn't it *marvellous*!"

7:00 a.m.

With the section and the carrying party combined there were twenty-two men as well as Robert and Corporal Bates. Bates was all right. He was stocky and round and came, like Regis, from Regina. "Well, well, well!" he kept saying. "I ain't seen a place since home with so few trees." And later—"Honest, sir! This is worse than the cyclone of 19-0-12." And—"Honest! It's worse'n a Wascana flood!" Robert liked him because he seemed to be genuinely overawed by the battlefield, whereas most of the men said nothing or were less impressed. It took them just exactly half-an-hour to go the distance. It was fully light by now, though the sky had filled with snow clouds—but at least the shell holes could be avoided. Those that already existed at any rate. Those created along the way by the continuing bombardment claimed two lives, but Bates just yelled out: "don't you stop for nothin' or I'll shoot youse myself!" Robert believed him and hurried forward with his Webley drawn lest he fall and have to defend himself from his zealous corporal. He led them to the Stained Glass Dugout, thinking if he could only get to some place he recognized he could pull himself together before the ordeal of putting in the gun beds.

7:30 a.m.

Levitt was stony calm. It was almost disconcerting. He only complained that Robert said he must remove his greatcoat. It could not be worn going through the mud, since it would tend to drag him down and might even cause him to drown. Then Robert did what he knew he must and turned the lesser assignment over to Levitt. Rodwell came to the door of the dugout to see them off.

"See if you and Poole can't get the brazier going again," said Robert. "Then we can have some tea when we're back."

Rodwell nodded, looking dour. "I wish those clouds would go," he said. "Then it might freeze—and get us out of this beastly mud."

Robert noticed he was caked with fresh, wet clay to his waist.

"What's the news with you?" he asked.

"Same's you," said Rodwell. Every last one of his men was dead.

8:15 a.m.

When they reached what remained of the forward trench they found it so shot up and so cut off from the rest of the line that none of the dead or wounded Robert had encountered there in the dark had yet been moved. They were sitting, squatting, lying everywhere you had to walk. Not a single man was on his feet. One man lay alive on a stretcher while at either end the stretcher bearers curled like caterpillars—dead. All the walking wounded had departed; these that were left must wait perhaps to the end of that day before anyone would come to get them out. In the meantime Robert and the others had to press forward. That was the rule. No one went back—even for a dying comrade. Only someone wounded could stay with another wounded man. Here, there were one or two who leaned side by side sharing a cigarette or who tried to dress one another's wounds but most were sitting separate, staring into space. No one spoke. The dead all lay with their faces in the mud or turned to the walls of the trench. This was the only way they could be told apart from the wounded. All were a uniform shade of grey. Even their blood had lost its colour. The air was green with the mist of dissipated body-warmth. And dark. The trench was like a tunnel with a black heavy layer of smoke as its roof. The barrage was bursting to the rear and seemed to be a long way off. Robert's footsteps and the water oozing from the wrung-out earth fell into puddles loud as clocks.

All at once there was a blast of cold air.

Robert stopped.

Bates came forward and squatted beside him.

The end of the trench had been completely rolled back and the earth folded over, packed with bits of timber and corrugated iron. There were also sizzling braziers, wheels, tin hats, and blasted sand bags—*backs* that must've been men; boots and rifles and someone's hand. Robert dared not look at the earth. He wished he was myopic. He was glad he wore gloves.

The "fold" was maybe five feet high and over it—beyond it in the open—lay the crater. All they could see from where they lay was the distance they had to go. A hundred and fifty yards. One hundred and fifty paces, Robert thought. *Seconds, if I could run it.* He and Bates crawled to the lip beyond the shelter of the trench. Robert scanned the edges with his field glasses looking for footholds. There were corpses—but not as many as Robert had imagined. Maybe only a dozen scattered around the sides. The bottom was filled with water. He could see the water rising. There was no way of knowing how deep it might be—or would get. The whole St Eloi district was well below sea level. Before the age of dikes it might have been an inland sea.

Bates did not look at the terrain. He looked at Robert. Here was an unknown quantity—a child in breeches with a blue scarf wound around his neck whose job it was to get them out and back alive. This—to Bates—was the greatest terror of war: what you didn't know of the men who told you what to do—where to go and when. What if they were mad—or stupid? What if their fear was greater than yours? Or what if they were brave and crazy—wanting and demanding bravery from you? He looked away. He thought of being born—and of trusting your parents. Maybe that was the same. Your parents could be crazy too. Or stupid. Still—he'd rather his father was with him—telling him what to do. Then he smiled. He knew that his father would take one look at the crater and tell him not to go.

The gun beds would have to be cut at about ten feet below the opposite lip. *How* was quite another question. Here was the all too familiar case of an officer —(Captain Leather)—standing to the rear with a map and a theoretical crater in his mind and making use of it in a fine imaginative way that had nothing to do with the facts. A crater was just a hole in the ground. It might be ninety or it might be three hundred and ninety feet in diameter. Twenty or eight feet deep. What did it matter? A hole in the ground was a hole in the ground. In a battle they only had one use. You got your mortars into them and started firing.

Robert thought; in an hour—two hours at the most, I will have done this. Everything that's going to happen will have happened. I will be back in the dugout drinking tea with Rodwell and the toad and I will be sending a runner to say this has been done. It will be over.

"Are you ready, Bates?"

"Yessir."

"Do you see that thing that looks like a ski pole?"

"Yessir."

"We shall head for that."

"Yessir."

Robert told Bates to wait until he was over the edge and had found a foothold before coming out to join him. The men were not to follow until the route and its safety had been established.

"Yessir."

Robert lay out flat and started to swim on his belly through the mud. There was nothing left of the snow just here. It had all been blown away. He cursed his gas mask which was in a canvas bag around his neck. It kept sliding under his chest and pressing up against his breast bone. His field glasses beat against his ribs. The back of his neck was like a board—waiting for the shot that would kill him. Everyone said you didn't hear that shot. They said if it got you it was silent. How the hell did anyone alive know that?

He had to turn his back on the crater in order to get his legs over the lip. He could see Bates watching him—chewing at a thumbnail. He jack-knifed. Then he just let himself go and began to slide towards the bottom.

The gas mask came up under his chin and he thought it was going to break his neck or puncture his windpipe. He was clutching at the passing earth, desperately trying to slow his fall and bring it to a stop. He'd known it would be wet—but not like grease. Nothing he grabbed at held. He even inadvertently grabbed at an outstretched hand and sent one of the corpses sliding past him, head first into the water. At last his knees struck something hard. It was a Lewis gun imbedded in the earth. Robert gave a cry of pain. It felt as if his knee caps had been torn away. But his fall was over. He was more than halfway down the side.

Robert rolled over and dragged himself to a sitting position with the gun sticking out between his legs. He rubbed his knees. The pain was excruciating. He looked but could not see Bates which meant that Bates could not see him. In fact, there was no one he could see except the dead man down by the water with his arms stretched out and his head beneath the surface. Very slowly, Robert stood. The Lewis gun was so far imbedded he could push himself upright against it. This gave him a sort of ledge to stand on, so long as he could maintain his balance.

He must get somehow to where he could be seen so he could signal to Bates and the others to come down and join him. He began to edge his way along like a mountain climber, leaning in against the face of the crater with his feet turned out, using his heels to squelch-cut footholds in the clay. He bit against the pain in his knees. He was mostly afraid he would slip and drown. Being shot seemed the least of his troubles. The clay was so oily all he had to do was press his fingers against it to produce a putrid sweat of reeking water. Turning his head from side to side as he went, at last he saw Bates come over the edge to his right at an alarming distance above him. More than twenty feet. Robert saw him slide to the Lewis gun—saw that he had landed on his feet and proceeded on his own way.

One by one, the men came down after Bates without incident. They, too, landed on the Lewis gun and started across the face of the crater. Those who were carrying the mortars lowered the parts on ropes to their partners below. Those carrying shovels rattled down free style with the shovels clanking above their heads.

Still there was not a sign of the enemy. Not even shrapnel fell in their vicinity. Robert was nervous of this "silence"—thinking that at any minute the ridge might spring up—alive with Germans. If it did there wasn't a chance in a million of survival. They would just be sitting ducks and that would be the end of it. Robert was the only one armed—except, of course, for the fact of the mortars but these were useless until they'd been assembled and put in place.

Robert was now directly below the "ski pole." Luckily, the gradation here was not so steep as it had been where they came down. Robert clambered up quite easily until he was within an arm's length of the rim. Beyond the rim was the last twelve yards of No Man's Land and then the German trenches. The beds could be cut where he stood. It was not too bad a position, from a mathematical point of view. Robert looked down and gave a wave to Bates. This meant the sappers could come up and commence their digging. Then he turned and examined the thing they had thought was a ski pole.

It was a ski pole.

8:50 a.m.

Four men were digging. A second shelf had been begun six or seven yards to the left of the first, where Robert was sitting. No one spoke. Robert looked down and saw that one of the gunners was throwing clods of earth into the pool below—like a child in High Park on a Sunday afternoon.

He got his notebook out and a broken stub of pencil and, gauging the angle of the crater's edge, he began his calculations. He became so engrossed he was barely aware of the fact the barrage had ceased. He was halfway through his geometry when his ears popped and the silence poured in.

The gunner down below had already thrown another lump of clay. It landed in the water like a bomb. Everyone stood still, except that each man leaned in automatically against the earth at his shoulder. The silence could only mean one thing. The Germans were going to attack. All at once—a bird sang over their heads. Someone swore, as if the bird had given them away.

Robert gazed upward. The sky beyond the crater's rim was patched with blue. The flat, steel-coloured clouds were breaking up and easing apart. This was dangerous. The smoke had begun to drift. It was dispersing back towards their own lines. Their cover was being destroyed. Robert carefully put the notebook and pencil away and drew his automatic. He felt in his pockets for his reserve of clips. There were only seven of these. He fingered them—counting and recounting. Each clip had seven cartridges. *Seven. Seven. Seven times seven. Is forty-nine. Plus seven. Is fifty-six.* If he hadn't fired the gun—but he couldn't remember that. He'd fired it at a peach can. When?

"Sir?" said one of the men who was with him on the ledge.

"Be quiet!" said Robert. Both of them were whispering.

"But sir . . ."

The man pointed.

Robert looked.

Slithering over the crater's rim—a pale blue fog appeared. Like a veil his mother might've worn.

Robert blinked.

It tumbled over the edge and began to spread out over their heads—drifting on a layer of cold, dank air rising from the pool below them.

Jesus.

Gas.

Bates had scrabbled up to the ledge.

"Put on your masks," Robert whispered. The air seemed to be alive with sibilance. The cannisters were that close.

Bates just stared.

"Put your mask on, Corporal Bates!"

"I can't" said Bates.

"What the hell do you mean?" Robert turned and shouted hoarsely to the men below him. "Put your masks on!"

"We *can't* sir," said Bates. "They sent us up so quick that none of us was issued masks."

"*Every* man is issued a mask!" Robert shouted out loud. (It was like being told that none of the men had been issued boots.)

"No, sir," said Bates. "It ain't true." He was shaking. Shivering. His voice was barely audible. Robert might as well have yelled at God, for all the good it would do. He looked at the weaving strands of gas. They were spreading further out—like a spider's web above the crater—reaching for the other side. Some of it was spilling down towards them.

Robert didn't even think. He just yelled: "jump!" and leapt into the air.

Looking back at the gas and seeing nothing else was to be done, one by one the others also jumped. Some landed short and tumbled the rest of the way but most landed helter skelter on top of one another in the water.

In seconds there was nightmare. All too quickly they discovered they could not touch bottom. Three of the men could not swim. One man had broken both his legs in the fall. Two or three corpses that had lain nearby against the sides of the crater, slid down after them and sank like stones. But in moments they floated to the surface and when Robert and Bates began to struggle to the edge with the men who could not swim, Robert found he was saving a man who was already dead. He pushed the corpse back in the water but it wouldn't sink this time and he had to kick its hands away from his boots. Silence—and every other safety precaution was thrown to the winds. For a moment they ceased to be soldiers and became eight panic-stricken men who were trapped in the bottom of a sink hole, either about to be drowned or smothered to death with gas. Eight men and one mask. Robert had to fight to keep it and he ended up kicking both the living and the dead. At last, lying flat on his back, he managed to get the automatic out of his pocket and using both hands he pointed it straight at Bates. "Tell them to back off," he said; "or by Jesus I'll fire!"

"Back off," said Bates.

Robert sat—and used his knee to support the gun. He was shaking so violently the air was filled with drops of water spraying off his head. He swallowed hard and looked at the gas. "All right," he said. "You sons-of-bitches do exactly what I say." One of the men began to run. Robert fired. The man fell down but was not hit, Robert having missed him on purpose. "Now," he said. "If you want to live you have about twenty seconds. Get out your handkerchiefs."

"We got no handkerchiefs," said Bates.

"THEN TEAR THE TAILS OFF YOUR GOD DAMNED SHIRTS!"

To a man—like chastised children—they reached around and tore the tails from their shirts. The man with the broken legs was lying by the water's edge. He was already the colour of death. His hands were full of clay. He didn't utter a word. He'd bitten his lips until they'd bled and his teeth had gone through the flesh. Robert threw the gas mask at Bates. "Put that over his face. And remember this gun is pointed right at your back." Bates obeyed—crawling to the man on his hands and knees.

The rest of the men were waiting numbly, holding torn pieces of cloth in their hands—staring at Robert with their mouths open. "What are we s'posed to do?" one of them asked. "These won't save us. Not if it's chlorine."

"Piss on them," said Robert.

"Unh?"

"PISS ON THEM!!!"

The men all looked at Bates, who had turned again, having put the gas mask over the injured man's face. He looked at Robert and shrugged. He nodded at the men. Then he knelt and began to fumble with his flies. He was quite convinced that Robert had lost his reason—but you have to obey a man with a gun—mad or sane. Here was the terror. Bates was so afraid that he collapsed backward and sat like a child in the sand and dug in his underwear for his penis. It had shrunk with fear. The gas was reaching down towards them—six feet—five feet—four. Bates was certain he would defecate. His bowels had turned to water. He fell on his side. At last his fingers took hold. He closed his eyes. He prayed: *dear Jesus, let me piss.* But he couldn't. Neither could one of the other men and this other man began to weep, till Robert shouted at him: "damn you! *Damn you*! Give it to me!" and he ripped the shirt tail away from the man and urinated on it himself. Then, with it dripping like a dishcloth, he thrust it back at the other man and said to him: "put it over your face." But the poor daft crazy was so afraid and so confused that he put the cloth on top of his head and Robert had to grab it again and slap it on the man's face so that it covered him from eyes to chin. Then Robert said: "all you others do the same thing and lie down flat with your faces in your hands." They did. Without a word. The gas was now two feet above their heads. Finally, Bates let go. His muscles gave away like bits of yarn and he fouled himself as he peed. How could it matter? They were all going to die. He flattened the wettened tail of his shirt across his face and rolled to his stomach, pressing his face in the mud. His father's image deserted him. His mind was white.

In the meantime, Robert dribbled all that was left in his bladder into his handkerchief and he too lay down—like a pilgrim in the clay.

9:30 a.m.

They waited.

What would save them—if it did—was an image that had come unbidden into Robert's mind from a dull winter classroom long ago. It was an image clear and definite as the words themselves: *two tiny bottles poised side by side.* Crystals forming in the air. *Ammonium-chloride*—a harmless dusty powder blown off the back of someone's hand.

Chloride in one tiny bottle—but what was in the other? Clear as a bell—in fact, so clear he thought he'd heard it aloud—came the sound of Clifford Purchas, all of twelve years old, giggling and poking at Robert's ribs. "*Piss*," he'd said—and been dismissed from class for saying it. Now that one word might save them. The ammonia in their urine would turn the chlorine into harmless crystals that could not be breathed.

10:30 a.m.

Still, they waited.

The gas had begun to dissipate. More breeze had sprung up. More and more clouds were leaving the sky. It became very cold. But Robert and the men dared not move. At any moment the Germans would appear, for surely the gas had been the prelude to their attack. And if the Germans came, their only hope was to play dead and pray.

* * *

12:15 p.m.

The sun—at its zenith—died.

The crows began to call to one another.

It also began to snow.

1:00 p.m.

Robert slowly tilted his head to one side. He had lain completely still for three hours. The back of his neck was numb. He slid his hand up under his cheek. The glove made it feel like a stranger's hand. His hair was frozen into points that hung down over his eyes.

"Bates?"

There was no answer.

"Bates?" A little louder.

"Yes sir?" Somewhere to his left.

"I'm going to roll over now. Onto my back. I don't want anybody else to move."

"Yes sir."

Robert eased himself onto his side. So far—so good. There wasn't a sound. Then he rolled over with his arms stuck out above his head. He looked like a child about to make "an angel" in the snow. The handkerchief was frozen to his left glove. Looking back, he could see it way off down his arm in another country. A bird sang, something like a white-throated sparrow: one long note descending; three that wavered. This was the bird that had sung before. He waited for it to sing again. It didn't. Robert tried to focus every inch of the rim within his range. The bird had made him extremely nervous. *Rob the Ranger* always whistled like a white-throat if he saw an Indian moving in the woods. And the Indians hooted like owls and howled and barked and yipped like wolves. Robbers could *meow* like cats. Anyone in hiding was an imitation animal.

Once he'd rolled over, Robert was the only brown figure in the landscape. That could only mean one thing. He was alive. All the others, playing dead, were covered with snow. Robert thought: well—no one's shot at me yet. Surely if anyone's watching they'd have killed me by now.

Snow was still falling. It filled his lashes and turned them white. He could taste it on his lips. He could feel a single flake on the tip of his nose. He sat up, resting on his elbows, sweeping his arms to his sides and his right hand into contact with the Webley.

He lifted his gaze to the rim.

Nothing.

He angled his head to the left.

The bird sang.

Robert froze.

There was a German soldier with a pair of binoculars staring right at him.

Robert stared back—unmoving.

The German—who was lying down at the very edge of the crater—lowered the binoculars. Robert could see his eyes. He was very young. Maybe eighteen. He was not an officer and he wore no hat. He did not even wear a helmet. His hair was frozen like Robert's, but blond. He wore a pair of woollen mitts that had no fingers.

Robert could see him so clearly he could see him swallow, as if he was nervous.

Bates said: "sir?"

Robert tried to speak without moving his lips. "Don't move," he said. "There's somebody there."

Bates did not reply but Robert heard one of the other men cursing in the mud. "Be quiet," he said and, as he said it, he saw in front of them the dreadful phenomenon that could give them all away. His breath. He muttered: "don't anybody raise his head. Keep on breathing into the ground."

All this time, Robert had not moved. All this time, the German had watched him. Robert thought: there has to be a reason.

He sat up.

Nothing happened.

The German went on staring at Robert—not even using the binoculars. He seemed to be waiting for Robert to take the initiative.

Robert thought: he isn't armed. That's what it is. He isn't armed. He hasn't caught us—we've caught him. He's afraid to move.

Very slowly, Robert drew the Webley and held it in such a way that the German could not help but see it. He didn't want to point it at him yet. He waited to see what reaction the gun itself would get. The German raised his binoculars. Then he lowered them—but that was all.

Robert said: "Bates? Don't be afraid. There's only

one and I don't think he has a gun. Try rolling over and see what happens. I've got him covered."

Bates rolled over.

The German shifted his gaze—saw that Bates had moved and then looked back at Robert. He nodded. It was astounding. He nodded!

Robert did not quite understand at first and then the German lifted his head as much as to say: *get up*.

"Get up," Robert said to Bates. "Stand right up. He isn't going to shoot."

Bates had been watching the German, too. He stood up.

"Now what?" he said.

"Go to the top," said Robert. "Go the way we came. Just go. But go slowly. Don't alarm him."

Bates went around behind Robert—out of his sight lines—but Robert could hear him scrambling and squelching through the mud and then the sound of falling debris as he clambered up the face of the crater. Robert didn't take his eyes off the German for a second and the German didn't take his eyes off Bates. The tilt of his head was like a mirror. It showed Bates's progress all the way to the top. And when Bates had arrived and was safe—the German looked back down at Robert—smiling.

Robert stood up. He waved acknowledgement. Whatever his reasons—the German obviously intended them all to go free.

"I want everyone of you to go and join Bates," Robert said.

"Don't stop and don't look back. Go as far as you can with your hands in the air, so he'll know you're not armed. Maybe he's crazy—but he isn't going to kill us."

One by one, four of the men began to stumble to

the Lewis gun. "Get up," Robert said to the fifth, whom he thought must have fallen asleep. When the man did not respond, Robert went across to him and turned him over with the toe of his boot. It was the man who had wept and become hysterical. Dead. His eyes wide and staring. He had strangled on his shirt tail.

Robert rolled him back, face down in the mud, and went to the man with the broken legs. All this while the German was watching him but Robert felt entirely safe. He crouched by the water's edge and was amazed to see it was solid. In the three hours they had lain there it had got that cold. This man was also dead. Probably of shock. Robert could not see his eyes. The vapour inside the gas mask had frozen. The man's last breath was a sheet of ice.

It was now Robert's turn to climb.

He would have to turn his back on the German.

Well. There was no other way.

He began.

It was the sort of climb you have in dreams. Every step forward, he slid back two. He almost dropped the gun. His knees were in agony. Harris's scarf got caught on the Lewis gun and Robert had to tear it away. He kept falling forward, sliding in the snow. Once, he looked up and could see Bates waiting—watching the German. The others could not be seen. They were over the lip and safe in the trench. Robert had about six feet to go.

All of a sudden, Bates shouted: "sir!"

What happened next was all so jumbled and fast that Robert was never to sort it out. He fell. He turned. He saw the German reaching over the lip of the crater. Something exploded. The German gave a startled cry and was suddenly dead, with his arms dangling down.

The shot that had killed him rang around and

around the crater like a marble in a bowl. Robert thought it would never stop. He scrambled for the brink only in order to escape it and Bates had to pull him over the edge, falling back with Robert on top of him. The warmth of Bates's body was a shock and the two men lay in one another's arms for almost a minute before Robert moved. He couldn't breathe. He couldn't speak. He could barely see. He sat with his head between his knees. He didn't even know the gun was still in his hand until he reached with it to wipe the mud from his face. It smelt of heat and oil. He turned around and crawled to the edge of the fold where, hours ago, he and Bates had first looked out and seen the crater. He wanted to know what had happened and why the German had so suddenly moved against him after letting all the others escape.

He raised his field glasses and the first thing he saw was their counterpart lying in the mud about a foot from the young man's hand. Binoculars. He had only been reaching for his binoculars.

Robert sagged against the ground. It was even worse than that. Lying beside the German was a modified Mauser rifle of the kind used by snipers. He could have killed them all. Surely that had been his intention. But he'd relented. Why?

The bird sang.

One long note descending: three that wavered on the brink of sadness.

That was why.

It sang and sang, till Robert rose and walked away. The sound of it would haunt him to the day he died.

* * *

When they made their way back through the trench there was no one there alive. They had all been gassed or had frozen to death. Those who lay in water were profiled in ice. Everything was green: their faces—and their fingers—and their buttons. And the snow.

Tuesday, February 29th—Thursday, March 2nd

One day bled into the next. They melded. Day and night became inseparable—the nights lit up with the flames of a terrible new weapon and the days impalled in smoke. The ground was on fire. Troops were obliterated and the others brought forward. Companies were decimated to the size of sections. In the time since the battle had begun Robert should have shared the command of twenty men with Levitt, but he lost all count of the numbers that had come and gone. Maybe eighty—maybe a hundred. More. He would only know when he took his tally book to Battalion H.Q. at the end. If there was an end.

The weapon with which the Germans now attacked had been introduced at Verdun. It was something called a "flame thrower" and rumours had come down the line describing it—but no one had believed. Men, it was said, carrying tanks of fire on their backs came in advance of the troops and spread the fire with hoses. Water burned and snow went up in smoke. Nothing remained. It was virtual attrition. The ultimate weapon had been invented. Only powder and dust remained of trenches filled with men. These were the rumours. Some of the commanders laughed. Fire could not come out of hoses. Don't be ridiculous. If fire came out of hoses—the men who wielded them would be the first to burn.

(Dynamite and tanks and gas and aeroplanes had all been dismissed with the same reubttal. A: men would not do such things, and, B: they could not. Then they did.) The flame throwers made their first appearance at St Eloi on the evening of the 29th—a Tuesday. (1916 was a leap year.) Fourteen "carriers" had appeared in No Man's Land at about the time of sundown, wearing metal breast-plates with large red crosses painted on the front. These were not the crosses of mercy. They were the emblem of the units specially trained in "liquid warfare" and shown off only a month before to an enthusiastic Kaiser. The German High Command had invested so much faith in this new weapon that they dubbed the Verdun Offensive where it would first be used as Operation *Gericht*. The Place of Judgement.

Fire storms raged along the front. Men were exploded where they stood—blown apart by the combustion. Winds with the velocity of cyclones tore the guns from their emplacements and flung them about like toys. Horses fell with their bones on fire. Men went blind in the heat. Blood ran out of noses, ears, and mouths. Wells and springs of water were plugged and stopped by the bodies of men and mules and dogs who had gone there for safety. The storms might last for hours—until the clay was baked and the earth was seared and sealed with fire.

Rodwell and Poole had managed to shore the roof of the dugout back into place. Levitt had gone quite mad and sat with his books piled up on his knees until they touched his chin. Devlin, Bonnycastle and Roots made forays out from Wytsbrouk and one day Robert and Bonnycastle fought in confusion over who was in command of the guns. But there were no guns. They had been left in No Man's Land. *But Roots had brought them others. No. Yes. No.* How many gunners were alive? There was a man called Bates. Rodwell disappeared for twenty-four hours. No one could remember where he was—or if his section had survived or perished. The rabbit, the hedgehog and the bird had died—asphyxiated in the gas attack. Rodwell had saved the toad by putting it into the drinking water pail and placing sheets of Devlin's glass on top. It drank through its pores. The water was pure. It was a matter, Rodwell had said, of your element. The toad had a choice. Also, it only breathed about three times a minute in its winter torpor. "Some of us are lucky!"

Then—on the Friday—there was silence. It was over.

Robert went up and stood on the roof.

It rained.

The ground went out. It was hot to the touch for a day.

Friday, March 3rd

Rodwell reappeared.

He was being transferred.

He said goodbye to them all and said he wanted to write a letter. He ate a can of peaches. Bonnycastle watched him but only asked for some of the juice. Rodwell let him drink from the can. They cleared the table. Paper was produced (torn from the frontispiece of Volume Three of Clausewitz). They left him sitting there alone.

Captain Leather finally put in an appearance. "Uhm. Just so . . ." he said as he surveyed the battlefield. "Isn't that amazing?" Then he put his hands behind his back and looked the other way. Robert, Levitt, Poole and Devlin were to return to Wytsbrouk. Bonnycastle and Roots were to stay with the men. What a pity Ross had gone and lost those guns in the crater, he said to Robert—looking him straight in the face. "I am Ross," said Robert. "Ah yes. Well. A pity." Then he coughed. They all looked up and watched an aeroplane. "Free as a bird," said Captain Leather. And left them.

"You're going back," said Rodwell. He handed Robert his haversack. "These are my sketchbooks and the toad. Please release him in the mud as far behind the lines as you can get him. Preferably where there's something green. If such a thing as green exists!" He laughed. "This letter—" (handing over a folded piece of paper)—"Can you see that it arrives? I have no envelope. The address is inside. If you would post it, perhaps. Thankyou."

"Where are you going?" said Robert.

"I don't know," said Rodwell. "Down the line." He shrugged. "Take good care of toad. Goodbye."

He put out his hand.

Robert took it.

"I shall miss you," said Rodwell.

"Yes. Goodbye."

The letter was addressed to: "my daughter, Laurine."

Robert, Poole and Levitt stumbled back with Devlin carrying his glass to the Battery Signals office. There, they put Levitt on one of the flat cars with a number of men who had been wounded. Levitt was the only one sitting up. The books were piled beside him—scorched almost beyond recognition. Certainly, they could never be read again.

It was a clear, blue day and the air was cold as ice. You could see for miles. Robert walked beside the horse. Poole walked in front of him with the bugle bouncing against his back. It was tarnished a black.

Levitt said: "what's to be done with us now, I wonder?" and Devlin, walking beside him, answered: "we're to rest awhile."

Sunday, March 5th

Word reached Robert Saturday that Rodwell had shot himself. Apparently he'd gone "down the line" and been assigned to a company who'd been in the trenches all through the fire storms without being relieved. Some of them were madmen. This was understandable, perhaps. When Rodwell arrived, he found them slaughtering rats and mice—burning them alive in their cooking fires. Rodwell, being Rodwell, had tried to stop them. They would not be stopped—and, seeing that he took an interest, they'd forced him to watch the killing of a cat. Half an hour later, Rodwell wandered into No Man's Land and put a bullet through his ears.

On the Sunday, Robert sat on his bed in the old hotel at Bailleul and read what Rodwell had written.

> *To my daughter, Laurine;*
> *Love your mother.*
> *Make your prayers against despair.*
> *I am alive in everything I touch. Touch these pages and you have me in your fingertips. We survive in one another. Everything lives forever.*
> *Believe it. Nothing dies.*
> *I am your father always.*

Then his name and then an obscured address in

Listowel. Robert did not even know where Listowel was. But he would find out.

January—February—March—1916.

Mrs Ross began to seek out storms. That is to say, whenever there was rain or wind or snow Mrs Ross would call upstairs to Davenport and say to her: *put on your hat. We're going out.*

Sometimes they would walk in the valley—down the long ravine with its high, treed sides and bridle path and sometimes they would walk down the streets of Rosedale. Mrs Ross would wrap herself in veils and scarves and set her hats with long and vicious pins that sometimes pierced her scalp. Walking she kept a desperate pace and Davenport was often left behind a half-a-block or more.

Mrs Ross took pleasure in the rain and snow. She pushed her veiling back and let them beat against her face. She never spoke to anyone she met. If someone known should come along the street, she'd close her eyes and let them pass unseen. She carried a stick—(she refused to carry an umbrella)—and often struck the lampposts as she passed. Once, when they were crossing the Sherbourne Street Bridge in a blizzard, she paused and threw her stick way out above the tree tops and watched it whirling through the snow until it disappeared. "There," she said; "it's gone." Then she stood till her furs and veils were layered white and Mr Aylesworth stopped his motorcar to see if anything was wrong. Davenport wanted to accept his offer of a ride but Mrs Ross said no, they were going to walk to the corner of Yonge and Bloor and buy another stick at Ely's.

Early in February, when the Parliament Buildings in

Ottawa were razed to the ground, Mrs Ross read all the accounts of the disaster in the papers—cut them out and put them in her bureau drawer. She studied them like textbooks—making notes in the margins. She believed her country was being destroyed by the fact that when the bells in the centre tower fell they were in the process of striking twelve o'clock—but had only tolled eleven times when they crashed to the ground. She wrote in the margin alongside this information—*"No more midnight."* It was like a prayer.

In March, when the wind blew down the ravine in gales, Mrs Ross put on the gardener's rubber boots and walked in the mud. If the wind was particularly strong, she turned around and walked against it backwards all the way to the river. Davenport would follow (wearing buckled galoshes) high up out of the mud, slipping and sliding on last year's leaves; clutching at the maple trees, tearing off branches when she fell. Sometimes she just gave up and waited, terrified of tramps, in a grove of oaks where the leaves had refused to fall—watching her friend being blown away. When Mrs Ross returned to the oaks from one of these backward hikes she would call from the bridle path: "come down!" and Davenport would emerge from her hiding place to be chastised for having failed to brave the river banks in flood.

On days when Mrs Ross was drunk, she sat in Rowena's chair and Davenport would wheel her all the way to Chestnut Park and back because there were a lot of streets to cross and the bumping kept her awake. She dreaded sleep.

Robert's letters were read and re-read—numbered and catalogued and memorized. Mrs Ross would write him every day—long, meandering epistles angled down the pages of her blue notepaper—often (more often than not) completely indecipherable. Sometimes, only a single phrase or word could be read; "your father"—"ever"—"I have been to Cluny Drive and back" and "when the robins."

Mr Ross would look at his wife across the table at the evening meal and never ask her what she'd done that day. Though he missed her terribly, he never complained. Many nights they ate in silence. Mr Ross, in his mind would recreate the past and watched her as she was when they first met. He could see the very first day. She had driven round and round the park in a shiny black phaeton pulled by a spotted horse. She was wearing a brown velvet hat with yards and yards of tulle and Mr Ross had gone to stand beside the water trough, thinking she must surely stop before the afternoon was out. He was just eighteen and she was twenty-two. All her sisters had been married, but she was refusing every offer her father arranged. She wanted a man with very special qualities and, so far as she was concerned, this man did not exist. As every suitor arrived she became more and more intransigent. No one was going to push her around—and no one did. Then her brother died (was killed) and her father died of a broken heart. Her ambitions for independence were suddenly narrowed. Thomas Ross came into view. He was a carriage maker—shy and darkly handsome. She paused. She pondered. If she remained alone—the factory could drag her down. But marriage was dangerous. The part of marriage she mistrusted most was the part about being loved. The fact of being loved was difficult: almost intolerable. Being loved was letting others feed from your resources—all you had of life was put in jeopardy. Maybe you had to give yourself away. But young Tom Ross was persuasive in a way she could not resist. He did not ask for her. He offered her himself. In time, he was a gift she clung to. He urged her to be free.

On that first occasion in the park she had refused to stop. The sun had risen higher and the day got hotter and hotter. Tom went on waiting—even refusing the shade of the trees. Every time she passed, he raised his hat. She thought he had the finest legs and arms she'd ever seen—but still she went on going around and around the park—never seeming to look in his direction. He thought how marvelously cruel she was—to him and to her pony—not to pause to let it drink and not to let him speak her name. Now she went round and round in his mind, fading in and out of view, still not letting him speak her name. But his love was undiminished. She was still the single-minded girl he'd won. But he feared for her, now. Across the table, she was hiding: hidden by smoke and flowers and lowered lamps. He'd smile and she would stare as if he wasn't there. He became a portion of her silence. He was just another room through which she passed towards the dark.

Wednesday—March 8th

Robert was being sent to "Blighty." His present tour of duty was over. He sat on the train. One of Rodwell's sketchbooks was open on his lap. There was the toad. Quite, as Rodwell had promised, realistic—lacking entirely any sentimental nuance. Just a plain, bad-tempered grumpy toad. Robert smiled. He leafed through the pages. There were birds and mice. The rabbit and the hedgehog. More toads. A frog and some insects. Then, towards the back of the book, he found himself. *"Robert."* He was lying asleep by the candle-light in the dugout. His mouth was slightly open. One hand reposed on his breast. He was wearing Harris's bitten gloves. The other hand hung down towards the earth. The likeness was good. Unnerving. But the shading was not quite human. There was another quality—speckled and fading into brightness where his clothes touched his neck and cheek. Robert could not decipher what that quality was—until he'd finished leafing through the book and glanced through the others (there were five, all told). In all of them—on every page, the drawings were of animals. Of maybe a hundred sketches, Robert's was the only human form. Modified and mutated—he was one with the others.

What had Rodwell meant by this? Or was it just the way he drew?

Early that morning, Robert had released the toad beneath a hedge. Here, there was at least the promise of green. The toad at once had begun to burrow into the welcome mud. It threw the dirt in all directions—making a nest for itself until its eyes were all that could be seen. And the hump of its spotted back. Robert reached down. He touched it with his fingertips. "Be well," he said. And left it there.

PART FOUR

Access to the details of the affair between Robert Ross and Barbara d'Orsey was gained as the result of a second meeting with Lady Juliet d'Orsey in London at number 15, Wilton Place. The interview was given on a weekend redolent with English rain and potted hyacinths and the ever-present freesia on the mantelpiece. There is sometimes thunder on these tapes and one of them records, in the background, the progress of a wedding that took place across the road on the morning of the Saturday. On the Sunday the windows were tightly closed and the drapes were drawn against the noise of the storms and nothing was heard from St Paul's, Knightsbridge till Evensong when the drapes were opened and the sunlight and the singing poured across the terrace. Downstairs in the Ministry of Scientific Information everyone had mercifully departed for the suburbs and South Ken—leaving the premises vacant. Their telephones rang from time to time and the sound of the watchman's footsteps can be heard, but that is all.

There is an aspect of this interview which, alas, cannot survive transition onto paper—and that is the sound of Lady Juliet's voice. As already stated, she is now in her seventies and a very large portion of her diet consists of gin and cigarettes. The voice, at times, sails off in what can only be described as *song* and its resonance causes the crystals dangling from the chandeliers to vibrate. The voice then quavers—cracks and is reduced to a helpless whisper. The effect of this singing in the passages where Lady Juliet reads from the diaries she wrote when she was twelve years old is both magical and devastating—for you know that what you hear is the voice of someone near to death—and the wisdom remains a child's. Lady Juliet herself is not aware of this apparent contradiction. You know that by the intensity with which she reads. To her—the voice is just the voice of her mind and consistent with the sound of thought. Turning the pages, there is no amazement of discovery on her face. Only the delight of verification. It might be interesting to note that she read with great rapidity and that when she paused to comment—(her comments will appear in italics)—she inevitably used the pauses as an interlude for gin. At one point she raised her cup and in the accent of an actress born to play Eliza Doolittle she said: *"gin was mother's-milk to her"* and grinned.

Stourbridge-St Aubyn's, where the incidents which Lady Juliet's diary describes took place, is a village about seventeen miles from Cambridge on the river Stour. This river rises in Cambridgeshire and empties into the North Sea at Harwich. For most of its journey, it constitutes the border between Essex and the Suffolks. The countryside is among the most beautiful in the world—being flat and made up of those lush green fields and winding streams—hedges, spires and woods of dappled beach and oak that define the word "English." Spring, in this region, has no equal anywhere. The fields are filled with black and white cows—the riverbanks are spread with yellow flowers—larks fly up in endless song—and the rain, when it falls, is soft and warm. Here are towns with names like Camden Lights and Grantchester—roads that wind past canals and over bridges—whirl you round a hundred village greens, scattering geese and waving at children—whip you past the naked swimmers in the ponds and deposit you at inn yards where the smell of ale and apples makes you drunk before you've passed the gate. It is an old world—comforting and safe; defined by centuries of slow motion.

St Aubyn's itself is an abbey and has been the family seat of the d'Orseys since the year 1070, when it was consigned to the founder of their line by William the Conqueror. The abbey has long since fallen into ruin, but the house—begun in Jacobean times—has grown in size and been consolidated by each succeeding generation. It sits in the middle of a park, surrounded by lawns, and in the mornings (up until the time of Lady Juliet's childhood, at any rate) deer would come out of the nearby forest and wander through the flower beds eating the lilies planted there in honour of the d'Orsey's origins as burghers of Rouen.

At the time Robert Ross first met the d'Orsey family, all five of its members of his own generation still survived. Their father, the Marquis of St Aubyn's, lived in London at Wilton Place. He loathed the country. He loathed his children. He probably loathed his wife. Juliet barely remembers him. The salient fact of his existence, so far as she was concerned, was his funeral. This she remembers vividly, because at the time he died she was his sole remaining heir and it was left to her to get him underground. In her own words: "I took advantage I'm afraid, and gave myself the pleasure of the loveliest mass you can imagine! The poor dreaded man would never have forgiven me, of course,—but you have to understand what it means to be able to *order* a mass and I knew I'd never have the opportunity again—and certainly I'd never hear my own—so I gave him 'the works' as they say and it's lasted me all these years. Oh! I had bits of Monteverdi—Mozart—Bach all jumbled up. It was glorious. A gourmet's hash of music. Do you know—it made all the hell he'd put me through worth it? I mean the hell of his absence." He died in 1952 when Juliet was forty-eight years old. She had then not seen him for so long she didn't recognize his corpse.

Their mother, Lady Emmeline, often declared she would have been happy to be a dairy maid—although, her version of a dairy maid had little to do with the real thing. What she meant, undoubtedly, was that she longed for a simpler life than she had. She was both a good wife and a good mother—and delighted in being the second. Her children, her gardens and her belief in God were all that mattered to her. But she extended her energies to providing her husband and children with a life in town even though it was basically abhorrent to her because she believed it was her duty to keep every avenue of social contact open to them. Daughters could not have a social life if their mothers did not provide it. And sons could not make marriages where a mother was conspicuously absent. As for the Marquis—she knew he could not be happy with his mistress unless his wife was there to drive him into her arms. This gave him all the reputation he needed with his peers and it kept him out of her bedroom. The last time she had thwarted him and gone off to St Aubyn's in the middle of the season, he had become so disenchanted with his mistress that he followed Lady Emmeline home—bedded her and got her pregnant with Temple. Temple was now five—and had been a late child. The experience had nearly killed Lady Emmeline and both her doctor and personal love of life had warned her it did not bear repeating.

Now that the war had come and settled over their lives, there was more and more reason for Lady Emmeline to remain in the country without a bad conscience. Especially since the Zeppelin raids had begun. Juliet and Temple must be kept entirely away from London. Clive, who had already been in France, and Michael, who was about to receive his commission, needed a haven to which they could retreat from the horrors of Kitchener's army—(that was Lady Emmeline's way of putting it)—and Barbara needed the stability of country life to offset the increasingly free-and-easy tenor of life she led in town. Soon, however, St Aubyn's became much more than a haven for her sons and an anchor for her daughter. Once the reality of Flanders struck and it was clear that the horrors of Kitchener's army were real and omnipresent, a flood of Clive and Barbara's friends in need of rest began to give the place the feel of a hostel. In the end, despite the awesome invasion it would mean of her precious privacy it was the Marchioness herself who decided that her home could not remain a private sanctuary. Once she saw the good it did "those poor young men" —she went up to London and quickly got the Marquis to pull the necessary strings to provide her with a charter declaring St Aubyn's a convalescent hospital. Four doctors and ten nurses and several orderlies were brought in. Friends were solicited for the provision of ambulances and medical supplies. A Fund was established. Well into middle life, Lady Emmeline had discovered her vocation. This was not to be a "mother" and a "wife" but to be a matron in a home for wayward boys. By March of 1916 St Aubyn's had achieved such high standards it came under the patronage of

Queen Alexandra. Even the Marquis was impressed by that. He was of an age to have fallen under the spell of her beauty when she was still the Princess of Wales and now, though she was an old and lacquered woman, he was sufficiently impressed by the fact of her honouring his name to come back home and walk around the wards with his wife's hand on his arm. This was about the time that Robert Ross returned from the Battle of St Eloi and accepted an invitation to visit St Aubyn's. It was issued in Taffler's name—but it bore a forged signature.

Transcript : Lady Juliet d'Orsey—2

I must admit to a lifelong love affair with curiosity. There was never a question I wouldn't ask—and rarely an answer I wasn't given. I don't know why that was. When I think back and hear myself—some of the questions must've been stupefyingly rude—but it may be I was given the answers because I had no guile. I wasn't cute, you understand. Or coy. I was precocious —yes; but I had no awareness of that. I can't remember a single instance in which I was patted on the head. Perhaps I was rather life a dwarf. I never played with other children. The only child I ever had anything to do with was my sister Temple. She was five. My heart adored her—but I also recognized that she was strange. I respected her—but out of fear. She didn't say her first words till she was three-and-a-half years old. Not a single word till then—and then, in the nursery one afternoon at tea, she said: "I want another egg." Wilson, our nurse, was very wise. I saw her pale and then with hardly any pause at all she turned to Temple and said: "you didn't say please." "Please," *said Temple and that was that. She got the egg. We were all extraordinary. One way and another. I think the fact was, we had reached our genetic peak. Clive was a genius. So was Temple. Michael and Barbara were beautiful beyond compare. And—there isn't any point in modesty—I was this malapert dwarf with a notebook. At the end of every day, I put down everything that happened—intrigues—conversations—all my questions—all the answers and all the things I'd seen. The affairs of my brothers and my sister—all their friends and all my parent's friends provided me with endless pleasure. The folly and the anguish of the adult world was food and drink to me and I never thought for a moment it might not be my business. I never took part, you see. Not ever. I was a born observer. Boswell in bows. These diaries will tell you what you want to know, I think. But I warn you—I was ears and eyes and that was all. The conclusions are for you to make. These—(*THE DIARIES*)—begin in March. They end in May. Robert's leave was extended twice because of his knees. In the course of his time with us he went to London for consultations with a doctor there. The second time, he had a minor operation. Something corrective—the sort of operation performed in the doctor's offices. He was with us both as a friend and as a patient. As a friend, he was given a room of his own. I think that's all you need to know as a background—so, I'll start to read. I won't read everything. The dates are unimportant. You know when this all happened.*

We now have fourteen men. Seven want around-the-clock attention. Of the others, five are on their feet and they walk in the gardens. It rains a lot, but the daffodils have just begun to bloom and the vista down towards the lake is spotted with them bobbing in the breeze. I counted over a hundred yellow heads before they began to blur and I was afraid I'd started counting twice. There's a nurse I don't like called Babbington. She never smiles at all and calls me Lady *Julie.* What if I called her "Babbins?" I bet she'd stop—but I'm not going to stoop that low. The next time she calls me Lady Julie I shall look the other way. Robert Ross, another Canadian, came up from town today. Barbara was supposed to be here to meet him but she wasn't. She was off somewhere in the hinterlands. Mother was in her office when he arrived and she came out wearing her jumper. Really, she can be so exasperating. Then she didn't remember why Robert Ross was here and she said to him: "shall I call you a nurse to take you to your room?" as if he was a patient and I'm certain he thought she was peculiar. I was sitting on the stairs and I said that I would look after him. That was fine. Mother said she'd come along and see him later, once he was in his pajamas!!! What's the use, sometimes? He was jolly decent, though. He didn't even smile until she'd gone away. I said: "she's just preoccupied. At teatime, she'll be mortified and make a thousand apologies. Pay no attention. You'll get used to her. I have." I liked him at once. His jaw is absolutely square and he has the nicest hair that won't lie down. He limps and he told me it was in his knees. Going along the gallery he said he thought that Barbara must be with Captain Taffler and I said no, I didn't think so but maybe. The truth was I wasn't really certain where she was but I found it awfully embarrassing since it seemed from the way he talked that he didn't know about the captain and I decided I would play his ignorance by ear. His room is the one with Lady Sorrel's ghost. I told him to expect her every night at two but not to wait up for her since she isn't really all that exciting. I told him what to do when she lights, the candles—just to wait until she's gone and blow them out. If she comes and goes and he's sound asleep it's a waste of candles but that can't be helped. I told him if he could bear the draught he should leave the windows open and that way the breeze will blow them out. I told him nobody dressed for dinner. Army officers couldn't be expected to trundle their evening clothes around in those funny little bags. I sat on the bed and watched him unpack. He had a satchel full of books and I asked him what they were and he showed me: sketch books with toads and things. I said they were jolly good and he said thankyou but they weren't his own. A friend in France had done them. After that he set them open on the mantel and beside the toads there's a rabbit and a mouse. His friend is dead. I didn't ask. Then he wanted to know where my own room was and I told him down the hall. I said: "I sort of waver on the verge of the nursery so that Wilson can keep an eye on me. Most of the time I give her the slip. She doesn't care. Her hands are full with Temple." I told him who Temple is and he said it was nice to have a child around. He said he had a brother who was younger and a sister who was older and a sister who was dead. He said his brother was about my age and I just said *oh*. The truth is, I felt rather sorry for him having a brother my age because I haven't met a single boy of twelve I liked. Twelve is a dreadful age in boys. All they do is blow farts and giggle. They think they're all so dreadfully funny and haven't an ounce of taste or intellect. I don't know how they grow up into men. The thought that Michael and Clive were ever that age simply makes the mind boggle. Ugh! I'm glad I didn't know them then. Anyway, Robert Ross was mostly interested in

Barbara and Captain Taffler so I finally took the bull between the horns and said that Captain Taffler was just downstairs and why not go and visit with him now? That seemed the right thing to say because I could see a funny look pass through his eyes when I said the word *visit*. The penny hadn't dropped but at least it was rolling around and whether he knew it or not he was getting himself prepared for something to be wrong. He took his army jacket off and showed me an old woolly cardigan and asked if it would be all right to put that on and I said yes, of course. One look at mother should have told him that. Then we went and looked at Temple, who was sitting on the window seat. Wilson was trying to get the fire not to smoke but since the shortage of coal we've had to burn all kinds of things and whatever it was had an acrid smell and the nursery had a sort of layer of haze. The light outside was very bright and at first we couldn't see Temple's face. She looked like an angel sitting in a halo. Both of them just stared. It made me feel most strange. Then we left. When we were going along the gallery again towards the other wing so I could take him down the Parson's stairs to visit with Captain Taffler there was laughter in the lower hall and, looking over, there was Barbara. And Major Terry. They had been at Cambridge and their arms were filled with packages. It's odd to see my sister and my mother *holding* things. I'll never get used to it. Seems like yesterday there was a hand on every door and all you had to do was turn your back and someone took your cloak. I don't mind, of course. But Barbara never looks her best with packages. Anyway, there they were laughing and they hadn't seen us and I waited to see whether Robert Ross would make a move in her direction but he didn't. This time, the penny rolled towards the slot. I felt very badly. I could see he was dreadfully worried, wondering where Major Terry fitted into the scheme of things and what it must mean he would find when he opened Captain Taffler's door. Then we went down the other way by Parson's and came to the room. Poor Robert Ross. It wasn't fair. I'd bungled it and should have been more forthright when he'd mentioned Captain Taffler first. The shock was terrible. I tried to imagine someone like Michael losing both his arms and no one telling me and me just barging in and finding him that way. But Captain Taffler made things easier when he winked at me and said that I should stand outside the door and keep the baboon at bay. I didn't know what he meant exactly till I saw Nurse Babbington. Then I realized that Captain Taffler didn't like her either and that she was the "baboon." I decided I should call her that myself. It's so much more imaginative than *Babbins*.

Supper was *dire*. Mother prattled. There were six of us. I was allowed to stay down so there'd be the right number of ladies. This meant putting on the *dress* which I hate. The smocking pinches my breasts which mother won't admit I'm sprouting. The other day when Wilson was rubbing them with the ghastly oil she says will make them *peak*, mother came in and absolutely shrieked "what are you doing, Wilson?" and when Wilson explained mother went into another shrieking fit and, staring at my breasts she said "don't you understand she can't have breasts? She's only twelve!" Then she went down the hall and I could hear her telling Barbara and then she went and told Doctor Withrow. Now I feel like a freak. I'm supposed to eat a lot of spinach—whatever that means. Anyway—at supper tonight there was mother and me and Barbara and Major Terry and Michael and Robert Ross. Mother has a rule that men from battle won't be asked questions and another rule that Michael is not to "rave" about the war the way he does every chance he gets. It was ludicrous. There we sat—with Robert Ross still in shock I think—and everyone was talking about Marrydown Cider. Mother let me have a glass of wine. I think she thinks it makes me sleepy. Here I am—and the clock has just struck twelve. Sort of like me. Barbara spent the whole time watching Robert Ross and I guess that means the end of Major Terry. Clive is coming tomorrow, bringing friends.

Last night, very late, I heard somebody walking and I thought it might be Lady Sorrel so I got up to see. I was thinking that if I followed her into Robert Ross's room I could blow out the candles and tell him how sorry I am for what I did. I shall always feel guilty that I didn't prepare him for seeing Captain Taffler. And I wonder if there's something mean in my spirit that makes me do these things. Three times I had the chance to say he hasn't any arms and three times I didn't say it. Maybe I should ask Clive. Clive is lovely the way he forgives you. If we were Romans I could go and tell a priest. Maybe the priest would forgive me. That would be so much easier than having to go and apologize to Lieutenant Ross. Anyway—it can't have been two o'clock yet because it wasn't Lady Sorrel walking in the hall. It was Barbara. She was coming out of Major Terry's bedroom and I distinctly heard her saying: "don't be such a jackass, Ralph. Goodnight." Then she went along past me but didn't see me because my door was only open a crack and I saw her pause by Robert Ross's door and my hair just stood on end! He's only been here a few hours and they hardly even spoke at supper. What can it mean? She wavered there quite a few moments and I saw her put her hand out almost as far as his door but then she withdrew it and held it behind her back. Then she looked right at me, but again she didn't see me and then turned around and went down the hall toward the Parson's stairs and I thought this was just too intriguing so I slipped out and followed her. I was just too late. All I heard was a door clicking closed—but it must've been Captain Taffler's. Underneath, there was a sliver of light. But I didn't hear a sound. I waited quite a while but Babbington came around the corner and I had to shrink into a doorway. Then I got too frightened to stay and ran all the way back here. This morning I did another mean thing which I just couldn't help. I was looking through the toy box for some dominoes and found our old Pin The Tail On The Donkey game and—honestly—simply not able to stop myself because it was just too perfect—I crept around the corner and slipped it under Major Terry's door.

(*Really*! said Lady Juliet at this point. *Wasn't I an awful child! That poor man. He came down to breakfast absolutely ashen and hardly said a word the rest of the whole day. But what I'd done I think in the long run made things easier for Barbara and Robert. Major Terry accepted the fact—all too quickly I think—that Barbara had put the donkey under his door and he withdrew from her company as if he'd been stung. I don't think he ever mentioned the prank to Barbara because I'm certain she'd have come to me about it. After all, who else had access to the toy box except Temple and Wilson and it was hardly likely they'd have done it. At any rate, the fact was Major Terry took the hint and was gone by the end of the weekend.*)

Clive arrived with masses of people. All his pacifist friends. I think they want to persuade him not to go back—but he's going. At least he says he is. Michael loathes and detests them. He says they're ruining the war. It's supposed to be very bad for everyone's morale to have them about. This afternoon he had a fight with Clive in the nursery. They fought in there because there wasn't anywhere else they could go where the pacifists couldn't hear them. The fight was about Mrs Lawrence. Mrs Lawrence is a German lady (Fat!!!) and Michael says they want to put her in jail. He says it is because she and Mr Lawrence signalled to the Zeppelins from their garden in the dead of night. And Clive said that was just a horrible rumour and no one had proved a thing. And Michael said even if it was a rumour her brother Baron von Richtofen had killed a lot of brave British airmen and it wasn't right and proper to have such a woman in our house with men like Taffler lying downstairs without arms. And Clive said if that's the way Michael feels then what on earth is the war about? And they went on *hours* like this till Wilson said if they didn't stop she'd have to ban them from the nursery and the whole thing was very bad and upsetting to "my lady"—meaning Temple, and I thought there's a fat chance of that, the way Temple sat there beaming at them both. She thought it was marvellous. Afterwards, at tea, Michael made a lot of noise stomping around the drawing room with his riding boots and every time one of the pacifists started to speak Michael called across the room to someone else and asked them at the top of his voice if they wanted more sandwiches or cake. Mother sat in the middle of it all trying to persuade Major Terry there was "absolutely no reason in the world she could think of why he should leave so suddenly and wouldn't he change his mind . . .?" All of this gave me the giggles and I thought one other thing was sort of strange. I mean that I don't understand why Clive wears his uniform when the pacifists come. Shouldn't he wear a suit? Later, all the pacifists went and sat at the bottom of the garden by the hedge. Looking down the lawn, you could see them there in the shadows leaning their heads together, smoking cigarettes and talking very seriously. Then every once in a while Mrs Woolf would throw back her head and laugh. Mrs Woolf is my idol. She wears such marvellous clothes and hats. I like the way she sits, with her knees drawn up till they nearly touch her chin and she smokes at least a dozen cigarettes just sitting on the lawn! We were standing on the terrace and there they all were at the end of the garden—about eight or nine of them with Clive—and Michael said to mother: "why do they *huddle* like that?" And mother said: "I think it's because they're literary, dear."

Robert Ross came back quite late and missed all this. He came inside from the terrace and mother said: "why where have you been Mister Ross? You look exhausted." Robert Ross said he had been for a walk and had seen three foxes in the field. He seemed to be quite excited by this but mother said to him: "please don't mention it to Michael or he'll have the whole house roused at five in the morning and all those horns going off and the dogs out baying in the yard." I considered for a while that I might write a little note and leave it under Michael's plate at supper but then I thought of all the soldiers lying in and I persuaded myself it was one mean thing I should avoid.

This afternoon I picked some daffodils because I wanted to take them down to Captain Taffler. This was after tea and about an hour before it was time to go and dress for dinner. The light in Parson's was golden—partly because of the sun going down and partly because of the Morris glass in the windows. The stones on the floor were warm for the first time this year. I had on canvas shoes and I didn't make a sound. I felt like

Lady Sorrel but it wasn't just because I was wafting over the tiles. I had on my pale blue dress and my navy jumper and everything was blue and gold and yellow. That's what she's like in the night—except she carries her tapers and I was carrying daffodils. . . .

(Let me just interrupt to say that Lady Sorrel d'Orsey was the daughter of the Marquis in Carolian times. Her lover, the Earl of Bath, was dreadfully wounded in the Civil Wars and was hidden in the room I have described where Robert slept at St Aubyn's. Her portrait shows she was immensely beautiful. The dress she wears in her appearances is indigo. The golden light is from her hair and the yellow from the candle forms that were painted in a later age to depict the legend. She was damaged in the Second World War when the buzz bomb fell on Parson's wing. Still—there she is! Bruised—but salvaged for all to see. The Earl of Bath ultimately perished of his wounds. By all accounts it was a lingering death. We were Royalists, of course, and the lands around St Aubyn's were taken by the Roundheads which meant that all through his dying he was also in hiding: hounded by Richard Cromwell of whom he had made a personal enemy. The legend of the candles had to do with the long and desperate nights Lady Sorrel sat with her lover and nursed him and, the story goes, even after his death she continued to light the candles and keep her vigil. She died at the age of sixty-five and was found in the chair by his bed with her candles burning all around the room. Needless to say—the candles have burned there ever since.)

. . . I could smell the prussic acid and whatever that other thing is they use in the dressings for the wounds. Something herbal but I don't know what. There was a nurse voice off in one of the rooms with the doors closed. Babbington or Colt or one of the others was talking to a man. I was standing on the third step from the bottom and I think I must already have come to a stop because what happened next is sort of like a photograph in my mind and I see myself in the picture. Robert Ross came out of Captain Taffler's room and the door, as it opened, gave a kind of click like a shutter of a camera. I suppose I must have been startled because I took a quick intake of breath and got a terrific whiff of the flowers in my hands. Then Barbara came around the corner—also from Captain Taffler's room. Neither Robert Ross nor Barbara saw me. They stood together in the hall and Captain Taffler's door was still partly open. Neither one spoke. They were very tense. Then Barbara turned and took Robert's hand. She leaned against his side. At first, he didn't seem to know what to do—but finally he put both his arms around her shoulders and held her for a very long time with his chin on top of her head. At last they stood apart and Barbara put her fingers on his face and then he walked away. Her hand remained in the air and she put it against her lips when he was gone and then she closed her eyes. Her head bowed down a moment and the dimple pulled at her smile and I was certain any second she was going to look at me. But she didn't. All she did was stare at Captain Taffler's open door. Then she closed the door and went away outside. Everything they'd done was like a dance between two birds. Barbara never cries.

I sat on the steps exhausted from having tried to hold my breath so long. I didn't know what to do. I still had the flowers and I wanted to give them to Captain Taffler but I didn't think I dared go down just yet. I waited almost half-an-hour. When the clock struck, I got up and went the last two steps and knocked at his door. There wasn't any answer so I knocked again and just went in. I wish I hadn't and I'm glad I did. I guess it saved his life but I don't think I'll be forgiven for that. Captain Taffler didn't want to live—and, in my bungling way, I made him. Why do I always end up being mean no matter what I do . . .? He was kneeling on the floor in a pool of unravelled bandage with his forehead touching the stones. The end of the bandage was in his teeth. One of the walls was covered with great wide swipes of red at shoulder height where he must have been rubbing his wounds to make them bleed. The stumps where his arms had been were raw and one of them was pumping blood in spurts across the floor. I dropped the flowers. I think I must have cried for help because I was standing there still when Babbington came on the run. After that I don't really know what happened. Mother was suddenly there and two of the doctors and Clive. I was taken away and given what they call a *sedative* and left in the nursery with Wilson. Next thing I knew I was waking up with Temple staring at me. Mother was saying: "Michael will carry you into your room if you want him to." But I said no. I asked where Barbara was and Robert Ross—I don't know why—and Michael said that they were walking in the park and I said: "how can they walk in the dark?" and Clive said: "not in the dark. The *park*. It's morning-time" and they pulled the curtains and a flood of light came in. Captain Taffler's had an operation and will live—but I'm not allowed to go to the wards any more so I sent him flowers by Robert Ross. Tonight I prayed and prayed. I want to be a nun.

After that, the affair between my sister and Robert Ross developed very quickly. I was shocked, of course. Dismayed. It seemed inhuman. Barbara never went again to Taffler. But Robert did. Thank God. It was now, in this period, that I heard the story of Robert's meeting with Taffler on the prairie and how he had thrown the stones at the bottles. Also the story of Harris—Harris's death and what took place at Greenwich. This is when I fell in love with Robert Ross myself—if I may put it that way. After all, we mustn't forget that I was only twelve years old. Still, it was love nonetheless and it hurt me greatly to see him so much with Barbara. Barbara was totally possessive of Robert just as she was of everyone she claimed. He found this difficult no doubt. Robert I discovered was a very private man. His temper, you know, was terrible. Once when he thought he was alone and unobserved I saw him firing his gun in the woods at a young tree. It was a sight I'd rather not have seen. He destroyed it absolutely. Other times he would throw things down and break them on the ground. He broke his watch that way. I don't know why. But he had a great deal of violence inside and sometimes it emerged this way with a gesture and other times it showed in his expression when you found him sitting alone on the terrace or staring out of a window. Still he was not at all times angry when alone and it says here: Robert went running today. I watched and so did Barbara. He was running in the paddock. We'd gone down with Clive and Honor to see the new foal in the barns. Coming out, we saw that Robert was running with the horses. He'd borrowed a pair of rugger shorts from Michael and that was all he had on. He was even in his bare feet. The horses seemed to love the race. They won—but Robert didn't mind. The running was what he wanted. You could tell that by the way he smiled. *This was between his trips to London to see the specialist and I think what he was really doing was finding out what condition his legs were in. Not good, according to this:* Robert went to London today to see Doctor Giles. Once he gets back there are going to be two weeks convalescence. *That was when he had the operation. In the interim, Michael went away to his training camp near Liverpool. Mother was in bad shape and she wrote to father begging him to come. This was around the time that everyone was going away. Clive would soon be gone and Lady Holman's son—a neighbor—went and was killed the first day he got to France. Father refused to visit us and it says here*: his excuse is a dinner party Mrs Dolby—(*his mistress*)—wants to give for Kitchener. Father is partial to Kitchener. He says that he owes it to the old man to see him rightly entertained in a time when Kitchener is on the outs with everyone else. Mother wept all afternoon. She told Lady Holman she thought Mrs Dolby must be mad to encourage father not to come and say goodbye to his sons but to stay in town instead to entertain their murderer. *Mother, you see, was blind enough to blame Mrs Dolby. She was never—even when she was dying herself and father refused to see her—reconciled to the character of the man she had married. She could not believe that people didn't love one another in their hearts. When my father failed to appear at the time of her dying she said to me: "he would come, if she would let him." Clive made a point of going to Wilton Place—coming here, in other words, to say goodbye to father but Michael didn't imagine he was going to die so he went off blithely without farewell and he and father never saw one another again. I suppose there is some poetic justice in the fact that shortly after Mrs Dolby's dinner party given in his honour, Lord Kitchener was embarked on his voyage to Archangel and the first week in June he was drowned. My father, at least, had got to say goodbye to someone.*

* * *

You must want to know if Robert's affair with my sister had a physical aspect. Yes it did—there being an instance of it that I knew at first hand. But I will only tell you this because it seems to me to have some bearing on the mood in which Robert left us and went back to France. Otherwise, I should not forgive myself for having told it to you. Many times, I have wanted to destroy this portion of my diaries but I always remind myself it is a part of someone's life: someone I loved and respected. I will tell you this and then one other thing and that is all. The rest you will get from other sources.

(LADY JULIET PAUSED A GREAT LONG WHILE BEFORE SHE READ THE LAST TWO ENTRIES. SHE READ THEM BACK TO BACK—TAKING TIME BETWEEN THEM ONLY TO FIND HER PLACE. THE FIRST ENTRY FOLLOWS ROBERT'S RETURN FOR CONVALESCENCE FOLLOWING THE OPERATION ON HIS KNEES AND THE SECOND ENTRY—SOMETIME, ONE GATHERS, IN JUNE OF 1916—MUST HAVE BEEN WRITTEN THE DAY CLIVE LEFT FOR FRANCE.)

I doubt that Wilson's wise—but she is Yorkshire honest. She'd rather "hurt thy feelings than find thee at the bottom of a well." She's never minced her words. She told me once that children of our class "lack of graces something disgraceful!" Isn't that a lovely pun? But Wilson wouldn't know it. She says it's because we've all these rights we take for granted, whereas *other* children ("other" means "proper" in Wilson's terms) know their rights are limited and "keep their little places to themselves." She says I am a blunderer. She's right. I've blundered into everything I know. I've blundered into rooms and I've blundered into danger and I've blundered into other people's lives. I've blundered into all my favourite books—like *Turn of the Screw* and *The Picture of Dorian Gray.* There isn't a single piece of even half-decent information I'd have if it wasn't for blundering. Mrs Dolby's children may be my half-brothers—but no one would have told me that if I hadn't been hiding in the sideboard. Blundering on Michael taught me all I need to know about boys—and no one would have told me *that.* Blundering saved Mrs Grimshanks. Otherwise she might have died of debt. And it was blundering that put a stop to Captain Taffler's suicide, though I know he didn't want to be blundered on. And now I've done it again. This time I doubt that I shall ever be forgiven. By myself.

Last night I was sitting on the stairs in the black hole of Calcutta. Everything's gone wrong. Michael's gone and Clive is leaving. I'm in love with Robert Ross but he hardly ever wants to sit and talk the way he did before he went away to have his operation. Now all he wants to do is sulk at the end of the terrace rubbing his knees. Father has been fierce to Mother. Jamie Villiers died of his burns. Clive is in a funk. The pacifists came and made an awful fuss. Lady Holman and Caroline Tedworth spent the entire morning in mother's office weeping and wailing. Major Larrabee-Hunt, who at least has a sense of humour, said it sounded like the chorus from the *Trojan Women.* Temple has a spot (just one) but Wilson started boiling herbs and moaning over the fire "father, son and holy ghost! Please don't let it be the German measles come to disgrace us just when the Kaiser's winning the war!" And my breasts feel funny. Sometimes they tickle way inside and other times they ache. Now I have to eat spinach twice a day and take a tonic full of rust and I hate it. Soon I will be a woman but they go on dressing me up as a child.

So—I was sitting there on the stairs, after dark, with all this on my mind when Barbara came along the hall and went into Robert's room. She didn't even knock. Slowly, it dawned on me that here was my chance for every kind of revenge I was dying for. Barbara has never believed in Lady Sorrel. Robert has been sulking and neither one of them will talk to me or spend any time being decent to me so I thought I could kill a lot of birds with one stone. I went downstairs and raided the dining room for candles. Then I went to Barbara's room and stole her silver dress. I put it on and a pair of her evening slippers with heels and I got my wide straw hat and put that on and tied it with the blue scarf that Wilson gave me for Christmas—lighted my candles and looked in the mirror. This was not exactly what Lady Sorrel looks like—(*by a long shot!*)—but what did it matter, since Barbara had said she'd never seen her? Maybe Robert had—but he didn't know her well enough to know she never changes costume. So I wafted down the hall—or sort of—and got to Robert's door. For a moment, I was nervous. I don't know what I expected them to do—but I thought they'd accept that I was her and not myself. All I meant to do was open the door and go to the mantel and light Lady Sorrel's candles with the candles in my hand and leave. Outside of that, I'm afraid I didn't really have a plan. Maybe growing up makes you muddled and you do most things unthinking.

What I did was worse than blundering. I'll never understand. This was not like Captain Taffler where at least I could see what he'd done. It wasn't like Michael where his being naked explained itself. This was a picture that didn't make sense. Two people *hurting* one another. That's what I thought. I knew in a cool, clear way at the back of my mind that this was "making love"

—but the shape of it confused me. The shape and the violence. Barbara was lying on the bed, so her head hung down and I thought that Robert must be trying to kill her. They were both quite naked. He was lying on top of her and shaking her with his whole body. That was really all I saw. Except, it was so vivid that I went on seeing it—even after I'd run away. Robert's neck was full of blood and his veins stood out. He hated her. And Barbara's hand was in her mouth. All last night I didn't sleep. I hid the candles under my mattress. Barbara's shoes and her dress I hid in the toy box and I'll have to pray that Temple doesn't want to play today. Maybe the spots will spread and she'll have to stay in bed. Neither Robert nor Barbara looked this morning as if they knew that it was me, and Robert even said to Honor, who is here, that Lady Sorrel must have been about last night since his door was opened and the draught was filled with the smell of snuffed-out candles. Barbara was pale, as if like me, she hadn't slept—but nothing was said. I feel a dreadful loss. I know things now I didn't want to know.

Later: Just about noon, I started to cry, I don't know why. It made no sense. I was sitting in the ballroom all alone and the doors were open to the garden and Barbara had ordered pots and pots of freesia from the greenhouse for tomorrow (*she must have been giving a party*), and they were sitting on the floor in the sunshine. I was sitting on one of the little gilt chairs with Amanda (*my doll*) and the tears just started and wouldn't stop. The things inside my head were the shape of Robert's shoulders and the whiteness of Barbara's skin . . . Amanda's face and the stitches coming open where her hands were undone—me in the mirror looking at my breasts . . . and Temple's stare. I don't know why. And the golden hairs on Michael's legs. I don't know why. And Barbara's head thrown back. And the dark surrounding everything. I don't know why. And I sat and sat and cried. Just cried. I didn't make a sound. Amanda seemed to be the only friend I had and I held her very tight. I'd been so mean. I'd left her on the window sill for weeks. Her loneliness was just unbearable. Me. She was lonely for me and I'd deserted her. I don't know why. Her hands were coming apart because I hadn't cared enough to sew her up. But now she was warm and safe and all I had. Just me and she and that was all. I don't know why. I don't know why.

Honor came and stood in the door. Clive came after that and Honor went away. Then Clive said: do you want to go outside or shall we sit in here? And I said: here. It's safe.

After that we sat a long, long while—Clive on the floor and me in the chair and Amanda on my lap. Then I said: why are Robert and Barbara so afraid? And Clive said: everyone they've loved has died. And I said: everybody dies. And Clive said: yes—but everybody isn't killed. Then I said: that's why Lady Sorrel lights her candles, isn't it. So the Earl of Bath won't perish. And Clive said, yes. He said that in a way being loved is like being told you never have to die. And I said: yes—but it doesn't save you, does it. And he said: no—but it saves your sanity. Then I said: are you afraid? And he said, yes. And then I didn't cry any more. Because he smiled.

Robert went away yesterday. Clive goes today. Robert walked. I thought it was so strange that Barbara didn't come. Instead, she stood at the top of the stairs and watched him from behind the glass. I was allowed to go to the end of the drive. I took his hand. He had on gloves. I loved him more than I could bear. He didn't say a word. All week I've wondered what I should give him to take away. He's already given me the sketch books with the toads and mice and himself asleep. Then the night before last I knew what it was and I wrapped it for him in a package. Today I handed it to him down by the gate and I said he mustn't open it just yet. I said he had to wait till he was on the train. Maybe he won't understand—but I think he will. It's one of Lady Sorrel's candles wrapped in tissue paper and a box of wax matches I stole from Wilson. Maybe he can use them in his trench. Right on the box it says: "WAX MATCHES—FOR ALL KINDS OF WEATHER!" And the candle has only been lighted once. By me.

Someone once said to Clive: do you think we will ever be forgiven for what we've done? They meant their generation and the war and what the war had done to civilization. Clive said something I've never forgotten. He said: I doubt we'll ever be forgiven. All I hope is—they'll remember we were human beings.

So far, you have read of the deaths of 557,017 people—one of whom was killed by a streetcar, one of whom died of bronchitis and one of whom died in a barn with her rabbits.

PART FIVE

1: Robert left Waterloo Station at 11:55 on a Saturday morning. He arrived in Southampton at 2:30 that afternoon and put his luggage on board a dirty, crowded little steamer which didn't sail till 6:00. In the meantime he sent a postcard to his mother declaring that his leave was over. (When she got this message Mrs Ross retreated with him into France.)

The crossing was rough till the sun went down and then the wind dropped. Robert leaned against the railings wondering how he was going to find his way back to Brigade H.Q. coming at it from such a roundabout route. He would normally have sailed from Folkestone to Boulogne but some ships had been sunk near the harbour off the English coast and for a while those ports were closed. The steamer arrived at Le Havre about 1:30 a.m. Robert and some others had to wait around the docks in the dark for two hours but they were finally given transport to the Canadian Base Depot and arrived there just as reveille was blowing at 4:30.

On the Sunday, Robert slept until noon. He kicked around the base till supper time and still had not received any word about leaving that night, so he went back into town and had his supper at the Metropole. The whole of the next day he sat in the sun against the wall of a transport garage. At 4:00 p.m. (Monday) his chit came through and he returned to Le Havre. Through a foul-up on the part of one of the Sergeants at the Depot, Robert was sent to one station and his kit bag was sent to another. The kit bag contained his socks, shirts and underwear, his binoculars and the Webley. He hastily left word with the local R.T.O. (Railroad Transport Officer) asking that the kit bag come on after him as soon as they located it. It was strangely disconcerting to have lost it. He felt as if he'd left his face behind in a mirror and the Webley in a stranger's hand.

The following morning (Tuesday) Robert was in Rouen. He sat in the cathedral, had some lunch by the river and returned to the station at 3:00 p.m. The train wound down through evening and the dark until at 6:00 a.m. it arrived at a town that apparently had no name. Here they were told they could not get off and had to sit on board until 11:00 a.m. When, at last, the trained pulled away it plunged almost at once into a thick green wood. This was now Wednesday. The nightingales sang in the wood at noon.

After the wood it rained. The darkened sky leaned down above a countryside the colour of chartreuse. Robert dropped the wooden slotted window into its gutter and rolled up his sleeve and let the rain beat down against his arm and his face. The air was filled with a sharp electric smell and Robert was briefly gentled back to the screened-in porch at Jackson's Point where, even now, his family might be seated staring off across the lake at a late spring storm like this while Meg stood stoic over by the cedars with her ears laid back and her eyes half-closed. Bimbo would be lying on the glider while his father and Peggy scratched her ears—one on either side. Stuart would be back in the shed, no doubt, as he was every spring—hammering nails into his wagon—altering its sides and windbreak. One year it had been a Roman chariot. Another it had been some mad machine from Jules Verne. This year it would doubtless be a tank. His mother . . .

It got dark.

Thursday morning Robert got off the train at a town called Magdalene Wood. This was still twelve miles from his destination at Bailleul. It was now about 4:00 and an hour before sunrise. Robert decided he would not proceed until there was daylight. He sat on a bench with his collar up and settled down to sleep. When he woke there was an old white dog at his feet and he shared his rations with it. Then he got up and went and tapped at the station master's window through which he could see the R.T.O. was boiling a kettle. Robert received a cup of tea and was told he would have to walk the next seven miles if he wanted to arrive in Bailleul before nightfall. There would be a wagon detail passing through Magdalene later that would bring his luggage—but if he waited for it, he would not arrive till midnight and that might mean he'd lose his chance at a room in the small hotel. Robert thanked the man and petted the dog goodbye and walked down the road with the sun coming up on his right-hand side.

The country he passed through now was beautiful and utterly peaceful. The guns had not yet started their pounding, but even when they did they were so far away they seemed to be in another world. The trees were just in the process of shedding their blossoms and the roadside was littered with white and pink petals. The air was filled with the sweet, sad smell of pollen and the bees had begun to buzz. Robert saw a small white farm with a cow in the yard and he thought: there cannot be a war. The barn was low and wide and thatched and there were bleating sheep inside. A man was standing on the stoop of the house preparing pails for the milking. Robert waved. The man waved back. The only signs of war were the ruts in the road. Robert hoisted his haversack and strode through the grass. He did not really know where he was. He passed a number of deserted buildings. It was suddenly an empty landscape. Where had all the people gone? Robert felt abandoned. He had lost his pistol. He had lost his clean white linen. The sun grew hot—then hotter. He hadn't had a proper sleep since leaving St Aubyn's. He walked in a daze of blazing light and sweat. He wanted only to arrive. He would eat, sleep and bathe in that order. Then he would find his gun. But it seemed a long, long way to go. At La Chodrelle he doused his head and neck with a pail of water—joined with two other horsemen and rode the last five miles to Bailleul. On arrival, Robert had a blinding headache. He had gone over two hundred miles in circles to get there from Le Havre. It should have been about a quarter of that. When he fell on his bed, fully clothed, he fell through a clouded countryside of small white barns and cows in yards and he slept to the sound of the water lapping his mother's feet and of nightingales in an unnamed wood.

2: He woke in the dark. There was a candle by his bed. He lighted it. He looked at his watch. 1:30. When? He crossed to the window, strapping the watch to his wrist. He had bought it—after breaking the other—in Cambridge. No. He hadn't bought it. Barbara had bought it. Robert had been embarrassed. Barbara had said: "don't be ridiculous. I'll buy you anything I like." He pulled the curtain. It was pitchy black outside and the courtyard was filled with noise. There were horses there and a large Ford motorcar. Robert watched, looking down, till his eyes became accustomed to the light—or lack of it. He heard women's voices. The women's laughter. Nurses. The door of the hotel opened and a spill of golden light raced out across the stones. One—two—three nurses. And two men. There were also some orderlies trying to calm the horses. Robert felt as if he had been drunk and a long way off. He even wondered if he'd lost a day. His stomach was empty and his beard felt six weeks old. Where had he been? In dreams with his father. He opened the window to let in some air. The women were now inside—downstairs. He could hear them talking to the concierge—asking for food. Robert thought: it's perfect. I will go down and join them. Then he saw himself in the mirror and remembered that he hadn't bathed in days. His father told him women demanded two things of men before they would sit with them, eat with them or sleep with them: a clean body and a clean breath. Robert turned back from the door and sat on the bed. He would not go down. He could not present himself like this. He lay back and reached for his flask. He took a long, slow swallow of brandy. It made him shiver. Then he lighted a cigarette. He wondered where his kit bag might have got to by now. He'd been sleeping in the same shirt and underwear for days.

Lying there—listening to the mingled sounds of horses down in the courtyard and the women in the dining room—he slid his hand across his stomach and down between his legs. Bang-bang-bang! went the guns at the front. Robert didn't listen. He undid his trouser buttons almost languidly—one by one. He was watching the ceiling through half-closed eyes. The women went on chattering and someone called for wine. A gramophone began to wobble out a song. *"Lil—Lil—Pica-*

dilly Lil— sitting on the hill—spooning with her honey —on a bright and sunny afternoon . . ." Way off up the line, the guns kept thudding their monotonous rhythm and the smell of gasoline and sweat blew round the room. Robert undid all the buttons on his shirt and took it off. That was better. He stood up and slid his trousers and his underwear to the floor. He could see himself now—pale in the aureole of candlelight in the mirror. It was a shock. He seemed like a fugitive. His beard and the shadows round the sockets of his eyes made him look like an old, old man. He smiled. He'd thought he would stand and see himself like a god in the glass—and there he was: a scarecrow. Downstairs, they began to dance. *"Lil—Lil—Picadilly Lil—don't you want to hold me—tell me what you told me—on our Picadilly honeymoon? Oh Lil—sitting on the hill —spooning with her Bill—through the bright and sunny afternoooooon!"* Robert collapsed on the bed. He was out of breath and dizzy, though he'd stood quite still. A cool breeze swept across his chest and thighs. His groin was wet with perspiration. The soles of his feet were cold. He drank again from the flask. His eyes wouldn't close. They looked up—sideways—at the ceiling. He made a fist around his penis. He thought how small it was. He drew his knees up. He felt—all at once—appallingly alone. The bed seemed just a shelf on which he lay above a vast and whirling chasm. A sudden vision of obliteration struck him like a bomb. The women laughed. The music played. The horses whinnied softly in the dark. The candle guttered out. Robert heard a long white noise. Oblivion. He slept with his fist in its place and the cold, wet blooming of four hundred thousand possibilities—of all those lives that would never be—on his fingertips.

* * *

3: Robert woke to find that it had rained. It was sometime after noon. A bent old woman brought him a jug of tepid water and a yellow cup of tea. He shaved. It was only a token. He would shave himself to the bone when he got to the baths. His hair was full of fleas but fleas were not so bad as lice. You could drown the fleas when you washed your hair and make a sieve of your fingers and scoop the corpses into the slop pail. You were given a bottle of strong, green liquid soap when you got to the doors of Desolé and if you used it directly on your skin it burned.

Robert was looking forward to his bath. He was going to treat it as an entertainment and revel in the water and the steam and afterwards he would buy himself an expensive meal, with a chicken, and sit downstairs with the gramophone music and a bottle of the local wine. He put on his riding breeks and boots and he wore the khaki sweater Eloise Brown had knitted for him. She'd sent it in a package with her photograph. Eloise Brown had always been in the background so long as Heather Lawson was around, but now that Heather was engaged to Tom Bryant, Eloise took a giant step forward. She was shy and sort of pretty in a pale, blonde way and Robert didn't mind her attentions. The sweater was well made.

He paused on his way out to tell the concierge he would pay for a chicken that evening. The concierge could speak a little of every language: French and Dutch and German—Flemish, Walloon and English. He even had some Spanish that had lingered in the district from a time four hundred years before when Philip of Spain had lain his claim on the lowlands.

The pullet would cost Robert dearly, he called out. But Robert said he would pay the earth.

He took his time as he walked through the town. There was transport of every kind lined up along the roads—some of it moving forward, some of it stopped. Ammunition wagons, guns and limbers, lorries and motorcars, motorbikes and ambulances vied for a place in the traffic. There were convoys bearing food and others bearing straw and hay for the horses. There were water convoys and convoys of medical supplies and long trains of horses and mules being herded up as replacements for those at the front. Troops mobbed forward, each man heavy with sixty pounds of equipment—with shovels and tin hats clanking on their backs. Officers rode in Daimler Limousines and Robert even saw a pair of RAYMOND/ROSS steam-driven tractors dragging a 12-inch howitzer. The noise was deafening along the roads—and the air was filled with the sound of songs that would intermittently drown out the neighing of the horses and the clatter of harness and the high pitched whine of the motors. *"Keep your head down, Fritzie boy! Keep your head down, Fritzie boy! For all last night, in the pale moonlight I saaaaaaaaaaa-aw you! I saaaaaaaw you!"* Robert began to sing along with them under his breath. *"You were fixing up your wire—as we opened rapid fire—so if you wanna see your mother or your sister or your brother—keep your head down, Fritzie boy!!!!!!!"* Robert thought of a Saturday crowd at a football game where everyone would link hands on the cold, fall afternoons and the long chains of singers would weave back and forth in the stands till the whole arena would be swaying from side to side. *And his run to the ball! The kick . . . and the long, high arc with the roar of the crowd as the ball was lifted between the posts! Rah! Rah! Rah! Yea, St Andrew's! Rah! Rah! Rah!* Robert hadn't dreamt of glory since he was ten or twelve. Now, it refreshed him.

He cut off down the road through the fields that would take him to Desolé. Its ditches were filled with bright yellow cowslips and paddling ducks. He wondered how the ducks had survived with all the hungry soldiers foraging for extra rations—and then he saw there was a child of about eight with an enormous blunderbuss sitting on a stile. Robert raised his hat to show that he had no designs on the ducks—but the child did not wave back. It scowled till Robert had passed and then it spat on the toe of its boot.

4: The yard at Desolé was crowded with inmates wearing their distinctive sky-blue smocks and with clusters of attending nuns. Robert had discovered that the nuns were deceptively sweet. They smiled a great deal and nodded a pleasant greeting when you passed but if there was a ruckus amongst the inmates, they rolled up their sleeves and waded into the fray like gladiators wearing skirts. Under their habits, they were strong and beefy as a horde of wrestlers. Robert had seen them throw the inmates up against the walls and batter them senseless with their fists. Then they would kneel and sweetly attend to the wounds they had inflicted as if a natural disaster had struck and they must do their best to revive the victims.

The baths themselves were located in what might have been a kitchen in the dark ages. Its high, vaulted ceilings could barely be seen except for the light that broke through the rusty panes of glass. You stripped and left your belongings in one of an old row of cells abandoned over a hundred years before. These cells were windowless and were it not for the single lantern hung from the wall, they would be as dark as caves and just as wet and filled with the possibility of rats. Iron bars closed the ends of the corridor and there were iron doors that could be pulled shut on each cell, closing out all external light. Robert had never much liked it there and was always glad to leave his clothes behind and take up the towels you were provided with and beat a hasty retreat to the open cavern filled with steam. He hated small rooms—he hated being enclosed. He'd grown afraid of walls that pressed too close since the dugout had collapsed. He almost ran to the bathing room.

The attendants were chosen from the best adjusted patients and often they would be no more than retarded. Sometimes patients were allowed to bathe with the soldiers, depending on how many soldiers were there. They sat about the walls, wrapped in white sheets to keep them from catching a chill. Many of them didn't want to bathe and were afraid of water. Every once in a while there might be a fracas when one of these recalcitrants had to be forced to remove his sheet and step up into the tub. On this particular day there were a dozen patients or more and with them a brace of male attendants strong enough to keep them under control. It seemed there were also men of every rank—whereas, in the past, the baths at Desolé had been the exclusive purview of officers.

Robert languished in his tub for almost an hour. He shaved again and washed his hair and lathered his body with the green lye soap from one end to the other. He scrubbed his toenails and fingernails and scoured his wrists and his shoulders with a brush that might have done justice to a wall of stone. When he was through and had lain in the water till the pads of his fingers and the soles of his feet were wrinkled, he got out and rinsed himself with four wooden buckets of clear, tepid water from the cistern. He'd just finished towelling himself dry and begun to walk to the cells for his clothes when one of the patients started to scream and yell obscenities at the attendant who was trying to manoeuvre him into a tub.

It began like that. As nothing more than an angry man who was slightly crazy.

Robert paused and watched for a moment—vaguely amused by the sight of the flailing arms and legs and the sound of the invective pouring from the man's lips. Then he walked on with his towel around his head.

By the time he'd reached the corridor the noise had swollen to such a degree that he turned around for another look. Five or six more patients had joined in the fray and most of the soldiers were standing up in their tubs and yelling at the combatants and waving their towels as if they were at a boxing match. Robert thought it would be a good thing if some more attendants were to come down and control the situation but his mind had already turned to thoughts of his chicken dinner when he entered the corridor and turned towards his cell. It was not till he was two or three steps inside that he noticed the lantern had been extinguished—and then it was too late. Someone was in there with him and the door was swinging closed behind him, shutting the sound of his cry in with him and cutting it off from the men outside.

His cry was nothing more than a startled response to the sound of the door clanging shut. No one had touched him, though he knew he was not alone. He stood absolutely still in what he thought must be the centre of the cell. All he could hear was breathing and a very slight rustling sound. He thought of the rats—but there was nowhere he could climb. He tried to adjust his eyes to the dark but the dark was complete and not even mitigated by a crack beneath the door. Robert was blind. He could not see at all.

"Who's there?" he said.

Someone was moving.

So was someone else.

There were two.

Almost at once, Robert heard a third sound that told him he was surrounded. Three at the very least and more than likely four were hidden in the dark. Robert felt a tug—very light at first—at the end of his towel. He pulled back and the pressure at the other end increased. He was afraid to put his hands out. He was certain he would touch someone and the thought of this was unbearable—not knowing who was there or why they had closed the door and locked him in.

The towel was suddenly yanked from his hand and he stood there naked and defenceless. He put his hand down to cover his scrotum, which suddenly felt as if it were going to be hit. His eyes felt the same and he wanted to cover them for fear he would be blinded but he didn't dare. He needed his other hand to defend himself. He feared an attack with weapons. His throat was constricted and his mouth had gone completely dry. He could barely breathe. The dark was terrible and seemed to invade his brain. The cell had become instantly humid, like a hothouse or a steam room. Robert's body poured with sweat. His mind went stumbling over a beach of words and picked them up like stones and threw them around inside his head but none of them fell in his mouth. Why? he kept thinking. Why?

Someone brushed against his side. Robert cringed. A hand reached underneath his arm from behind and caressed him just above the groin. Fingers dipped down through his pubic hair and seized his penis. Robert felt the length of a naked body press against his back and a mouth press down against his shoulder. The fingers holding him started stroking him very slowly. Robert pressed back as if to escape the fingers but someone kneeling in front of him grasped him around the knees and began to rub their cheek against his thighs. Robert threw his head back and tried to scream but a hand went over his face and fingers were inserted in his mouth. They pulled at his lips until he thought his jaw was going to snap and the scream made a knot in his throat and began to choke him.

He struggled with such impressive violence that all his assailants fell upon him at once—still without a sound—and holding his legs and arms out wide, they jerked him off his feet.

He was spun around in the dark so many times he lost all sense of gravity. Then he was lowered onto his back and held there by someone who was lying underneath him. His legs were forced apart so far he thought they were going to be broken. Mouths began to suck at his privates. Hands and fingers probed and poked at every part of his body. Someone struck him in the face.

Robert began to pass out. He could feel himself being lifted into the air again and turned around and made to lie on his face with one man still underneath him and now with another on top. All he could feel was the shape of the man who entered him and the terrible strength of the force with which it was done. Robert desperately tried to sink his teeth in the man underneath—but someone grabbed him by the hair and pulled him back so quickly that Robert lost his breath and fainted. A pale, mean light enveloped him. His brain went silent.

After a while—(it might have been an hour or a minute)—he could feel the others retreating. He felt their bodies going away and his own being rolled and dumped face down on the stones. He heard them pulling the bolts on the iron door and he tried to lift his head to see who they were but his neck wouldn't function. He felt himself passing out again—but just before he did he distinctly heard one voice—and the words as clear as a bell: "don't touch his money, that's a dead giveaway."

His assailants, whom he'd thought were crazies, had been his fellow soldiers. Maybe even his brother officers. He'd never know. He never saw their faces.

5: Robert stood in the centre of the room.

He wanted a clean shirt.

He wanted a clean pair of underwear.

He wanted his pistol.

He looked behind the door.

He looked underneath the bed.

He pulled out the drawers of the dresser one by one.

He dumped them on the floor.

* * *

He lifted the mattress and pulled it sideways across the bed.

Nothing but an old magazine.

He looked behind the washstand.

Dust.

He tipped the water jug.

Water.

He threw the jug in the corner.

It broke into sixteen pieces.

He tipped the dresser.

Nothing.

He knelt beside the bed and ripped at the mattress, pulling out great loops of horsehair and dropping them onto the floor.

He tore the ticking off the pillows and the air filled up with feathers.

Gun. Gun. He wanted his gun.

Somebody knocked at the door.

Robert could barely speak.

The knock came again.

"Who is it?"

He was afraid to open the door.

"It's me, sir," said a voice he recognized but couldn't place.

"Go away," said Robert.

"No, sir. I can't," said the voice. "I have something for you."

"What?"

"Your kit bag."

Robert wrapped a sheet around him—just like a madman—and opened the door.

It was Poole.

"Good God," said Robert. "Where did you come from?"

"I'm only passing through," said Poole. "But this came to Battalion H.Q. and I knew you'd want it." He showed the kit bag.

"Come in," said Robert.

"I can't stay," said Poole. He was looking at the shambles of the room. "I have a boat train to catch."

Robert said: "stay for a moment. Please."

Poole came in and Robert closed the door. He took the kit bag—perhaps too eagerly—almost grabbing it from Poole's hands.

There was a long, awkward silence.

Robert said: "you're looking well."

"Thankyou," said Poole.

Robert smiled. "Your voice has changed."

"Yes, sir. I guess so."

"Well—it happens to the best of us." Robert tried to laugh. Then he didn't know how to go on—or what else to say. "So you're going to Blighty," he tried.

"Yes, sir."

"How are the others? Bonnycastle? Devlin? Roots?"

"I'm afraid Lieutenant Bonnycastle . . ."

"Oh."

"The others is fine. When I left them. . . ."

"Yes. I understand. And you have your leave now. Well. I wish you good fortune, Poole."

"Thankyou, sir."

"I'm glad you brought the kit bag. I wanted it."

"Yes."

They stood there. Robert wished with all his heart that men could embrace. But he knew now they couldn't. Mustn't. He said goodbye quite suddenly. Poole simply walked away. Robert heard him going down the stairs. Then he heard him in the courtyard and went to the window to watch. He wished that Poole would wave—but he didn't. He went away and disappeared in the crowd.

Robert sat on the mutilated mattress and opened his kit bag. Everything was there—including the picture of Rowena.

Robert burned it in the middle of the floor.

This was not an act of anger—but an act of charity.

6: It was to be the most determined push the British had made on the salient. Masses of material and men were being moved up the roads. Robert joined them in the early morning.

He was riding with an ammunition convoy with thirty-five mules and a hundred horses in the rear. His sleeping-valise, his pack trunk and his kit bag and haversack rested where he could see them in the back of a wagon. The Webley rode in its holster, pressing up against his ribs.

They began to pass the marshes where Robert had nearly drowned in the winter. It was not the same place, he thought. Blackbirds sang from the tufts of last year's rushes. Barges moved along the canal, three of them being pulled by old men and children—only one having the luxury of a horse. It was all so incongruous. A woman waved from one of the decks. Less than a mile away—shells were falling.

At a fork in the road there were Military Police. They wore red armbands. Their holsters were open. They were directing traffic and also keeping their eyes out for possible deserters. And, of course, for spies. Often, when there were large-scale movements of troops lik this, renegades would make an attempt to get to the rear posing as wounded or sometimes as messengers. Spies, too, could infiltrate the ranks—usually posing as local peasants or refugees from near the front. The job of the M.P.s was often quite brutal. In the trenches before an attack it was their responsibility to see that everyone went over the top. Their orders were to kill any man who refused. It was done, from time to time, but Robert had never seen it.

The road went off in two directions here. One fork led to the north-east and Ypres—the other angled to the south by a very few degrees and led to Wytsbrouk. It was this road that Robert's convoy took. Most of the large guns and nearly all the troops went on to *Wipers* from where they could be deployed in the regions of the Menin Road and Hill 60. These were still objectives. Nothing had been won.

Within ten minutes they had reached yet another crossroads—this time with a fork leading off towards St Eloi. Robert felt as if he had come home.

It was 11:45 a.m.

The sky was dotted with small, bushy clouds.

It was odd.

Robert looked up.

There should have been birds.

He was riding near the centre of the column.

Out of the corner of his eye, he saw a rabbit beside the road. Then he heard a rush of wings.

Something exploded.

The rabbit disappeared.

Robert ducked as a whoosh of air threw him forward. His hat fell off. He opened his eyes to see the wheels of an aeroplane clipping the driver of the baggage wagon. They severed the driver's head from his body and his arms went up as if to catch it.

A bomb fell. It exploded to Robert's right.

He fell to the left, but somehow he fell on his feet and still had the reins of his horse in his hand. His horse began to rear. Robert grabbed at the halter and pulled it down. Another bomb fell. The air was alive with planes—so many planes that Robert had no time to count them.

Horses, men and mules were running in every direction. Robert seemed to be standing at the centre. All around him everything was in motion as the men and the animals floundered into the ditches. There was so much screaming and so much roaring of fires that Robert couldn't hear the planes when they returned or the next string of bombs when they fell.

They came back along the road, flying so low that Robert thought they must be trying to land. He could even see the faces of the pilots. This time, the bombs fell into the thick of the column, exploding outward towards him. Then there was silence.

The planes were gone. The road and the ditches looked like the entrance to a charnel-house. Robert put his foot in the stirrup. His horse began to walk in circles. Robert could barely get up. All he could see from the height he had gained was the distance the carnage had been spread. Other men were rising from the ground. A very few horses and mules were running back and forth in a maddened condition—trying to find some way to escape from the scene but just as unable to do so as if a fence had been put around the road.

At the last, a circle of survivors gathered at the centre. There were seven mules, fifteen horses and twenty-three out of sixty men. When Robert bent down to collect what remained of his kit bag—which was practically nothing—Juliet's candle was wedged in the earth in an upright position. Somehow—it had been set alight. Robert blew it out and put it in his pocket. Then he turned around and began to help the other survivors extricate themselves from the dead.

7: Robert spent the next six days riding with the supply wagons. Sometimes there would be a consignment of animals as well, but it was not inevitable.

Some of the journeys were made at night. Sometimes it rained. Always, they were shelled or bombed. In places the ditches were literally piled with corpses and carcasses to a height above the level of the road. There was also a growing static convoy of vehicles and wagons and guns that had been destroyed. The Pioneers worked the roads from dawn to dusk but the most they could do was keep them open. They could not do more than remove the bodies and the wrecks to the ditches. Nothing could be buried—nothing could be salvaged. There was neither manpower nor time between the attacks for this.

Robert had not yet been to the trenches. All his working hours were spent with the convoys. But he heard many stories of what was happening there. In a few places, the German line had been broken and captured. The trenches south of St Eloi had been taken and the crater where Robert had shot the German sniper was no longer a part of No Man's Land. It was now a hundred and fifty yards behind the British line.

But the advance and its success was ragged. The Germans had counter-attacked in places and many prisoners had been taken. It was also said that a number of British troops, including many Canadians, had surrendered. No matter what the numbers thrown against the enemy, German numbers and tenacity seemed to be greater. Nonetheless—there was a steady stream of reinforcements constantly coming forward from the rear and Robert found himself always a part of a general counter-movement—like a gigantic conveyor belt that ran between the front and Bailleul—back and forward and forward and back. There was always a convoy or a staggered line of troops or a train of wagons and ambulances moving against him. Back and forward—forward and back. It was just a muddy circus and sometimes Robert hardly knew which way he went. The only orientation at night was the guns, whose emplacements were more or less constant.

To the south of Wytsbrouk, the line was particularly weak. This was in the region where the ridge, which the Germans still held, took its turn to the north towards Passchendaele. There was an *elbow* in the ridge just there and this elbow gave the Germans a double advantage. They could fire on anyone advancing from two directions; which is to say where the elbow jutted forward over No Man's Land, they could fire at the backs of troops advancing against the opposite corner of the ridge. The casualties were terrible, rising in numbers by the hundreds by the day. It seemed to be an impossible objective and it was here that many of the troops surrendered to the Germans rather than press on with the hopeless attack. A road came up from this region, cutting into the road to Bailleul to the rear of Wytsbrouk and this road was filled with exhaused troops and with a steady flow of walking wounded. As almost had to be the case where so many men had been completely demoralized, there were, among these wounded, some deserters. The Military Police were stationed where the two roads met and, from time to time, a single revolver shot would ring out—mostly in the dark.

One night, just about an hour before dawn, Robert was riding on this stretch of road in the fore of an ammunition train. It was raining. The mud was just beginning to be tiresome. His horse had sunk down twice into pot-holes and for a while, Robert had been forced to walk. But now he was back in the saddle—almost asleep—and the guns had fallen quiet. The rain beat down in squalls and there was hardly any light. The only sound was the falling rain and the grinding of the wagon wheels. All at once, Robert's horse shied and refused to proceed. Robert was jarred into wakefulness.

He tried to coax the horse forward but it was useless. Robert got down to see what the problem might be. He shone his torch at the mud, in which he was wading up to his shins, and he saw there was a body lying in the road. It was a man without a trench coat. An officer. He had been shot in the back and was sprawled face down. Robert rolled him over carefully thinking he might still be alive. But he wasn't. He was quite dead and had been for more than an hour. It was Clifford Purchas.

* * *

8: On the seventh day since his return to the front, Robert was caught with a fresh supply of horses and mules (some thirty of each) in the stables at Battalion Signals when a barrage was commenced that was to last for fourteen hours. This time, the German guns had found their mark. There was hardly a shell that burst to the rear or in front of the line.

Robert had only taken eight hours sleep in the last three days. He was living on chocolate bars and tea and generous portions of rum which he took from the supply wagons. His body was completely numb and his mind had shrunk to a small, protective shell in which he hoarded the barest essentials of reason.

Not all the shells were falling in their vicinity. The barrage was being laid down for a mile either side of the Signals Office. Robert went inside at one point to request of Captain Leather that he be allowed to take the horses and mules he had just brought forward and make a strategic retreat with them so they might be saved. But Captain Leather, who was underneath a table at the time (as was Robert), was adamant in his refusal. "What would it look like?" he said to Robert. "We should never live it down." Robert returned to the stables where he crouched in a stall with Devlin—both of them rolled like hedgehogs with their heads between their knees.

Finally, when the shells began to land in the barnyard, Robert couldn't stand it any longer and he said to Devlin: "I'm going to break ranks and save these animals. Will you come with me?" Devlin wanted to—and said so. But he was afraid of Captain Leather. "Leather is insane," said Robert flatly. "It cannot be called disobedience to save these animals when they'll be needed, for God's sake, half-an-hour after this is over. And if we stay here, how can they avoid being killed?" Devlin concurred. They both stood up and began to release the horses and mules and to drive them into the yards. Robert sent Devlin running so that he could open the gates and let the animals escape. Then he returned himself to the barn and released the remaining horses.

While he was inside, it was everyone's misfortune that Captain Leather rose from beneath his table in the office and looked out of the window long enough to see what Devlin was doing. He raced outside, in spite of the shells, and started yelling at Devlin, who by now was at the gates. But Devlin was forthright. Once he had made his decision to go with Robert—he stuck to it in spite of his fear of the captain and the consequences.

Leather called for an M.P.

None came.

He ran towards Devlin brandishing his revolver.

"Shut those God damn gates!" he screamed. "Shut them! Shut them! You traitor."

But Devlin went on driving as many horses through as he could until, inevitably, Captain Leather shot him. Then Captain Leather ran to the gates and dragged them closed himself.

There were now between thirty and forty mules and horses in the yard—milling about and running in a circle.

Robert came out of the stable and saw what had happened.

Captain Leather saw him and brandished his revolver and began to shout at him just as he had at Devlin. "Traitor! Traitor! You'll be shot for this!" He was waving the gun in the air and trying to get through the circle of horses and mules so that he could draw a bead on Robert. Robert, in the meantime, had begun to make his way towards the gates.

The shells began to make direct hits at this moment. One and then another fell on the Signals Office. Robert paid no attention. He just kept running for the gates. He could hear the men who were trapped inside the ruin screaming to be let out. Everything was on fire.

Another shell landed on the barns. They too began to burn. Some of the horses ran back inside. Robert could not prevent them. He was too far away. "Just keep going," he said to himself out loud. "Just keep going."

Captain Leather was now about ten yards away. The gates were five.

"Stop!!!" Captain Leather screamed.

As if the word had been their cue—three shells burst in order—all in the yard.

Robert was blown out into the road. When he got to his feet and started back towards the barnyard he had left—it wasn't there.

The barns were a heap of burning rubble. So was the Signals office. In the centre of the yard, there was just a smoking hole. All the horses and mules were either dead or were dying. It appeared that only Robert had survived.

He got out the Webley, meaning to shoot the animals not yet dead, but he paused for the barest moment looking at the whole scene laid out before him and his anger rose to such a pitch that he feared he was going to go over into madness. He stood where the gate had been and he thought: "if an animal had done this—we would call it mad and shoot it" and at that precise moment Captain Leather rose to his knees and began to struggle to his feet. Robert shot him between the eyes.

It took him half-an-hour to kill the mules and horses. Then he tore the lapels from his uniform and left the battlefield.

* * *

9: The day that Mister and Mrs Ross received the news that Robert was "missing in action" Mrs Ross refused to dress. She remained in her nightgown and wandered around the house on South Drive with a bottle in one hand, a glass in the other. Miss Davenport locked her door and sat in a chair with her back to the window. The sound of Mrs Ross's cries to heaven rose up through her room and made her stop her ears.

Peggy and Mister Ross sat in the drawing room where Mister Ross had drawn the curtains. Out beyond the windows, the robins sang and the sun shone and the lilacs were still in bloom.

Stuart sat on the bottom step in the front hall with Bimbo at his feet. His mother's appearance alarmed him. Frightened him. But his brother's apparent death was strangely exhilarating news in itself. Not that Stuart wished Robert ill. But the thought of going to school and saying: "Robert is dead. He'll prob'ly get the Victoria Cross"—this was marvellous to contemplate and it sent a shiver down his back.

The cable had arrived just after lunch. Now it was early in the evening. Mrs Ross had wandered the length and breadth of the house. She was in her bare feet. Her hair, in a plait, hung down her back. Stuart went to the drawing room and sat on his father's other side. A strange and terrible silence descended. Even Miss Davenport became alarmed enough to unlock and open her door.

Mrs Ross stood on the landing of the stairs. The bottle fell from her hand. It was empty and it rolled to the bottom step. She gave a final agonizing cry.

Everyone froze. Even the neighbours, listening through the open windows.

Mrs Ross put her hands out and started forward. She found the banister and leaned against it all the way to the bottom. At the bottom, she just avoided stepping on the bottle. She sat down beside it where Stuart had sat through the earlier part of the afternoon.

"Help," she said.

Nobody moved.

"Help," said Mrs Ross.

Mister Ross, in the drawing room, stood up.

He advanced towards the hallway.

"Help me," said Mrs. Ross.

Mister Ross put out his hand.

"Where?" said Mrs Ross. "Where? Where are you?"

Mister Ross said: "I'm here."

Mrs Ross said: "I'm sorry. Please. I cannot see you."

Mister Ross went across the parquet floor and sat beside his wife. He put his arm around her shoulder and held her against his side. She was cold.

"I'm blind," said Mrs Ross. "I've gone blind."

There was not a trace of emotion left in her voice, But she fumbled with her fingers and found her husband's hand.

"Never mind," said Mister Ross. "Never mind. Here we are."

Peggy came and stood in the doorway. Mister Ross signalled for her to get her mother's coat. Peggy brought it from the cupboard and Mister Ross put it around his wife's shoulders. Then Mister Ross sent Peggy and Stuart and Bimbo away. They all went off and sat in the garden.

Upstairs, Davenport looked from her window.

The ravine was full of mist.

The sun was descending. It was cool.

In the distance, the traffic on Yonge Street and Bloor

Street rumbled and clattered. Everyone was going home. All the clocks were striking.

Mrs Ross began to fall asleep. Mr Ross held her and rocked her from side to side. The house began to darken. They sat there, silently singing. Finally, she slept.

In the drawing room, sitting in its silver frame, Robert's picture started to fade.

It got completely dark.

This was the sixteenth of June.

10: That night the sun fell down through rolling palls of smoke. The road to Bailleul was clogged with horses and machines. The army in retreat had swollen to three times the size of the columns stumbling forward to the front. The earth had baked beneath their feet and the air was filled with a fine, grey powder that matted in their hair and scoured the rims of their eyes. The only water to be had lay out in the marsh beyond the flaming hedgerows of abandonded carts and lorries. No one dared to leave their place in line for fear they would not be allowed back in. If a mule or horse fell down or stumbled in the traces, the wagon it was pulling was rolled aside and its wounded occupants surrendered to their fate. The fallen animals were dragged, still living, to the ditches where unavoidably they burned or were drowned. There were no acts of mercy. There was no ammunition to be spared.

It became apparent the Germans meant to raze Bailleul to the ground. Their long-range guns had begun to fire that afternoon. At first these shells fell only in the orchards on the outskirts but through the night they probed wih deeper and deeper bursts into the heart of the marketplace and the railroad yards. Here, there was a trick of timing that had disastrous results for the British.

For weeks Bailleul had been shut down as a reception depot. This was because of the ships that had been sunk at Folkestone. But three days before, because of the superhuman efforts of the Canadian Reserve contingents stationed just a mile-and-a-half from Folkestone at Shorncliffe—the ships in the harbour had been raised. This meant the channel crossing to Boulogne could be put back into operation and in turn this meant the railroad line to Bailleul had been re-opened. For the past two days troops and horses and supplies that up till then were being diverted through Le Havre and Rouen—(far behind the lines and utterly out of the range of the guns)—had been arriving by the trainload. Now, as the Germans turned their guns to its destruction, the British filled the town with their entire reserve for the battle.

Bailleul's facilities were swollen with hordes of soldiers—some in retreat without commanders—others standing rigidly in place waiting for their orders to advance to the front. When the shells began to fall in the ranks, there was instant panic. The narrow streets filled up with running men. Convoys of ammunition and petrol were abandoned where they stood. Drums and tanks of gasoline spilled to the stones and spread through the town in rivers of fire. Men, machines and houses went up like torches. It became a holocaust.

This, too, was on the 16th of June.

* * *

11: She was standing in the middle of the railroad tracks. Her head was bowed and her right front hoof was raised as if she rested. Her reins hung down to the ground and her saddle had slipped to one side. Behind her, a warehouse filled with medical supplies had just caught fire. Lying beside her there was a dog with its head between its paws and its ears erect and listening.

Twenty feet away, Robert sat on his haunches watching them. His pistol hung down from his fingers between his knees. He still wore his uniform with its torn lapels and burned sleeves. In the firelight, his eyes were very bright. His lips were slightly parted. He could not breathe through his nose. It was broken. His face and the backs of his hands were streaked with clay and sweat. His hair hung down across his forehead. He was absolutely still. He had wandered now for over a week.

Behind him, the railroad track stretched back towards the town. In front of him, it reached out through the fire towards the open countryside and the road to Magdalene Wood. On one of the sidings there was a train. Its engineer and crew had either abandoned it, or else they had been killed. It could not be told. Robert appeared to be the sole survivor.

He stood up. The engine hissed and rumbled. The train was about a dozen cars—no more. They appeared to be cattle cars. Robert walked to the horse.

He had feared she might be lame, but as soon as he approached she put her hoof back down on the cinders and raised her head. Robert petted her, slipping his arm around her neck and drawing the reins back over her ears. She greeted him with a snuffling noise and looked around to watch him as he adjusted her saddle and tightened the cinch. The dog, in the meantime, had got to his feet and was wagging his tail. It was as if both dog and horse had been waiting for Robert to come to them.

The horse was a fine black mare, standing about sixteen hands. She had been well cared for up till now and someone had obviously ridden her every day. She was in superb condition. The dog apparently was used to her company and she to his. They moved in tandem. The dog was also black. One of his ears fell forward in an odd way, giving the appearance of a jaunty cap. Robert did not know what sort of dog he was, but he was about the size of a Labrador retriever. Before mounting, Robert reached down and rubbed his hand across the dog's back. Then he said: "let's go" and swung into the saddle.

They rode down the track towards the road to Magdalene Wood passing, as they went, the engine in the siding. When they got to the first of the cars—the horse stopped. She threw her head back and whinnied. Other horses answered from inside the car. "All right," Robert said. "Then we shall all go together."

Half an hour later, the twelve cars stood quite empty and Robert was riding along the tracks behind a hundred and thirty horses with the dog trotting beside him. They were on the road to Magdalene Wood by 1:00 a.m. This was when the moon rose—red.

12: Here is where the mythology is muddled. There are stories of immediate pursuit. But these are doubtful. Some versions have it that Robert rode through La Chodrelle at a gallop—all of the horses running in front of him, stampeded. There are several "witnesses" to this. They describe Robert as some sort of raving cowboy—giving the Rebel Yell as he flew past—driving the horses deliberately through a cordon of soldiers hastily thrown up to prevent his escaping —killing three—five—nine and even a dozen pickets. None of this is in the transcript of his court martial—but the "witnesses" insist it was the case.

Far more likely is the version that describes the horses making a detour out around the woods lying west of La Chodrelle and waking, in their passage, the troops who were under the command of one Major Mickle whose bivouac was in the field of flax on the other side of the wood. Here, it is said, Robert shot Private Cassles and this is more probable. Private Cassles was certainly killed by someone and there are two witnesses—(one of whom testified at the court martial proceedings)—both of whom claim that Cassles went out—unarmed—to prevent Robert's passing and that when the private made a grab for Robert's reins, Robert shot him in the face. What has never been made clear is why Private Cassles felt compelled to challenge Robert in the first place. After all—Robert was an officer of the Field Artillery and had every right to be in charge of a convoy of horses. The obvious answer to this is that Cassles was alert enough to perceive how unlikely it might be that the horses should be driven *away* from the centre at Bailleul—but no one has said for certain this was the case.

At any rate, what happened was that Major Mickle went himself immediately to his signals office at La Chodrelle and sent word back to Bailleul that an officer of the C.F.A. had shot and killed one of his men and had then made off with a great many horses in the direction of Magdalene Wood.

It took some time, due to the confusion at Bailleul, to discover that the horses were indeed missing and that no authority had been given *anyone* to remove them from the "Military Compound" (a euphemism for the station yard during the state of emergency.) Once this was established—Mickle was commissioned to give pursuit to the renegade horse thief and, within about four hours of Robert shooting Private Cassles, Major Mickle and forty men had taken after him on foot.

13: They found him in the abandoned barns he had first seen when he was walking to Bailleul. Of the hundred and thirty horses sixty had been stabled in the two smaller barns and about fifty were in the larger barn with Robert, the black mare and the dog. Twenty others had wandered back through some trees towards the river—and these were never found. From this point on, all that happened is very clear and precise.

The sun had risen. It was a cloudless, humid day. The air was filled with the sound of insects. Mickle deployed his men around the barns—with orders to shoot to kill if Robert opened fire. Mickle was adamant about this. Cassles had been shot. Robert had done it. But Mickle was also determined he should regain the horses for the army. He said as much to Robert—calling out to him from the barnyard.

Robert was inside—watching Mickle through a crack in the door. He had drawn the Webley and was quite prepared to shoot at anyone who came in to get him or to release the horses. There can be no doubt whatsoever that Robert meant the horses should not go back. His actions at Wytsbrouk preclude any other interpretation of what followed.

Mickle put his case: that Robert should surrender both himself and the horses—throw down his weapon and offer himself voluntarily for arrest. Mickle promised to take such "voluntary surrender" into account in submission of the case to the Military Police.

Robert refused.

Mickle countered by saying that in that case he had no choice but to come in and take Robert by force.

Robert's answer to this was to take a shot at Mickle—which missed.

Mickle was a brave man. He decided that, plainly, he was dealing with a man gone mad and that he must act in accordance with that interpretation. He must dispense not only with mercy—but with reason. That he did so, puts the state of his own mind in question—for what he did next cannot be interpreted as being any less "mad" than what Robert had done in taking the horses and deserting the battle. Mickle said: "we shall have you out of there, I tell you. Do not doubt me. I shall have you, even though you kill me."

He then offered Robert one more chance to come outside of his own volition and Robert's answer—just as before—was a shot. After he had fired this second time—and Mickle was in hiding behind the gate to the barnyard—Robert called out very distinctly (and there are *twenty* witnesses to this): "we shall not be taken."

It was the "*we*" that doomed him. To Mickle, it signified that Robert had an accomplice. Maybe more than one. Mickle thought he knew how to get "them" out.

He sent four men around behind the barn by a route Robert cannot have seen—behind the wall—and told them to set fire to the roof.

That is what they did.

Mickle claims it was only a ploy. He had no intention of destroying the horses. He could not, he said, foresee that Robert would not be able to open the doors in time to let them out.

The fire was set.

Mickle recounts that the dog could be heard at this point giving the alarm.

The roof, being made of thatch—and it not having rained for two days—went up in seconds like a tinder box. Within less than a minute of the fire being set, the rear portion of the roof fell into the barn—and, presumably, onto the backs of the horses.

Nobody knows what happened to prevent Robert from opening the doors. Perhaps he was injured in that moment (his collar bone was broken) by the panic-striken horses and perhaps he even lost consciousness for those few precious minutes when he might have got them out.

What in fact happened was that Robert began shouting "I can't! I can't! I can't!" and by the time Mickle realized this meant "I can't open the doors" it was too late. A man was sent running to pull them open—and he did so. Robert—riding the black mare—was seen trying to bring her under control in the middle of the barn. There were flames all around him and his clothing was on fire. Mickle admits that, at that moment, he said a prayer for Robert Ross—and the prayer was for a quick death.

But just as the walls began to fall in on top of the fifty horses—all of them standing in their places while they burned—Robert turned the mare and she leapt through the flames—already falling—with Robert on her back on fire.

Mickle and several others rushed forward to save him—and they did so by rolling him in the dust.

Mickle has stated that, looking down at Robert after the flames had been extinguished, he was barely able to recognize that Robert had a face—but that nonetheless, Robert was heard to say with great clarity: "the dog. The dog." And then he lost consciousness.

The dog was never found.

14: Transcript: Marian Turner—3

Language is a strange thing, isn't it. *Bois de Madeleine . . . Magdalene Wood.* Take your pick. Now, I say *Mag-daleen* Wood if I'm speaking what you call *Canadian;* you know, North American. But the English say it's *Maudlin* Wood. Maudlin-Mag-daleen-Madeleine. They're all kind of nice—but I like *Madeleine.* That is where I say I was, if people ask. I served at *Bois de Madeleine* from the spring of 1916 to the fall of 1917—roughly eighteen months. A lifetime. Here is a photograph. . . . *(*IT SHOWS MISS TURNER, IN HER TWENTIES, SEATED ON A GRASSY KNOLL WITH THIRTY OR FORTY OTHER NURSES—ALL IN DRESS UNIFORM WITH CAPES*)* Girls. You see? Just girls. And I am the sole survivor. That's Olivia Fischer there. My very best friend. "Fish with a *C*!" she used to say. (LAUGHTER) Fish with a C. (A PAUSE) She's lovely . . . wasn't she. Yes. (SHE PUTS THE PHOTOGRAPH AWAY. BESSIE TURNER, MARIAN'S SISTER, ENTERS THE ROOM AT THIS POINT AND THERE ARE BRIEF INTRODUCTIONS. BESSIE TURNER SITS NEAR THE WINDOWS, PUSHING AT THE DRAPES TO LET IN MORE SUNLIGHT.) Robert Ross was brought to us the 18th of June, 1916. I can tell you the date because two days before, the hospital was bombed. It had been my first experience of what was meant by "under fire." We nurses lived in tents, you understand, and these were all destroyed as well as the damage done to the hospital which was in someone's house. I remember the strangest sight when the raid was over. I'd been hiding under a bed and when I crawled out and stood up I looked down the rows of platforms where the tents had been and there, at the edge of the step, sat a pure white cat we'd had as mascot. It was cleaning its paws! Serenely cleaning its paws. Well . . . life goes on—and a cat will clean its paws no matter what. We had to go about our business and get the hospital back in working order. Not a pane of glass was left and not a jot of power. The situation then was terrible. The Germans were doing their best to destroy us all—and the whole of the salient sweeping down from Ypres through the St Eloi district to Ploegstreet and Armentières was going up in smoke. And this was a bare two weeks before the Somme Offensive, for which we were all meant to be in top running order, ready to receive its casualties, treat them and send them on to England. And there we were, as the young people say today, in a shambles! It was under these conditions we received Robert Ross. *Received.* The language again. Like a package. Or a message. Or a gift. We received him. Well—I've told you that: the way he was—the burns—the pain and the dreadful, dreadful silence that surrounded him. He was delivered to us in the dark. Sometime very early in the morning. I recall distinctly standing by his stretcher in the dark and saying to him: "I am here." I was surprised and angered that they kept a guard—a young M.P.—who never left his presence. Even when Robert Ross was taken to surgery, the M.P. stood outside the door. It was because he'd killed a man. I never fathomed that. There, in the midst of battle, a picket was posted to assure us that the killer-Ross would not escape. And where should he escape to? Death? A few brief hours of sleep? The painless tranquillity of morphine? I tell you, it nearly drove me mad—the sight of that spick and span young man with the armband, sitting in his wooden chair by Robert Ross's bed. (MISS TURNER IS ASKED IF SHE EVER CONVERSED WITH ROBERT ROSS. THERE IS A PAUSE ON THE TAPE—AND THEN BESSIE TURNER IS HEARD SAYING, FROM ACROSS THE ROOM: *"Why don't you tell him, Merni? Why don't you say it and get it off your chest?"* THIS IS FOLLOWED BY ANOTHER PAUSE AND THE SOUND OF MARIAN TURNER RISING FROM HER CHAIR. THE SOUND OF HER VOICE GROWS FAINT, FOR SHE HAS CROSSED THE ROOM AND STANDS BY THE WINDOWS LOOKING DOWN AT THE PARK BELOW, WITH HER BACK TO THE MICROPHONE.)

Yes. One conversation only. You see—it was almost impossible for him to speak. I could speak to him—and I often did—but I didn't expect replies, except this once. I'd given him some morphine. We were running low. This was after the first of July and the Somme had produced its influx of wounded. I kept some aside for Robert Ross—by which I mean I hoarded it: kept it in a secret place. (ANOTHER PAUSE. BESSIE SAYS: "*Say it.*" THE PAUSE LENGTHENS AND THEN MARIAN SAYS:) I wanted to help him die. (HERE SHE TURNED FROM THE WINDOW—BUT HER FACE COULD STILL NOT BE SEEN: ONLY THE BLAZE OF THE LATE-DYING LIGHT BEHIND HER.) I'm a nurse. I've never offered death to anyone. I've prayed for it often enough. But I've never made the offer. But that night—surrounded by all that dark—and all those men in pain—and the trains kept bringing us more and more and more—and the war was never, never, never going to end—that night, I thought: *I am ashamed to be alive*. I am ashamed of *life*. And I wanted to offer some way out of life—I wanted grace for Robert Ross. And, by then, I knew the young M.P. who sat by the bed and I sent him away—some errand

—water—the bed pan, I don't remember what it was . . . and when he was gone, I sat in his place—in the chair by Ross's bed—and I looked down through the lamplight and the bars—(there were bars on the bed to keep him from falling out in his sleep. In his sleep, he would dream—and try to rise)—and I said: "I will help you, if you want me to." And I knew he understood—because he said: "not yet." *Not yet.* Do you see? He might have said: "no." He might've said: "yes." But he said: "not yet." There, in those two words, in a nutshell—you have the essence of Robert Ross. And perhaps the essence of what it is to be alive. *Not yet* has been my motto ever since . . . and here I am. (*"No, dear,"* SAYS BESSIE TURNER. *"Here we all are."* AND THEN, TO THE INTERVIEWER: *"won't you have another glass of sherry?"*

(LATER, MARIAN TURNER SENT ALONG A PHOTOGRAPH IN WHICH HE IS SEEN WITH HER FRIEND OLIVIA FISCHER AND THE WHITE CAT. "I thought you might like to have this," SHE WROTE. "At my age, you don't need pictures any more.")

15: Robert was held in *Bois de Madeleine* hospital, under arrest, for two months before he could be moved. Towards the end of August, he was returned to England. In September, he was tried *in absentia* and—since he could not be kept in prison—he was allowed to go to St Aubyn's for convalescent treatment. This was allowed on the understanding that—according to the medical testimony—there was virtually no hope that he would ever walk or see or be capable of judgement again.

Barbara d'Orsey acknowledged his arrival and paid him one visit. She carried an armful of freesia—and was accompanied by Lieutenant-Colonel Albert Rittenhouse—an Australian who had won much praise and two decorations for valour at Gallipoli.

Juliet d'Orsey has said that she loved Robert Ross. There can be no doubt of this. She rarely left his side as he recovered from his burns. Every day she would take him flowers—summer and winter. In the winter, she cut the flowers in the greenhouse. And there was always an unlit candle beside his bed.

He died in 1922. He was not quite twenty-six years old.

There is a photograph of Robert and Juliet taken about a year before his death. He wears a close-fitting cap rather like a touque—pulled down over his ears. He has no eyebrows—his nose is disfigured and bent and his face is a mass of scar tissue. Juliet is looking up at him—speaking—and Robert is looking directly at the camera. He is holding Juliet's hand. And he is smiling.

Mister Ross was the only member of his family who came to see him buried. On the gravestone, Juliet had inscribed the following words—

EARTH AND AIR AND FIRE AND WATER
ROBERT R. ROSS
1896 1922

Epilogue

Robert is seated on a keg of water. This is at Lethbridge, in the spring of 1915. Behind him there are tent flaps—bedding—camp cots. Someone is lying down beneath a blanket, diffused by the lack of focus—but a human shoulder can be seen and a human hand that is dangling down against the shadows. You can tell what it is by the unmistakeable shape of its thumb. Robert's legs are wrapped in puttees and his uniform is done up tight. He is hatless. The eyes are staring straight at the camera and the lips are slightly parted. His hair is riffled with the breeze and it must be spring because the grass is short at his feet. He appears to be sitting on his left hand. Perhaps it was a chilly day. His right arm hangs down and the hand is making a shape, as if to hold some object. The object must be delicate. Robert's fingers are poised in such a way that you think he might be holding something alive or made of glass. But the object—once you have made it out—is nothing of the sort. It is white and slightly larger than his fist. Magnification reveals it is the skull of some small beast—either a rabbit or a badger. Robert's middle index fingers are crooked through its eyes. You put this picture aside because it seems important. To his left there is a fascio of guns: tall old-fashioned rifles stooked and bound as if for harvest. Then you remember something written long after Robert Ross was dead. It was written during another war—in 1943—by the Irish essayist and critic Nicholas Fagan. This is what he wrote: "*the spaces between the perceiver and the thing perceived can . . . be closed with a shout of recognition. One form of a shout is a shot. Nothing so completely verifies our protection of a thing as our killing of it.*"

The archivist closes her book. She stares into time with her hair falling forward either side of her face. Her fingers smooth the cover of the book which is hard and brown and old. She purses her lips. She rises. It is time to tell us all to go. Something prevents her—just for a moment. It is the sound of birds beyond the windows, making commotions in the dark. The archivist moves among the tables—turning out lights and smiling—telling us gently "late. It's late." You begin to arrange your research in bundles—letters—photos—telegrams. This is the last thing you see before you put on your overcoat:

ROBERT AND ROWENA WITH MEG: Rowena seated astride the pony—Robert holding her in place. On the back is written: "Look! You can see our breath!" And you can.